# THE EMPTY ORCHESTRA

## Book V of the Troutespond Series

## Elizabeth Priest

*For Jane, the best writing buddy.*

# Contents

# Drowned Out

This might sound like excessive whining, but I was really bad at playing the mandolin.

This wasn't just because my boyfriend probably invented music and if you hand him a whistle he literally plays like a god. I knew people who were only moderately awesome at music, somewhere along the lines of competent, and other bad players. I was pretty sure I was the worst of the lot. After half a semester in the Music Society at my uni, I was still having trouble moving between one note and another, and I'd only been trusted with two of them in the piece we were learning at the moment.

"Allyyy," Molly sang, drawing out my name in a note far sweeter than the one I'd just played. "What are you doing?"

"Er, presumably not playing a C," I said, a blush creeping over my face. My sense of humour wasn't icy enough to make it go away. It was as bumbling and awkward as I was. Dad humour, in fact. For my bedtime stories, when Mum wasn't up to it, he used to read from one of those awful joke books (literally, "The Bumper Awful Joke Book") and we'd chuckle at the terrible puns and not-really-jokes-at-all together. My wit has never recovered since. A couple of people in the orchestra giggled. I really hoped it was at my terrible not-even-a-joke and not at my awful playing.

"What am I doing wrong?" I looked down at my fingers, mashed onto the strings at the top of my strange pot-bellied instrument.

"Still holding down all the strings for that D as well," she said when my contemplation stretched out into the zone of awkwardly long. I glanced up. She was still smiling patiently. The girl was a saint. Not literally.

I very carefully lifted one finger and looked back at Molly. She nodded encouragingly. I began to lift another and she shook her head ever so slightly. I hastily put that finger back down and tried another.

"Okay! Just keep strumming like I said, and let's try again! From the top! And one... two... one two three..."

With a mixed rate of reaction time the thirteen of us started up again, the rather more competent players filling the artfully muffled practice room with the orchestral take on a popular song with Halloween-themed lyrics, lost on anyone who didn't know the tune since we had no singers. Someone had conscientiously filled in all the lyrics on the battered photocopies the people who could be trusted with real music were holding. It was the thought that counted.

I hadn't even known how to hold the Mandolin of Motherly Guilt when I'd shown up on the first Wednesday. I'd been brought there by a mixture of good intentions and determination not to let the oddest parting gift between any university-going student and their barmy hippie mother just sit and rot in the corner of the room. Or possibly to sit in the corner of my room and stare at me with its weird, glaring eyes until I picked it up and practiced or else ritually burned it just to be really sure.

Because, yes, she had given me, the perpetually terrified and anxious creature, a musical instrument that not only could I not play but looked like some sort of folk art masterpiece, complete with huge stylised evil eyes either side of the fingerboard. All together the design definitely had a pareidolia of some sort of huge grimace in the flowers and leaves swirling in bright paint across the face.

It was pretty hard to feel homesick when your present burned fiery guilt into you with its cursed hoodoo face, forcing you to practice whenever the vast piles of reading and essays that I'd actually signed up for this whole experience to do weren't looming. Its fearsome look had even inspired me to do some of my university work out of sheer terror. Perhaps, then, this was my mother sending a glare at me to do my homework from all the way across the country.

I'd actually had my boyfriend check it for evil spells or some sort of nasty mandolin goblin trapped in it like a genie that would be released when I finally played the correct sequence of notes (little chance of that at the moment, at least), but he'd found nothing.

Apparently some odd artist on the internet who sold these things after painting up a plain old mandolin just liked adding frightening faces to things. I didn't want to know what my mum had been browsing for when she had found it. Or why she had immediately thought of me when my only past encounters with music could probably be measured on the Richter scale for how catastrophic they'd been.

Around me, all the players had managed to get back into the swing of things and, with some intense concentration, I'd hopped back onto the train with them. One thing that I had found was that once I managed to remember what I was meant to be playing the simple repetitive pattern meant that I was free to look around and let my thoughts wander, as they were extremely apt to do, occasionally letting them thump back into place when I messed up and missed a string or forgot what it was I was actually meant to be doing. I was fine once I got going... it was remembering how I had been doing it ten minutes later which was the problem.

In my first practice sessions I hadn't been able to look away from my literally white knuckling fingers on the strings. The next time I focussed my eyes determinedly on a knothole in one of the polished wooden beams above us in the tall, narrow room. I'd memorised a square of steel fixed to it, probably some part of a clamp for an overhead recording thingy that we were blessedly not using. But I'd got a bit more confident lately and now I could watch the twelve other people crammed into the sock-smelling practice room with me without instantly messing up what I was doing.

This was also inspired a little by Molly patiently explaining that I needed to be at least a little aware of the noises the people around me were making if I wanted to stay in time.

Amir was the best and worst to watch. Perpetually grinning, our token maths student in this creative ensemble had been as new to music as me to begin with, but rather less worried by this fact. He'd improved, like I had, but while it was handy to check my tune against his, his optimism and lack of deep-rooted shame meant he never made all the freezes and embarrassed stops I did. He just kept strumming away, whatever he might happen to be playing. Amir's instrument sported eyes drawn in an Arabic sort of style with permanent marker pen after the second week. He'd been pretty impressed with my instrument, and brought some books of Aztec and Native American art from the library to try and pin down what sort of curse I should be worried about. Er, I mean, to trace the origins of the weird eyes out of academic curiosity. Obviously not everyone assumed everything that looked at them funny was probably cursing them. I'd had a strange summer.

I'd asked him about the way he never seemed worried about messing up once, as we were packing up after a particularly brutal practice, and he had thought for a while and replied, "Ah... The guitar, it is a story." and he smiled widely and walked off, shouldering his acoustic guitar, to leave me to ponder that riddle and how much someone could think when they were chill and didn't spend all day panicking about little things. I didn't have to say a thing to know that my boyfriend would tell me I had as much to learn from him as I did from our super awesome orchestra leader.

Molly's favoured instrument was the violin, but she played many, and recently had been mostly using the keyboard that lived in this room gathering chewing gum so she would be freer to call things to us. Usually, "Ally! Chord change!" She was a very neat, well-dressed sort of girl, and it showed she'd been brought up rich (aside from owning a stupid number of instruments, all stashed in the nicest dorm building on campus). She wore navy-blue cardigans like she still had a school uniform; her very long shiny, straight hair was always held back with an Alice band, and she wore a pearl necklace and earrings every time I saw her. Funny, one of my bestest friends back home was from a wealthy family too, and it was just as easy to tell from how scruffy she was and how badly she dressed in the most current hipster trends of ancient second-hand clothes and leftovers from her early teen goth phase. She could afford aesthetics.

After staring at Molly, checking how I was doing, I found my eyes resting on the girl sitting next to me. Lucia was a friend who spoke fluent English though she was of French-Caribbean descent, and still had the gorgeous accent even though she'd lived in London a while. She was in most of my classes, as a fellow Literature student, and I didn't need to idolise her because, despite her excellent music skills, she could be as dumb and normal as me, albeit often drunkenly. She played violin and had started when she was six. Unlike Molly, she'd then put it down for ten years after achieving a few grades in it and not played again until she got to university, having discovered it while moving her stuff into storage. She'd been joking about selling it, but I'd convinced her to come with me to the Music Society for moral support and she'd got back into playing in a big way. Still, she wasn't very confident either and determinedly chewed her lower lip through the melody parts of the song, and thought she was a lot worse than everyone else said she was.

A wiggle of her masses of dark hair had escaped from her scrunchie and was resting on the end of her nose, and from her cross-eyed expression I could tell she was in trouble: her bow faltered, her head jerking to the side a few times in an attempt to dislodge it. Her nose twitched like a bunny rabbit's, and finally she dropped her bow and let out an enormous sneeze that shocked us all into silence, then into a burst of laughter. She tried to laugh along with us, hiding her face in her hands, and scraped her hair back into a new ponytail to avoid having to look at anyone, an awkward smile on her face.

"Hey, a song that didn't end because me or Amir messed up so bad we were playing Greensleeves by mistake!" I put in brightly, trying and pull the shame away from her and back to my heart where it belonged.

"Do not speak that name," Molly snarled. There was one rule: we would never, ever be required to play Greensleeves. I understand she learnt it devoutly for a performance, then the next month a different music tutor put her class through it all over again for two solid months of Greensleeves-based projects.

"Have we ever actually played the end of any of these songs?" Sam drawled. He was a violin player, perpetually wearing a trilby, who did philosophy because he thought it made him deep and interesting to girls. I had literally thought people like him were a joke and had met six so far this month, largely due to the proximity of the Philosophy department's offices to the Lit department. They gaggled around their tutors and asked deep questions which weren't about when assignments were due.

He was also working on a screenplay, and I only hoped he was better at writing than he was at sawing out violin noises.

"Like, we did a full run of a song five minutes ago?" Lucia said.

Sam ignored her because he already had the rest of his insult lined up. "Maybe we should just play the ends of some of these before Ally has a chance to ruin them?" He ran that icky wax thing over his bow with a scraping sound, attempting to look aloof.

I smiled at him, because after all I'd been through I was still not above laughing pathetically in self-deprecating agreement with someone being mean to me.

"Shush, we've got time," Molly said. "And there are some we can all play. Why don't we do one of those tunes we started with just to get our confidence back? It's nearly seven, so we can call it a night after that."

"Okay," we all chorused. In a minute we'd all tuned up for the song, Lucia had scratched her nose really well and Amir and I had confirmed that we knew our parts. I watched Molly and her nods that she conducted us with, knowing this was a bit more complicated (my part had actually been expanded from "here, pluck this one lonely string from now until we stop" after I'd mistakenly shown a fleeting bit of competence at it). I had to listen to the music rather more closely as well.

And what I heard when I actually put my mind to it alarmed me so greatly I almost squeaked out loud and ruined another song. I held onto it, though, and listened hard.

Our sound seemed oddly magnified, too much bass humming like a cello that definitely did not fit into this room was following our higher-pitched violins and violas. A stronger tone of the violins echoed intensely through what our orchestra played, a sound far too great for our small string section to manage on their own. There was a breath of extra wind to the two flutes, maybe even the sound of a clarinet or something in there (no, despite it all, I can't tell wind instruments apart). But the most striking part—the thing that had startled me the most—was the sound of a floating, sourceless note, which could have been vocal in its rawness, wavering pitch and feeling behind it. But not a one of us had our mouth open, except Lucia was chewing her lip again, sending the top of her violin bobbing madly about.

And the more I listened to it, the more I could have sworn I was hearing just snatches of someone singing the missing words to our song. That the sound really was a human voice that could not possibly have been in the room with us.

I made it to the end of the song without freaking out, but I didn't stick around long after that, though this was one of my few chances to socialise properly in a day if you didn't count complaining loudly in the five minutes between classes with Lucia. The longer I stayed the more I would think about it, and the more tempted I would be to blurt, "Who was singing?" and my tenuous status as not being catastrophically weird would be shattered. My tenuous status as a sane normal person, though… That was something a bit harder to handle.

Imagine it though! Here I could cultivate a whole room of people who thought I was only surface-level weird. A whole campus of them. I wanted to preserve that as long as possible. Come across only as strange as anyone else in a place with a vast collection of youths from all over the world, art students and musicians and so many different flavours of nerd… And not a single one of them thought of me as the girl who was weirdly obsessed with fairies and had the odd witchy mum.

It did mean, though, that there was only one person that I could talk to right now, and I was sure that he held all the answers, because, well, if he didn't then who possibly could?

While everyone was still glancing around in satisfied relief to hear the closing notes of a song, checking Molly's reactions for anything other than the same blind relief, I stumbled over to the pile of bags in the corner of the room.

"Sorry, got some reading I need to do for tomorrow!" I cried, ramming my mandolin into its case. It glared furiously at me for the treatment. I zipped the bag shut with a sharp tug.

"What reading?" Lucia demanded at once, rightly freaked out. I'd forgotten my excuse already had more holes than the socks Mum had lovingly knitted me before I left.

"Er… Not sure. That's part of the problem! I mean if I knew I'd be a lot more calm about it but I need to go find my reading list and…"

"Calm down. It'll be *Wuthering Heights* still; we have two more weeks of it."

"Oh *no*," I groaned. "What part?"

Lucia shrugged. I felt guilty for giving her yet more reasons to chew her lip, especially since I was not sure I wasn't just making up the reading. It was Schrödinger's Homework: I had no idea if it existed or not and until I went back to my room and opened my notebook. It wasn't like I enjoyed being absent-minded, but on the other hand I did get great big chunks of blissful forgetfulness between moments of stress.

"Right, well then, I'm off!" I cradled my mandolin in my arms as I barged open the door of the practice room with a shoulder. "See you!"

Everyone called confused and amused goodbyes as I legged it. I was so obviously the weird one.

*

Bursting from the stuffy, well-padded practice room to the theatre's outer shell, I abruptly smacked into a huge space, cold and blue and echoing. Like

I'd stepped from a room with a roaring fire to the cold castle battlements that lined it. 'Tis bitter cold etc. Large windows filled the spaces between thick columns in the rounded wall—brick but carved into the shape of pillars out of antiquity. While the terrible fake-classical look was just disheartening from an emotional and aesthetic viewpoint, it was also crap for insulation. The Ancient Greeks had not had the same need for double glazing and moderate window placement that we modern peoples did, what with being in Greece and all. Trying to make up for the lack of Mediterranean warmth with fancy blue-tinted glass just did not work once it was under ten degrees.

This building was like a Russian doll: the round, red-brick theatre in the middle, with the columned outer layer surrounding it in an echoing, airy space five stories high, full of metal fire escape style paths and hanging spiky art pieces donated by graduating students who realised the spare bedroom at their parent's house didn't have room for a two-storey naked lady made of dented cast-iron pots and pans. Through the floor-to-ceiling outer windows I could see the dark campus, a little hazy mist hanging between the soft yellow lights, looming dark shadows of other monstrous red-brick buildings. It looked damp out there, and some of the lamps were blocked by shaking cloaks of leaves, shining with a recent rainfall, swaying in and out of shot. An altogether calmer, less alarming world, but what would be the landscape to match this strange building?

I circled the round theatre placed like a squat tin can in the middle of this weird edifice; a walkway ran right the way around it on all the balcony levels, with an icy railing that I didn't want to touch without gloves for fear my hand would freeze to it. As I jogged around, looking for the nearest stairs down, the whole structure clinging to the sides of the theatre clanged and shook and wobbled. Of course I had to climb up and down the most stairs possible... The fake temple was ringed at the top with practice rooms.

The automatic doors in the atrium slid open for me as the metal stairs were still recovering from my cacophonous descent. A gust of icy air washed over me even before I could step out into what was more like a young storm. I took a deep breath like I was going to dive into a swimming pool and forged ahead. This was no time for being sissy about the weather. The little café, hardly more than a doughnut stand and espresso machine in a nook between the bookshop and cloakroom, was calling to me with the thought of hot chocolate, saying this was the perfect time to dally by the heated glass, to get a nice hot cardboard tube of nourishing liquid chocolate to make the walk bearable...

I closed my eyes and ran a few steps before I gave up and settled for a fast stride. There was the clear, green smell of rain at night and though I was pretty sure in a five minute hurry I wasn't going to get washed away by a flash flood... it could happen, and if there was anyone it would happen to it was me. I had got away from the practice rooms, out of the theatre... Was I sensibly putting space between myself and the weird ghostly voices, or was this exactly where

I wasn't supposed to go? No spectral monsters lurking in the undergrowth to grab me and devour me for a more fitting hero to discover in the morning.

The lights over the paths were bright, but for large parts of the walk I felt like I was in a tunnel through darkness as I crossed what was more of a park than a university campus. Sherrick Campus, of a larger county-wide university organisation, was particularly well-funded and picturesque when not in the middle of an autumn storm at night. The music rooms were open later than most lecture halls: even if the Literature Society wanted to meet past seven it would just use the common rooms in the Students' Union building. For some reason though, everyone was perfectly happy letting the noisy students who wanted some time with their band and some high-end amplifiers do it in the expensive sound-proofed rooms at night. It was a great deal of trust that I was not totally sure should be extended to all these budding starving musicians.

(I was a literature student, obviously I was going to fare better than them in my career.)

As I drew closer to Students' Union territory the sound of the bars—thumping dance music, yelling students, the football playing somewhere—washed over me. With it came light and I could see beyond the path to more than shadowy branches: there was the awful, probably racist Mexican-themed bar ('L Bar'); the sleek building of the nightclub with the dark blue-tinted windows that disco lights were rolling across; an old-school pub that was actually a concrete block of a building, painted white with abstract wooden beams but with a gorgeous sign proudly swinging outside it. It was nothing like home, which would have been utterly dead by six p.m. I don't think loud dance music had ever echoed around our part of the valley. Who would emerge from the ancient woodwork to boogie?

But in its own special way the campus was sort of like my town. There were parts of it that were dead quiet at night, but the size of it was similar, if you ignored the monolithic buildings and all the space in between them. If all of Troutespond's quaint little houses were stacked together at the corner of the high street they'd probably make a pile about as big as the blocks of halls that nestled behind this social area.

The thoughts of building Tetris and how you would fill a complete row with what was available on campus, with plenty of L-shaped blocks but not a whole lot of the T-shaped ones, distracted me almost until I forgot much of the reason that I was rushing and probably only carried on instinctively because, though I might be a bit dumb, my body does know it's not a good idea to freeze to death.

I came stumbling up to the door of my building at last and stopped, panting, on the sheltered doorstep to dig out my key card. Beyond the cold metal frame the garish hall lights weren't exactly a welcoming shade. It wasn't going to be any warmer until I got through one of the heavy sealed fire doors and onto my corridor, where the heat and smells of the kitchen, showers and bedrooms with clanking radiators and closed windows all mixed together to form a particularly sweat-and-gravy tropical atmosphere. With big puffs of my breath pouring out of my mouth I was actually longing for the muggy atmosphere, though I had been predicting mushrooms would be growing in my lungs by Christmas after my first whiff of the halls.

The red light on the door glared at me as I dipped my card key in and out a couple of times until it went green, then I rammed my shoulder into the heavy thing to get it open. I was pretty worried that I'd end up with a dislocated shoulder, but the other option was hypothermia from a night spent out in the cold.

After that it wasn't so hard to leg it up the stairs and slip through the door with the big B on it, permanently left unlocked. It was not just because the key cards were rubbish; our floor were a sociable lot and, whatever the hall wardens said, we were happy to let anyone wander in and out of our private living space. After all, with a front door so impenetrable anyone in here would have passed a pretty basic security check.

Corridor B was quiet at the moment: I could hear conversation from the kitchen but only a couple of doors were wedged open and I could quite clearly make out the sounds of the song that room B6 was playing, since no one else was contributing to the usual cacophony of music and TV noises.

A rather more obnoxious security check had me rattling my lock and jabbing my key in and out of it for a minute before I was actually in my own room. I stumbled into the tiny centrally-heated bubble and groaned in relief as I stood there dripping and steaming. This little beige box with itchy blue carpet and furniture identical to the other three hundred rooms on campus might have been bland but it was a very welcome sight. Something like cold weather really makes anything seem like home if you get to put your hands up against a radiator.

I'd done my best to make it more cosy and familiar, but I'd been alarmed to discover that no amount of cushions and throws make up for having a mother like a hyperactive five-year-old running around spilling poster paint and sequins on everything. I had a feeling the wardens wouldn't like it if I added a liberal sprinkling of glitter to everything to get rid of my homesickness.

While she might have been separated from me by a hundred miles, there were some people it was impossible to be rid of. As I leaned my mandolin up against the desk, someone said "Well met," behind me.

I squeaked with surprise, even though I should have been used to it by now, and turned to see the Piper sitting on the comfy chair wedged between the window and my bed. I don't know how I'd missed him before if he *had* been sitting there when I first entered – his long legs were sprawled most of the way across the room.

"Hi," I replied, immensely relieved but also standing like a total dork in the middle of my room, arms folded, trying to shuck my damp trainers off my feet without bending over and unlacing them. I wobbled and hastily flopped down on my bed since he'd taken the only other bit of furniture which wasn't apparently constructed from coat hangers and an old tea tray (I'm looking at you, "desk chair").

"I do like how your door won't let *you* in, but I can come and go as I please," he commented, looking maddeningly smug.

"You watch out I don't start phoning you up just to grab something from my room I forgot," I warned. It was a valid threat: most days I had to double back halfway to the lecture theatre because I'd left my books behind or forgotten to grab my photocopy card or something. I pulled off my coat, hopping up again because I had been sitting on the trailing ends. I contemplated moving closer to him, but threw the coat at him instead. "Hang that on the curtain rail, would you?" There was a distinct lack of storage space in this room, and a floor-length black and white coat that weighed almost as much as I did was not going to take up half my closet if I had a say in it.

"Are you alright?" he asked, not needing to be magical to work out my mood. The end of the curtain rail groaned under the weight of the coat, but I think he glared it into not breaking, at least while we had this moment. With all the tea stains I'd already added to the carpet, I was pretty sure I wasn't getting my deposit back no matter what else happened here.

"I thought I... Well, I heard something really odd today when we were playing."

"And you were worried that you're going crazy, even though just the fact that I'm here in your room talking to you should reassure you that stuff like this can happen without being a product of a fevered mind? It's rather adorable." He chuckled very rudely, I thought. Maybe fondly, from an objective standpoint.

"Shut up," I grumped. "It wasn't like I thought that Molly was a pixie or something like that. It was a lot more subtle. It was just a lot like more people were playing than were actually in the room."

He shrugged and stretched out his stupidly long arms. "Well, I'm stumped."

"*What?*"

"Doesn't seem to be hurting anyone, does it?"

I resisted the urge to pathetically thump him and try to prove him wrong. "But that's it? 'I'm stumped'? I could have got the same answer from anyone!"

"It doesn't mean more coming from me?" he laughed. I scowled until he made even the barest atom of an effort. "Well... Did you check if there were some extra people in the room that you might not have spotted right away? You're not always very observant."

"I'm very observant! If anything, that's the problem! I can't believe you'd be so... so... dumb!"

I folded my arms, turned my back on him and sat heavily on the bed.

He kept on laughing, that stupid infectious laugh. Even calling it 'hearty' would be underselling it. It faded a little as he realised that I still hadn't turned around and intended to keep on freezing him out as long as it took. He stood up, his shadow momentarily looming over me, and then there was a crunch of bedsprings as he settled down behind me. Even without his arms snaking around my waist his weight tipped the horrible mattress enough to make me flop against him.

"Oh, go away," I grumbled as he pressed his lips to the side of my neck and gave me a squeeze, like he could squish the grumpiness out of me.

I felt a tickle as he laughed against my skin, and was rather annoyed to find that I was beginning to smile as well.

"Is it that you're worried about the upcoming show?" he asked, still trying to work out my bad mood (because of *course* it was not his fault for being an unhelpful ignoramus).

"Not, it's fine... Molly's given us small parts it's hard to mess up, but even if we do I think she's the only one who would actually hear us and know that we'd done it wrong. I'm pretty confident the violins will drown us out." (especially if we had some extra mysterious ones playing along...) The hamster in my brain was still scrabbling around for the exact words and approach to asking about what the hell I'd experienced and actually make it sound like... anything. So I sought to get the topic of conversation away from me and into something I could just nod along to without having to contribute too much myself. "How was your day?" Could have been a boring question for anyone else, but he was on another whole sphere of existence so it was kinda fun.

"Funny you should ask. I happened to be in Severstrong Abbey so I dropped by to catch up with your friend Teb."

"Oh! I haven't talked to her all week. How is she?"

"Well she wasn't pleased to see me! She threatened me with a trowel before I could even start talking and told me to shove my advice and let her dig in peace. She has always been like that, right? I don't want to overdiagnose the effects of selling her name."

"Oh, no, that's classic Teb. If anything she's been way more quiet and chill since she's been a goddess."

I cuddled up to him and let him distract me with a tale of my righteous friend indignantly giving the Piper what for. I was totally rooting for her while he told it. Serves him right. For being useless and not answering the question that I hadn't asked him.

Around nine my stomach made a loud, embarrassing rumbling noise and the Piper shooed me out into the kitchen to feed myself, determined that I'd not waste away on his watch. Originally I'd assumed what he meant by "you need me around to protect you" was "you almost got sacrificed to a barmy dragon-worshipping cult in August and I don't want that to happen again." But now I understood it to be more, "I'm here to save you from yourself, even in the most mundane aspects of life where you fail a lot harder than normal people."

Still, I guess after seeing how many cups of tea I made he trusted me to heat things up for myself, so he made his excuses. Well actually, he said that he had to go stop some goblins taking advantage of the thinner veil between worlds around Halloween and acquiring the fairy equivalent of weapons of mass destruction, which they'd put on the market to the highest bidder. Having seen the kind of people in positions of power in the fairy world, I let him go without complaint.

Our halls of residence were set up so ten bedrooms and two big communal bathrooms flanked the hall down either one of the wings of the T-shaped building (Sherrick Hall was pretty central to the building Tetris around here). The end of the hall opened into a lounge and kitchen area with bean bags and simple, brightly-coloured furniture which must have looked brilliant in the brochure and brand-new in the eighties. By now the cartoonish kitchen counters were stained with the surfaces peeling off, the sofa's back was a little loose and cracked ominously when you leaned on it and the carpet was sticky and static-y like we'd got our own cinema experience with added soy sauce from the hordes of Chinese students who flocked around the campus and took it in turns to have huge groups crowd into a residence to make food and hang out. As for the surface of the hobs on the oven… Or the egg-splattered innards of the microwave… Or…

Maybe it was a good thing that Teb, neat freak of our group, was still living safely at home and not with between three and fifty other people.

Right now the only people hanging in the communal area were the guy from B3 and his stoner friend. I slouched past them with a wave and mumbled hellos. The kettle went on as a first point of action even before I decided what I wanted. Even if I wasn't going to cook with it I was long overdue my tea fix.

Just to give an example of the criminality of my peers, every single item in the kitchen was theoretically meant to be stamped with a big red B, but this kettle had a yellow C on the side in peeling plastic lettering. The C lot were pretty friendly (it probably helped with their crimes) and I'd gone upstairs to say hi… And observed they had more blue-marked As and red Bs on their kitchen appliances than their own yellow. In fact, their communal TV had a red B on it, which explained why we were using Angie from B7's TV from home and also doing her dishes. I supposed the friendliness and willingness to party over in C played some part in breaking all their stuff then mounting a midnight raid on other corridors to replace it instead of just asking the hall stewards for a new one. I was just smug we'd taken anything back, which meant the tribalism of lettering us had got to me too.

I may also have been reading Angie's psychology textbooks.

Between the parties and the thieves, this probably explained why everything constantly seemed to be missing, or in the wrong place, which for a scatterbrain like me made cooking and sustaining myself next to impossible. All of us asked daily, "Did you move my…?" or "Was the kettle always in the…" or "Who ate all my…?" Sometimes it felt like the combined efforts of thirty people using one kitchen had created a poltergeist that hid behind drunken antics and forgetfulness to create the most thorough confusion ever beheld.

I got some pasta cooking in one of my pans, which I had located in the washing machine (no, not dishwasher. Washing machine. I shared a floor with stoners. This was the only explanation that didn't involve ghosts) and then drifted out to see what Michael and his friend were talking about while they were on my mind.

Avoiding social interaction was acceptable, and there were a couple of people on the floor I hadn't said a word to after group circle time on day one induction, but if I ever were to announce battle plans to steal our television back from floor C I needed to be on good terms with at least some of the people on my floor. There were only so many times Angie could dramatically flop down in front of her TV, sighing with the woe of having to share, before someone either killed her or would listen to my plans.

Michael quite cheerfully rotated his lanky frame in the little creaking chair and filled me in: "Hey Ally! Bus was just telling me about this party in his first year, right, where he and these two other guys got wasted, right, and…"

It wasn't hard to realise what sort of story this was going to be, so I grinned, nodded and half-diverted my attention to waving to Bus Stop to continue with his tale as I let the anecdote about his strange midnight adventures wash over me. They couldn't be half as strange as any of mine, although I did keep an ear out for key phrases such as "accidentally threw up on a goblin" or "tripped and fell into a portal to fairy land". Sadly, I'd heard a few of these now and I was starting to think the chances of this ranging into my territory were pretty low.

Bus Stop was a third-year friend of pretty much anyone with so much as a casual interest in weed, and certainly, as it seemed, the life of any party. I was not entirely sure how he'd made it to his third year while devolving into someone who couldn't start the day without a spliff, but here he was, still hanging around first year halls trying to sell pot to the curious and carefree, making a lot of casual acquaintances to further his adventures of getting into trouble with golf course owners and later for unrelated reasons spending the night up a tree. I excused myself when it turned out this was only the first act, saying I could hear my pasta boiling over, and rushed off to tend it.

When I came back to sit with them, spooning cheesy tomato pasta goo into my mouth at an alarming speed, Bus leaned back and gave me his big happy stoner smile. I remembered the stories my mum had told me about her time at university (and how she'd ended up having a tangentially substance-related breakdown afterwards), and wondered if his ease with the world was anything like her happy hippie ways. They seemed pretty far apart, but I could easily dread the way she would obviously strike up a conversation with him, become best friends and probably ask in an undertone how much he was charging, and if there was a student discount, because she did technically attend the Open University, you know…

While I was busy internally cringing at something that hadn't even happened, Bus said, "You should come to some more parties, Ally. I've never seen you cut loose and it's already, er... a couple of months into term, right? There's one on campus in a couple of days"

"When exactly?" I asked, mostly to be polite, really hoping that "in a couple of days" meant "Halloween," so I had a ready-made excuse.

"Er..." He looked thoughtfully up to the damp ceiling tiles, counting on imaginary fingers. "The day before the day before Halloween, right? Friday?"

"Right," I agreed, feeling a heavy weight settle on my stomach at the thought of having to half-promise him to go, or to babble around the subject until I found a loophole. I didn't think I even had that much homework to do seeing as until November all our course wanted us to do was read a couple of the old classic novels. And, sad to say, I'd read most of the Austen, had enough of a stab at the Dickens in the past to know what they were talking about, and had been so excited to study Wilde I'd checked his complete works out of the library in the summer and was most of the way through two weeks before the rest of the class would even consider looking inside the front cover of *Dorian Gray*. Even *Wuthering Heights* wasn't giving me as much trouble now I'd got into it. I'd dreaded it when I first reattempted the opening since a disastrous attempt during the GCSEs, when we were stuck with a substitute after one of the various non-demonic teacher burnouts our school weathered, and they hadn't read it, couldn't be bothered to start, and decided to teach us the text using Wikipedia.

"Well... I might be able to come? Maybe?"

He and Michael looked delighted. "Great! It's over in Bradley Halls. Third floor."

"It'll be every floor," Bus promised, practically hopping with excitement. "Bring your boyfriend, he's way fun."

"He's... what. Oh, never mind." It was a mistake to let him hang out here when I wasn't around. He was making *friends*. I put on a smile, then thought that it looked like one of those big fake smiles chimps use when they feel threatened, and hastily removed it from my face. They'd both already sort of lost interest in me anyway, getting back to watching some videos on their phones, so I was glad to take the cue to go.

"I have some reading to do," I said, gratefully scooping up the last of my pasta and hiccupping a little. I left with no further words, since politeness wasn't really a ritual observed among the people of our halls.

I made tea with the water left over in the kettle and sloshed past them with hot tea running down my sleeve in my haste to get back to my room and put a barricade between myself and the rest of the world. I thought I was doing really well with coping with all this socialising and existing outside my previous bubble of two to three people, but I was glad to not have to do it all day long.

Sitting back at my desk, I faced the empty chair the Piper had chosen as his usual perch whenever he was here and sipped tea. For a while I considered picking up my mandolin and having a go, but I still felt weirdly disconnected from the whole thing. A little scared that playing it would draw monsters down on me where I sat in my room. Which was ridiculous, because I'd been practicing in here the whole time and nothing dramatic had changed in my life that might have started a whole… thing. I hadn't done a thing out of my boring ordinary schedule and something weird had still snuck up on me. Perhaps what I was feeling was offended that I hadn't even deserved it this time.

Instead of sulking all night, I tried to remember more about the odd noises I'd heard while we had been playing. Memories of sound can be so weird; I had to try hard to capture all the little shards of voices and weird feelings and low notes that couldn't have been there. Stitch them back together in my mind and make a real effort to be sure I wasn't adding more in my memory for the melodrama of the whole thing, as I was so often accused of doing. I wanted to have it as clear as possible. It was a good sort of mental exercise to keep my panic in check. To try and make this as grounded as possible, since I hadn't had a chance to whip out my phone and record it.

So far, I thought, I had done a very good job of not freaking out or overreacting. If Tanya was around she would tell me thirty things in one breath that it could be, but I was waiting for her to phone me, and it had been two months and she hadn't, so I wasn't going to break that impressive streak of not talking to her since it was clearly her problem to sort out and therefore she had to call.

What other resources did I have to call on? Surely more than enough. Okay, Teb was incredibly busy being the new goddess on the block, as well as taking archaeology on the side. I think she was much more bound to the valley than she wanted to admit. Her choice of university had been far on the other side of the country and it must have hurt to turn them down. I was glad she was keeping busy, but like Tanya, she was terrible at initiating conversations and hard to talk to when I did. Besides, she had a good but limited set of knowledge based mostly on being a goddess back home, and would probably still try and rationalise it. "You said it was windy. Maybe you were hearing the wind howling outside?" her voice echoed in my head. Imaginary Teb was bored of me already. Assuming I'd made a ridiculous leap from a standing jolt of anxiety.

As for Alana… After the events of the summer she was the only one I still enjoyed actually talking to, and she had slacker hours at university so was always online, or at least happy to answer her phone. But Alana was coming to visit me in a few days, and I didn't want her to think that it was a job that she had to do all of a sudden, or that I'd known all along and lured her there. The last thing I needed was for her to think this was all some new thing that she had to protect me from after my damsel in distress moment in the summer, or, well, anything that she needed to stick her nose into. She would make it into a huge deal or get worried about me, and before I knew it she'd be dragging out literal skeletons from closets.

With none of my friends except Alana easy to contact, I was left to try and puzzle this out the way my much smarter friends might.

What helped a great deal with my deductions was that without Tanya, Alana and Teb around, my chances of meeting aliens, fairies, goblins, Martians, mermaids, pixies, trolls, vampires, werewolves, witches or interdimensional travellers from our parallel lives was greatly lessened. While with them we'd stumbled across ancient gods, odd cults and the occasional dragon on a monthly basis, here I was nice and safe away from their determination to poke and pry in what they really ought not to poke.

Therefore, I told myself, ignoring how much of the poking I had done myself in moments of overcurious madness, I should write off any freaking out on the basis that while I may be hearing an unnatural phenomenon it was not at all as likely to want to sacrifice me as other things we'd met.

Instead, I could focus on the real issue: raw, primal survival.

It was sort of strange to discover that what I had originally developed as coping mechanisms for my family and friends were basically the sort of survival life skills one needed at university. I had been amazed to realise that a little bit of clumsiness and ineptitude at things where one is meant to use their brain did not actually spell certain doom in the same way that forgetting to turn your mobile phone off before going to spy on cultists did.

For a month or more now I had cooked and cleaned, remembered to change the sheets on my bed once, and even nominated myself to go talk to the wardens on the first week when the light bulb in the communal bathroom broke and no one else knew where to go or could be bothered to do it. After all, when you have seen a giant star boar come smashing through your sixth form prom, going to ask a guy to come fix the light so we don't have to pee in the dark was rather not frightening, and the dark itself only a mere inconvenience, especially in an era where we all just had torches in our pockets.

By-and-large I'd made it to my lectures on time, done my few early assignments with a day or so to spare and kept up with the reading. I had joined the Orchestra Society, though I hadn't gone to the chess or video game or— well, any of the other societies I'd signed up to. I saw my boyfriend regularly without interrupting my study/sleep time (helped by the fact I rarely sleep more than four hours a night). In fact, if it weren't for the fact said boyfriend was a being of immense cosmic power then I would have been living an utterly normal, magic-free life. It wasn't like the disastrous time when we'd tried not to talk about it despite all of my friends being walking time bombs to a magical event. And that had ended amazingly well: at least we were all alive to not talk to each other.

It was safe, it was quiet, and it was really quite nice.

With no goblins to chase I opened my laptop, looked up a documentary of suitable dullness about something tangentially relevant to my degree on iPlayer and settled back on my bed right as the Piper appeared to hug me until I was asleep.

# Revenge of the Grimy Flip-Flops II

All through my early teenage years I'd been mocked for wearing this ratty old pair of flip-flops constantly. When I say pair I mean there were two of them, not that they were matched. Now that I was at uni they had actually become one of my most prized possessions.

The floor in the bathroom was theoretically clean, but I didn't want to find out what sort of super-evolved verruca germs were growing there, so I'd never dared set my bare feet in it, wearing my flip-flops right into the shower. I was just annoyed that Teb, who'd done all the mocking, wasn't even at any university and sharing this experience so I could say, "*see!*" to her after she had to look for a discounted pair in the piles of leftover summer stuff in stores.

I usually also made a great effort not to forget I was wearing them and keep them on all the way to the lecture halls. I could tell I was having a slow day this next morning, though, when I got most of the way across campus before realising that my toes were a bit nippy and my feet were squelch-slapping their way along the scenic paths of the campus. A night of disturbed sleep, worrying about what I'd heard but still not being sure enough that it was anything to warrant action, while having the Piper right there to ask if only I felt sure enough of myself to do it...

I took it as an ill omen. I'd done very well so far, and the flip-flops in bad weather had become rather symbolic of my luck with stumbling across odd supernatural happenings. I almost went back to change before sensibly realising that would make me stupidly late, and not even for something worthwhile like my notebook. Superstition being allowed to rule my life was what got me into trouble with fairies.

So I sneaked into the lecture a few minutes late and sat with my usual group. Since I wasn't great at having more than two friends at once, the "group" consisted of Lucia and Rose.

I liked Rose. Wearing a red university-logo hoodie, she kept a stash of cookies permanently in the pocket and wasn't stingy about offering them around under the desk so we could practice crunching in time with the lecturer's droning. Lucia and I had decided that despite a somewhat loud mouth and a lack of desire to do the reading assignments, she was a very welcome member. We'd convinced her to come along to orchestra with us a couple of times since she played guitar very well (as we'd discovered when she and Molly wasted the best part of the evening rehearsal trying to outplay each other). Since the showdown Rose had admitted preferring rock to classical, even classical medleys of popular rock music as some of our songs were, and she only made sporadic appearances to play with us.

As I sat next to them Rose slipped a biscuit (Jaffa Cakes today!) my way with minimum rustling noises, and I sunk down into the uncomfortable chair and let a weight of silence and stillness descend over me. Morning lectures always had at least one guy slumped over the table, a can of foul glucose-y energy drink cuddled up to him like a baby with its bottle. That morning he represented everything I wanted to do with my life: namely, go back to sleep. It was amazing how priorities shifted around when exhausted. Suddenly "get a top class degree and go out to fight crime and save the world!" turned into "I'd be happy to snooze until midday without there being repercussions".

I sat there fidgeting with my pen but not taking any notes down, my mind still drifting about without really crossing paths with the words of the lecturer. I thought I could hear someone listening to music through headphones, a tiny beat vibrating through the air as vague as a fly buzzing at the back of the huge room. But after I suppressed a yawn until my ears popped, my hearing cleared. And just like that the sound was gone, though if anything it should have been louder. A little shiver ran through me, tiny crackles of nervousness that began to wake me up a lot more. I focussed hard on trying to hear imaginary sounds for the rest of the lecture, but I didn't catch a peep. Or a word of what the lecturer was discussing.

After the lecture we walked to our seminar room. Lucia was on my case at once, since I'd come to the lecture late. "You rushed off pretty quickly last night, didn't you?"

"I was seeing my boyfriend," I replied primly. Seeing as they never announced my role in the group repeatedly like Teb would (she liked sorting things), I had no idea how they saw me, but it was worth trying for somewhere along the lines of "respectable and well-adjusted" instead of any of the alternatives.

"Ooh," Rose sang, and giggled. "This is the mysterious stranger you won't tell anyone the name of?"

What did I say? 'He doesn't have a name'? I suppose if he went by anything it was Troute or St Troute, if we were looking for a human name once given to him, but that was worse than trying to explain how he was called the Piper to them. The other option left open to me was to casually explain it away like, "He's called Tedd," but I didn't think I could manage it with a straight face.

"It's not a big deal," I mumbled. "You guys just haven't met him yet."

"Will we?" Rose asked, enjoying this interrogation. I may inadvertently have come off as 'mysterious', of all things. Me, who usually babbles every thought on my mind before I can stop myself...

"Teeeeell!" Lucia begged.

"Not if you ask like that!" I tried a desperate stab at changing the topic of conversation: "Did you hear anything strange at the practice last night?"

"I think there was a moment where Amir invented a new chord that was until now unheard of in music."

I grinned. "Okay, aside from our awful playing."

"Like what?" Rose put in. "How did it sound?"

"You should come along more often if you care."

"Maybe I will if you tell me what was weird."

I backed off a bit because I didn't know how much more banter was acceptable between us as newly established friendos. "Well... it was just... like there were more musicians joining in on the last song."

Lucia shrugged. "It was the one we're all more confident on. Maybe everyone was just playing louder. I mean, I've noticed you sometimes *pretend* to play along when you're stuck. Did you feel how thick that article was they gave us to read by next week? And on *top* of having to read *Dorian Gray*." She hoiked her bag further up her shoulder and groaned at the weight of all the books padding it.

Rose smiled sympathetically at me and offered me another cookie. And just like that I'd lost any hope of being the normal one, and once again I was Weird Ally again.

We reached the seminar room where the smaller groups were gathering and, being some of the last people in, we were herded in together to sit and start our group work. Maybe it was my imagination, but I thought that Rose was still looking at me strangely as we dragged out folders and notepads and books (and then tried to balance them all on the square inch of desk attached to the chairs in these rooms). It was a sidelong look and I couldn't tell if it was curious or suspicious because it lasted barely a millisecond.

Then the tutor gave us some questions and we got into our groups to discuss them. Before anyone else could get a word in edgeways Lucia proposed, "*Wuthering Heights* was well shit, right?"

Our discussion went downhill from there.

*

Fifty-five minutes and one browbeaten seminar tutor later we were free for the afternoon. Rose hung back as Lucia groaned overdramatically and shoved papers haphazardly into her overlarge yellow pleather handbag. I let her go on without me, since we had no plans to meet up until the orchestra practice later, to see what Rose wanted to say.

I mean, she stood there raising her eyebrows and miming packing a bag really slowly, so I hoped I was reading the signs right. Maybe it was a "hurry up and move so we can get to lunch" mime?

But then she double-checked to make sure Lucia was gone and asked me, "When is the orchestra playing again? Wednesdays?" as we stepped out into the balmy October afternoon. The trees on campus hadn't really begun to turn properly autumnal yet, and there was a disappointingly thin layer of leaves to crunch through despite the wind last night. Wasn't this meant to be the month they were willingly leaping from the twigs like lemmings over a cliff?

"Every day from six to seven in the run-up to our first public performance. You'd have to start coming to all of them if you want Molly to let you play in the show, no matter how good you are. She was going on about teamwork last time. She must be serious." I pulled a face.

Rose nodded. "Okay. Well... we'll see."

"She's hoping we might nail down the classical version of 'Thriller' in time for it? That is, just a version that a group mostly composed of violins can handle."

There was more of a smile to her as she answered. "Okay. I'll come pad out your string section with some real talent. See if I can't hear this ghost orchestra for you as well."

"I never said..."

"What?"

I shook my head. "Just... weirded out by your turn of speech. I *hope* it isn't that. It meant nothing."

"O-kay." She drew it out worryingly disbelievingly.

"I mean, obviously ghosts don't exist... ha ha!"

"You should probably stop talking, Ally."

"I get that a lot," I replied, hoping that was just a generic "you so weird, Ally." I glumly watched my feet in the cracked plastic flip-flops as we trudged along in silence until Rose peeled off into the student shop to get more biscuits.

# Mangling my Mandolin

I continued aimlessly for a while, then realised I needed to get a book. I went to the library to check out some critic's snobby opinions on Oscar Wilde and got totally sidetracked reading *An Ideal Husband* standing up in the middle of the Drama shelves. By the time I snapped back to reality I had just enough time to drift to my room to dump heavy bags, make a late lunch and eat it while dropping sandwich crumbs all over my poor laptop and finally, a few paragraphs deeper into an essay, it was time to pick up my instrument and go. Just a normal day in Ally Land.

Everything is fine.jpg

As I crossed campus a little more purposefully, the big ugly music building rearing its head behind the twin Arts buildings, my phone rang in my pocket. I jumped and veered to the side of the footpath, almost bumping into a small huddle of Argentinian students on the way. They hastily moved on as I began swearing weakly and emptying out the contents of my bag, my mandolin hanging off one shoulder, probably leering at them because it was not a very polite instrument.

I finally found my phone in my pocket, answering it while shovelling receipts and train tickets back into the bottom of my bag, where they created a lining worthy of being a nest for some sort of bag-living bird. Or perhaps those little bag-sized dogs nested? I wasn't sure what odd evolutionary turns such a creature would take. I wasn't exactly looking to get a Chihuahua to find out however much the thought of having a pet alien amused me.

"What's funny?" Alana greeted me.

"Never mind," I said, trying to keep my Snickers down as I imagined a rucksack full of Chihuahuas in space helmets. "What's up?"

"Nothing much. Going mad on my own waiting around for next week."

"Er... You're coming *this* week, right? I've got it written down and everything so I don't forget."

"Yes, of course I am, you moron. It's when I go to America next week that I'm worried about."

"Right." Now I remembered her accusing "*your boyfriend* bullied me into going to visit Greg on my half-term break!" Somehow the Piper was only "your boyfriend" when he'd done something to annoy her. I hadn't asked him about it, mostly because I'd instantly forgotten, but he'd probably had a good reason. I was fairly certain (not a hundred percent but close) that he didn't just wind Alana up because he could.

"So you're still coming here this week?"

"*Yes*. I need to take my mind off things. Like what the hell you do when you spend a week with your previously presumed dead father. I mean... Are there self-help books for that?"

"Probably," I said, not really listening and pushing things back into my bag.

"Okay, well I can't find the section in the bookstore," she snapped.

"Bet if you went shopping with Tanya you could." I regretted teasing about her—Alana went cold for a long second after and I also felt the stab of guilt in my guts.

"Well anyway," she said. "When do you want me to come visit you?"

"Uh, I have no idea. I thought we sort of agreed something anything."

"Sort of. You said come before Halloween!"

"When is it good for you?"

"I already said, I'm on half-term right now for two weeks. Any time is good as long as it's before Sunday. I can come whenever I like."

"Then do that?" I suggested desperately, my voice a wound-up squeak by then.

"Yeah, but when is a good time for me to show up? You always seem to be running around—I can hear you doing it now! So tell me a time when you're not going to be mangling your mandolin or discussing dire Dickensian dramas."

"Nice alliteration."

"Thanks."

"They're really not that bad, though..."

"Ally! Focus!"

I thought long and hard as I scurried along the path. "Well... The trains don't run from about one am to seven am, so maybe not then."

I heard a slap on the other end of the line, and I guess it says something that I'm so experienced with interpreting smacked foreheads down the phone. "And I'm in practice from five to seven in the evening, so not around then," I hastily added.

"And your classes?"

"Usually over by two or three."

"I'll aim for three then. I can probably start walking to the uni from the station without an escort if you're still just coming out of a class then... Not that I trust you to find me and lead me safely back to your halls anyway."

"Okay. Well, the performance is Halloween, so why don't you come the day before? Then you have a couple of days, or you can leave when you get sick of me and still have time to make it to the airport?"

"This is what I'm talking about. Organisation! See, it wasn't that hard, was it?"

"No," I admitted. "Well, thinking of being organised... I don't think I've got much chance of making it to orchestra practice in time now."

"Oh, run along then. Just... Before I hang up... Are you okay? I mean I just burst right out into all my own stuff without even being halfway polite and I am really bad at being polite, but I should, especially when I'm coming to visit you and—"

"I'm fine," I said to stop her talking before she could challenge me for my mad babbling crown. The next thing I thought was asking myself if I should tell her that I was seriously considering that something odd might be going on here, whatever the Piper thought.

I still didn't want her worrying, sure, but now I was thinking about it, I *really* didn't want her to get all enthusiastic either, poking around my new friends and insulting them and asking obnoxious, embarrassing questions like she had done to insinuate herself with us when we first met her. It would ruin everything nice that I had going here. I might be odd, clumsy and frequently late, but my reputation was no greater than anyone else's: those things were just something cute about me, rather than something that they planned their lives around. And I was doing my best to keep it that way.

"How are you?" I extremely lamely concluded when I could think of nothing else to say.

"Yeah, I'm good," Alana said with an equal lack of enthusiasm. There was an awkward silence filled with exactly the same sort of melancholy quiet as I'd just projected at her.

"Okay then, I'll see you soon!" I babbled down the line and hung up before I could even hear her response.

I legged it across campus to the music rooms.

*

Even though I got there five minutes late, I was still not the last person in: as I was trying to tune up my mandolin as fast as I could while it scowled at me, unamused at the treatment, the practice room door creaked open again and Rose poked her head around it.

"Oh good, you're all here," she said, a grin breaking out on her round face. She sidled in, hoiking her guitar through just before the heavy door closed itself with a sticky sealing sound.

"What are you doing here?" Molly asked flatly, scowling over her viola, which she already had resting on her shoulder.

"Ally said you were practising tonight?" Rose said innocently, edging towards a seat on the end of the row.

Molly turned to give me a look that almost matched my instrument for unwarranted fury, but she attempted politeness again as she returned her gaze to Rose, though her displeasure at her unzipping her guitar case were obvious. Molly was still a decade or so from being one of those women who were always running around local community centres and churches organising things, but she was already radiating the same energy as someone who sat on six different boards.

"I'm sorry, but we've been learning these songs all month... I just don't think you could pick up the whole set before Halloween. Why don't you come back next month to learn our Christmas songs?"

"Aw, fuck *Jingle Bells*... I like the songs you're doing now. Come on, I can play them all, and you know it."

Molly had gone so rigid I thought she was rocking slightly on the spot, but she knew she didn't have the authority to tell anyone to leave for empty personal reasons... And Rose had paid the two pound membership fee to the Students' Union. Legally, *anyone* with an SU card could crash this society and demand to sit on stage and pluck a rubber band stretched across a jam jar and Molly could only nod and smile and find them the right rubber bands to be in key for each song.

"Well, try to keep up, then. And for God's sake, I know you bragged about your collection... Get yourself a more classical instrument for the performance. This isn't a rock band."

Rose plucked a string, producing a muted twang from her electric guitar. "It's not even plugged in, Molls."

Molly blocked Rose out entirely and began quickly talking us through the next song that we'd all forgotten since last week, the end of her nose a distinct shade of pink darker than it had been earlier. She got to work making groups of us play our individual parts so she could pinpoint who was making us sound bad.

Rose came and plonked herself down on the end of the line. "Well, that wasn't too bad," she said, grinning casually like she argued with people like that all the time. Someone who smiled like that could never lose. Just like someone who ended up cringing in the way I did never truly won. I could only be grateful Rose didn't feel like bossing me around.

"You shouldn't wind her up," I said, and because of what I'd just been thinking was immediately aware of how whining and prissy that sounded.

Rose didn't seem to care that I was being a snivelling suck up, though, and just offered me a cookie. She was so freaking cool.

Molly picked on Lucia to play a few lines, and with her eye turned our way I quickly dropped eye contact with Rose in case she felt like saying anything else and getting me in trouble with Molly and oh my gods Ally you can be pathetic sometimes.

I leaned across to see what Lucia was playing, to take my mind off things, and did my best to follow the tune on the sheet music, since I was also just now learning to read sheet music again after a decade break when I stopped taking keyboard lessons with Teb on account of still being grade zero when she was grade two.

The photocopied sheet music propped up on Lucia's fancy music stand was actually sort of yellow and battered, the corners bent and the edges soft. A name that was not Lucia's pretty French name was scrawled across the top in mostly-faded pencil.

When Molly turned her attention to Amir, next down the line, I had a Topic of Conversation (capitalisation required) on hand. "Do you think Molly's done this before?" I whispered to Rose and Lucia. "The sheet music is all second-hand."

"Maybe she killed the last group because they weren't playing to her standards," Rose suggested sourly.

Lucia twiddled a loose curl (she still hadn't learnt) and seemed unimpressed with my Topic of Conversation, even though she deigned to reply. "She found it when she was getting us music stands in the first week. There were piles of music for a Hallowe'en theme, and thirteen parts as well. She just had to change a couple around because of the different instruments and, well…"

"We have fewer violins and more… you," Rose gestured at me as she finished that thought for Lucia.

"*Thanks.*"

"Come on, Lucia makes fun of how you play all the time."

I shrugged. Somehow, coming from Rose, it meant more. She wasn't capable of joking around in the same way. She was someone who everything seemed so certain. She never doubted anything she said, and jokes seemed flat coming from her mouth, because you had to take a few steps back to see she'd not meant it seriously. After waiting three seconds to laugh, a laugh never sounded genuine either.

"I suppose it saved us some money in photocopying," I eventually whispered, feeling I couldn't just leave the conversation there or it would get all awkward and I was trying so hard not to be awkward here. "About enough for…"

"A packet of biscuits?" They were out again. Maybe Rose offered them when she thought she'd offended me, but they certainly eased things a bit, and I happily took one. She definitely seemed to care about us, at least in the sense that we three needed each other's snark and perspective to survive the seminars together.

I looked up and saw Molly watching us, and I could tell her patience was wearing a little thinner. She wasn't looking at me: it was Rose she was saving her glaring for.

As I was trying not to crunch my cookie disruptively loudly, Rose carried on a thought: "You know, using the old sheet music, the old stands... It's almost like the old orchestra is still with us."

"Don't be so morbid!" I complained, spraying biscuit crumbs, surprised into a too-loud yelp. I guiltily wiped down the Mandolin of Motherly Guilt with my sleeve. It scowled back at me.

Lucia gestured her music. "The last person wrote their name on this sheet; they were called Sanchez."

"Well that ruins things," I complained. "Can't be mysterious now. It's almost like they're in the room with us." I glanced over at Rose and, thinking of being mysterious, she was grinning in an awfully dark way, like we just amused her. The devilish look made me wonder what it was she had really been thinking. She had said "ghost" first, and now this? If we were playing supernatural chicken, seeing who would say something that showed we *knew*, then she had lost. But if she wasn't playing chicken in the first place...

And if that was the case...

"Alright, stop chatting," Molly complained. "Let's get a run-through of this all together now... And I *mean* that. Ally, pay attention to the chord changes."

I nodded, and lifted my mandolin. "Ready."

"Not if you're holding it like that. That's better. Okay, I'll count in two for you, then another three for everyone else."

You know what? People *were* changing their behaviour to make room for my incompetence. I had already lost that battle.

As we began twanging and screeching our way through the opening notes (okay, maybe that was just a select few inept players), I closed my eyes and concentrated on the music, paying more attention to what notes were dancing all around me than any time we'd played before. I hadn't listened this intently to a song since perhaps the first time the Piper had played for me.

Now that I was trying to hear something strange it didn't seem hard at all to make out the extra voices around us. They were actually playing a lot better than us: I wished Molly could hear them and then maybe she wouldn't be so harsh on us.

Surely, despite the creepiness of this, there was nothing inherently wrong with them? I hoped? I couldn't imagine a group of mysterious music players deciding to join in with us being a bad thing, since I didn't *think* they were enchanting me. I didn't feel any urge to get up and dance and not stop, and aside from all the anxiety, which I could fully credit to my own personality, they weren't sending me into any melancholy or whatever else dramatic emotional swooning that would be suitably poetic for this concept.

We'd see how I was after this session. If I fell into a dreamlike state where only listening to more of their music would satisfy me, refusing to eat or sleep and so on, then we probably had a problem with them.

I mean, maybe there was just a group of goblins who really liked music and wanted to join in with us. I couldn't complain, not with the performance looming over us and needing all the help we could get. Maybe they'd elves and the shoemaker our playing style for us or something. Tune up our mandolins in the night to sound perfect. I wasn't going to be the narc who spied on them and left a bowl of milk and ruined the whole thing.

"Ally! Are you going to keep playing all night? The rest of us stopped three bars ago!" Molly snapped, cutting through my daze. Hehe, oops. What did I say about being enchanted?

My eyes refocused on the room to find everyone staring at me, but by now I could only go a little pink: if I crawled under my chair to die every time I messed up I really would have spent most of my time down there. Molly had her hands on her hips, but there was an exasperated smile on her face, a bit of the kindness which, despite how virulently annoyed she got at Rose, had tempered her into someone who had helped me learn to play and I did sort of see as a music mentor.

"At least you've got the hang of it now."

"I was playing it right?" I asked, amazed.

"Mostly," she admitted. "After we finish focussing on this show I'll definitely give you some more complicated parts to do. I was thinking if it goes well we will definitely have a go at a Christmas recital."

"Oh... Yay." I tried to give her a big wide smile, but I don't know how well it came across.

"Come on, everyone can play *Jingle Bells*," Lucia said encouragingly.

My mind set at ease for having come up with a nice simple solution for what the strange extra music was all about (definitely some bored goblins), I got my smile back quickly enough and enjoyed the rest of the music we played a little more normally... And messed it up a bit more normally too.

# L Bar

After practice Rose called quite loudly, "We're going to the bar! Anyone who wants to join is welcome!"

"Who's 'we'?" Lucia asked snidely, raising both her thinly-plucked eyebrows quizzically. No one around here seemed to have learned the trick that Teb had spent hours honing in the mirror of only raising one at a time. Effort, yes, for quite a silly thing, but the resulting expression had a great deal more practical application. I think I just really missed Teb's sarcastic look right about then.

"Well, you guys are coming, right?" Rose asked, not bothered by the less than interrogative stare.

"Oh, why not," Lucia sighed, because unlike my friends who stand rabidly by a principal that they have declared themselves for, people in the real world were often quite flexible and subtle in their approach to situations.

"I can come," Amir said at once. It really seemed like the squad was assembling. Except I was borderline stress meltdown from balancing the whole goblin thing with… reality for starters.

"Uh, sorry to ditch you all a second night running. I'm meeting with my boyfriend later," I said. "I need to make him dinner or he never eats." The fact that he didn't need to was completely by the by. I liked doing it.

"Pfft, he should be left to starve then," Lucia replied. I'd heard her feminist views before as she sounded off on a particularly misogynistic text our lecturers found, and I did sort of agree when it didn't apply to me. Or my weird boyfriend.

"Trouble is he won't," I grumbled, more to myself than to them as Amir went for a high five at that. Lucia looked at me all confused, but Rose clapped me on the shoulder. "Phone him up and he can buy you food at the bar. We'll go to L Bar since they do food. Settled!"

Sam joined us as we went to the door, I think just because we were proposing something social to do and he didn't want to miss out on a chance to drink. Or make fun of me. "Someone has to keep you girls out of trouble," he said, grinning at us.

"And I look after you so you don't do karaoke again," Amir laughed. Sam scowled as Amir winked at me—I took that to mean it was payback for Sam laying all the blame for our bad playing on me. Happy as he may have been, Amir had to know that he still had a lot of work to do if he wanted to play well. I just struggled so hard to understand those who were perpetually chill.

As we went down the rattling stairs, Lucia cleared her throat. "Ally? Aren't you going to call your *mysterious boyfriend?*"

"Oh, right," I said, completely lacking any convincing acting skills to make it sound like I'd just forgotten.

Of course, he probably already knew where we were heading and that he was invited along: it wasn't like he read my mind all the time, but shortly before he was meant to meet me he would be keeping an ear out to see if I was running late (likely) and if I was still up for seeing him, or if I was in a bad mood and just wanted to sink into bed with Oscar Wilde (um, his complete works, that is, not the long-dead gay playwright himself, which would be extremely odd and disgusting for him if he were fully resurrected and even more disgusting for me if he were not).

I took out my phone and, feeling rather strange about calling the Piper when I never normally bothered, selected the number that I had him saved under. I sometimes wondered if he actually had a phone. I'd never seen him with it.

The Piper answered right away, but the echoing Latin service in the background made me think that this may not have been the best time to drop him a line.

"Busy?" I asked.

"Give me a minute to poke this Cardinal awake before he has a dream encounter that will lead him to write a book on the true language of the angels that will plunge all religions in the world into a bloody global war," he hissed.

The mumbling sermon rambled on in the background and I almost missed my footing on the metal stairs as I wondered if he was crashing midnight mass in the Vatican. Much closer to the microphone there was a rustling nudge, a snort and the beginning of a confused foreign expletive (did you have to swear in Latin in Vatican City?) before an embarrassed silence. The Pope kept on mumbling, seeming not to notice. The noises cut off suddenly to be replaced with a background noise of campus chatter and the sound of the annoying Latin music (the other sort of Latin) that L Bar played. "I'll see you in a minute," he said.

"Okay!" I said brightly and hung up. Hey, he averted the war... What was there to freak out over? Some variation on this was definitely an uncomfortably common coping thought I had every day or so.

Lucia was looking at me in an *extremely* confused way now. "He can't come?" she guessed, from my extremely limited end of the conversation.

"No, he'll be there!"

"But... You didn't say where we were going!"

"Oh... Oops!"

I put my phone back into my pocket.

*

He was sitting outside L Bar on the cold, damp grass, eyes closed, face turned up to the sky. Outdoors was much more his sort of place, and I felt almost guilty at the thought of dragging him into a hot and cramped bar.

"There's no one sitting at the outside tables," I started to say.

"Because it's *freezing*," Lucia said at once, cutting short my proposition that we sit there.

"Ew, no surprise. Look at that weird hobo sitting there as well," Sam explained, pointing completely unsubtly at the Piper. There was the slight matter of his glamour spell which made introducing him to other people a little awkward. While it made working under the radar very easy for him, it did get a little embarrassing in social situations. I knew he was a clean, well-employed guy, but to others...

"Just because he has dreadlocks does not make him homeless!" I burst out. "He's wearing perfectly normal, clean clothes and *happens* to be my boyfriend!"

"Dread—" Lucia said, making a double take. She blinked uncomfortably, then shrugged it off, telling herself that he had looked like my interpretation of the Piper all along. Rose burst out laughing at this social awkwardness, punching Sam playfully on the shoulder. Sam at least looked a bit embarrassed, but he also looked rather less like he was going to chase my boyfriend away.

At least none of them had ever seen him before (I assumed so), leaving me free to shape their first impression as much as I liked. Alana had known him longer than I had, and I was pretty sure saw something completely different. Teb had met him around the same time as me, but since she'd lost her memory of all that, likewise had her own version of the Piper that she used to fill in the blank. Usually with weird comments about celebrities he reminded her of that day.

Hearing that I'd dealt with the sticky business of introductions, the Piper opened his eyes and stood up. I skipped over and hugged him. "Hey!" I said, turning to gesture broadly at my friends. He'd know which was which. "This is Lucia, Amir, Rose and Sam... Guys, this is my boyfriend, um..."

"Call me the Piper." He glanced at me, a sly grin coming to his face. "Hippie parents."

I pulled a face at him. I don't know how he could joke when he obviously had the worse deal: even my middle name wasn't as bad as trying to pass off his title as a given name, and my mum had been obsessed with this book about the Classical world when she'd been pregnant with me.

"Come on," Lucia said, hopping from foot to foot. "It's cold enough to freeze your bum off out here."

"Only if you sat on the grass like the Piper," I said helpfully.

My contribution to society did nothing to stop us from all being herded into the warmth of the bar. Lucia visibly deflated in the muggy nacho-and-beer-smelling air. The boys both instantly walked up to the bar to begin elbowing their way to the front of the queue.

"Are both of you going up?" Lucia asked, looking between me and the Piper. "Only it'd be nice if someone could save us a table. It's filling up fast."

"Oh, um, aren't I?"

"Dinner's on me," the Piper said, taking me by the shoulders and rotating me in the direction of an empty table long enough to accommodate our group. I went off to spread out as many of my possessions as I could to ensure that it remained free, like a dog scent-marking the table but nowhere near as gross because we were going to eat here.

Some guys dressed as sexy (female) nurses, with the obligatory L Bar sombrero on, came and sniffed at our spot, but I gave them my best weird bug-eyed stare and they decided that they were too drunk to make the required fuss to get me to surrender the table. They moved on, followed a minute later by a gaggle more of what I took to be the hockey team in their downtime, from the way some of the sombrero-sporting nurses also had their hockey sticks still with them. I was pretty sure the visuals in a student bar were enough to make me think that the world really had been slacking with what odd stuff I'd seen before I left home. Baseline normality was resetting every day.

The rest of my group came back wearing sombreros and carrying drinks. The Piper looked especially ridiculous with two of the hats stacked atop his head to leave both hands free for carrying our drinks. He'd got a black and a white hat, and a lemonade and a cola. Aww. After he'd put the drinks down he plonked the black sombrero on my head. It was made of cheap itchy paper or something, snagging my hair as it slid ill-fittingly down over my eyes. Truly it was a headpiece only to be enjoyed by the stupidly drunk. I figured all the food and drinks here would be a lot cheaper without Sombrero Tax included as well.

"Oh, don't give her the black one," Lucia complained. "It looks like a straw witch hat on her, and that's just tacky."

"It is nearly Halloween," I said, fingering the colourful paper ribbon threaded around the brim. "I could probably pull this out and put a few fake cobwebs on it... Instant costume." I followed it up with a weird witchy cackle. Lucia edged back in her chair.

"We should dress up for the performance," Sam said. "You'd make a good ghost, maybe. Drape you in chains or something..."

"Pfft!" Lucia said, pretending to smack him. Her elbow caught her drink: half of us seemed to dive for it at once, but it was over on the table, a long splash of sambuca down Rose's front.

Lucia froze and winced: she looked terrified. "Oh my *God*. I am so sorry, Rose... here, let me get some napkins..."

Pretending like it wasn't weird for someone to look far more terrified than embarrassed over an incident like that, Rose shrugged, "Don't worry about it." She brushed down the wet patch with her sleeve and wrinkled her nose.

"Are you just going to sit there dripping?" I asked, feeling somewhat dense. I mean, Rose was scary. I knew why Lucia looked so freaked out, but Rose was being way *too* calm.

She scowled harder, but by that point she was somehow making a scene by doing nothing at all except for being uncomfortably wet and sticky.

With a sort of implied "Fine!" in her actions, she suddenly ripped off her hoodie, bundled it up in her lap and folded her arms tightly across her chest, not even attempting to fix the mess whipping a jumper over her head did to her loose, wavy hair. She stubbornly blew at a strand of it hanging into her face.

There was one of those awful awkward moments where no one really knew where to look, because we'd all been looking so curiously at Rose, in a way we wouldn't have if she'd just squealed like a normal girl and flung her jumper at Lucia in revenge. Just for a moment we got a flash of pale arms as she yanked the hoodie off, before she folded them firmly under her chest, we saw there was something clearly wrong with them. The first two things that jumped to mind for me in that moment were serial self-harm or drug abuse, and that was why all of us were suddenly examining our coasters or drinks like they contained TV sets. Or a guide on what to say next.

It was Rose who saved us from speculating on what the flash of scars and discoloured skin might have been. "So, Piper," she said, leaning forward with her arms folded on the table and hands closed over the flesh on her inner elbows, "What do you do?"

"I don't study here," he said automatically. Of course, he wasn't shifting uncomfortably in his chair in the first place. He must have seen worse every day.

"You and Ally are awfully good at not answering questions." She said it with a sort of smirk, like she was so proud to prove that other people had stuff to hide.

"I work in repairs," he said. "I travel around a lot."

"Repairs? You're a handyman?"

"I do a bit of everything. I'm also very good at music."

"Piping?"

"I'm cursed with it."

"You took up playing... pipes... because your parents named you Piper?" Sam said scathingly. "That's just sad."

The Piper shrugged it off with a mild smile.

"Wait..." Lucia said, squinting at the Piper. "When you say you play music... Are you a rock star? You look just like that guy in that band..." Oh dear, the glamour was beginning to shape him again to them. Why did people always insist on seeing such stupid things? Clearly my slightly hallucinatory vision of the Piper was the only true one. Whatever Alana had complained about cultural appropriation and projecting in some long rant she cracked out whenever the subject came up.

"Nah, they're a Scottish band," Rose said. "He's not got the right accent."

"What do you mean by 'piping'?" Amir asked, grinning and a few seconds behind as he translated in his head. He wasn't doing half-badly considering I'd basically witnessed his entire progress learning conversational English since he arrived in the country two months ago knowing what you need to be a maths whizz and not much else.

The Piper responded by pulling out a slim wooden recorder from the inside pocket of his jacket, pale wood at the mouth part, the body a dark, polished brown.

"Oh put it away," I laughed. "No one will hear you over *this* racket anyway."

He just seemed to take that as a challenge and blew a dozen quick, high notes in succession. The thumping music faded out and, proof of miracles, the eighty drunken, laughing, self-absorbed students in the bar all shut up, even the hockey team. The Piper didn't stop to admire his handiwork, even as all our mouths dropped. Yes, even mine. I'd accepted he was magic. This was just... unreal. I mean, pixies were one thing, but students? No one could control them.

He just launched right into a quick, jaunty tune, good for dancing. The beat had not vanished entirely... In fact, was it still playing, uninterrupted, outside the bubble of this table? No one in the room was looking around at us, and the sole source of sound in the room, to see why they'd been silenced.

Yet while no one had been really dancing yet, the evening still in a state of meeting friends, getting meals and ordering the first drinks, suddenly the dance floor at the back of the pub was filling up. Within a few seconds at least a dozen people were dancing in a manic way, as if feeling totally unobserved by the world. I grinned, though my friends were looking downright baffled.

The Piper wound up his song and the music resumed, rather a lot quieter than before. If that was just his way of calling across the bar, "Turn it down, mate!" then I was impressed. Most of the dancers staggered back to their seats and carried on their conversations from before, pretending like nothing had happened.

A girl with a ridiculous fake moustache and an apron tied in a way it might have been more appropriate to call it a corset came out with a plate of nachos for Sam. It shook us out of our music-induced daze. I don't think they realised quite how powerful the song had been. The first time I had heard him play I'd completely lost myself and I actually hardly remember the moment any more, no matter how central an event it had been in my life. It all drifted away like trying to remember a dream. Not to mention, you know. Tanya being punted into the fairy world for the first time as a result of it.

"Definitely should have a word with Molly about playing with us," Lucia said, stealing a nacho from Sam before he could crunch them all up.

"Impressive. Have a cookie." There was a smirk to the way Rose said that, and I realised with a start that I should have not been including her in the bedazzled section. Instead she was playing a solo piece of amusement. It was the same expression of "aw, how cute" that the Piper used on me.

The waitress (who, I think, was in my Modernism class) came back and announced some enchiladas with the least enthusiasm I have ever heard anyone ever use. It was like there wasn't even a single note to her voice.

"Here," the Piper said, and we got a plate of cheesy Mexican food to share. I dug in, and as soon as I had alarming spices dancing around in my mouth I felt genuinely contented. I've heard somewhere that the act of eating together bonds groups or something, and sitting here in the bar with a group of people who seemed to be, well, my friends... It made me happy. Huh.

"So why cookies then?" The Piper asked, and I felt a stab of annoyance. Wait, he was paying attention to Rose still? How dare he find her belittling amusement at him provocative! I'd always thought he had an ego problem. Which could be excused for what he was, but this was me time.

Rose was still giving him all her attention and a truly devastating grin as she shrugged. "I like them."

"A bit too much," I heard Sam mumble beside me. I turned and tried to give him Teb's look, but actually I found his criticisms quite refreshing when they weren't levelled at me. Due to a total lack of a bold and threatening aura on my part, he failed to notice my look anyway and got on with spooning salsa onto his plate.

I turned my attention to eating, trying not to look like I was watching the Piper and Rose talk back and forth. The enchiladas felt far more greasy and miserable in my mouth than they had before.

"And you're a part of this orchestra now?" he enquired.

Did he know Rose from somewhere? What did 'now' mean? Was she another Alana, scooped up from peril and turned into a cuddly, cookie-eating girl who did normal things like a Literature degree? It would explain her uncanny comments about ghosts she'd been teasing me with.

"I play guitar." She didn't seem too bothered by the questioning, or to have even noticed the Piper's interest in her, despite how he'd been showing off for her. She replied casually, rolling her eyes often, nibbling a breadstick. His performance was meant to have told her something, I realised. A business card pushed her way. She'd picked it up, I could tell that. I didn't know what she wanted from him... Or what he wanted from her. And that made me a little scared and confused. I mean, he was everywhere at once. He fixed everything. How could he not have met everyone at least once, even if they didn't know it themselves?

But she was carrying on now with an incredible poker face.

"I started with a lyre, obviously, but I didn't want to carry it around on campus."

"They sound expensive," Lucia commented.

Rose nodded. "Yeah, mine is quite an antique. So I got a second-hand guitar just so as I'd have something to play while I was here."

"Same guitar as Jimi," Amir put in.

I turned to look at him. "Hendrix?"

He grinned at me. Like, *of course* there's only one Jimi.

"Right," I mumbled. I looked over at Rose. "Not *the* same guitar?" I asked, my head still swimming a little with confusion. That old sense of believing anything was back.

She winked at me. "You never know, when you get something second-hand."

I looked down at my enchiladas, and decided I really just wanted to go to bed. I stood up. "I'm... I'm going to go," I said.

"What! No, stay!" Lucia protested at once.

"I just feel tired, sorry," I said. "I think it's too warm in here or something."

"We could sit outside," she said remorsefully, and I felt bad for making her feel like it was her fault for driving me away.

"No, I want to go lie down," I said, and before they could make any more protestations I grabbed my mandolin and fled from the bar.

*

"Ally, wait, where are you going?" The Piper appeared alongside me, skipping the part where he ran after me entirely. I had always felt like that was sort of a requirement for a situation like this, so I kept on walking, ignoring him. If he wasn't going to run he didn't deserve my attention.

I didn't want to go back to my room, where anything that I shouted at him would be heard by everyone on my floor, regardless of whether they believed in ghosts or not. So instead I headed for the one reliably soundproofed place that I knew. The Piper followed helplessly after me, but at least he didn't, like, teleport ahead of me.

The wrought iron gate between the theatre's rickety steps and the last flight of stairs to the music rooms weren't locked: perhaps Molly had forgotten, or perhaps someone was staying even later than we ever did. I stomped up the stairs and let myself into our practice room, flinging myself down on one of the creaking plastic chairs once I was inside.

The Piper followed me in, closed and locked the door, then knelt in front of me. He pulled one of my hands loose from my furiously folded arms and squeezed it.

"What's wrong, Ally?"

"Don't you know?" I asked, my voice wobbling. Forget everything else— this was shaking my faith in *him*. "Can't you feel it? I'm noticing weird stuff all over the place again! Who is Rose? How do you know her?"

"She reminds me of an old friend."

"Oh, so you were *just* flirting with her?" I sniffed.

"Of course not!" he looked horrified.

"And what about that weird ghostly music?! I've heard it both of the last times we've practised. And once in my lectures, I think! It was even stronger this time! How can you not know what it is?"

"I have never heard it myself," he admitted. "I don't come to your practices; you banned me in very strong terms. For all I know, it could be anything."

"But, but, but, you have to be able to sense all the things being out of whack all the time. Like, that's your job!"

He looked around the room thoughtfully. "Certainly there's no trace of anything magical in here right now. I'm sorry, I can only sense what things are wrong that I have to handle—cosmic imbalance, egregious magical justice errors, the flow and interplay between the many realms of the world. Sometimes I have to admit something isn't my business. This might be too small for it to get to my inbox."

I didn't know how harassing my old history teacher was of cosmic importance, but whatever. "Well fine, come tomorrow then. Tell me what you hear. I can handle anything if I know I'm not the only one."

"Ally…" Well, he sounded like he was about to ask the worst question ever, from the cautious way he tried to put it to me; "Is this about your mother?"

"You are *terrible* at this boyfriending business."

"It's just that you seem so certain that you are going to lose your sanity… Well, I'm worried that it's actually pushing you closer to the edge, just because you're so sure it's going to happen. You're like her but that doesn't mean you're the same person, or predestined to follow the exact same pattern as she did. You aren't doing any drugs, you already *know* about magic and spend a lot of your time in the presence of, well, me, and it's doing you no damage. I don't know what you *couldn't* meet these days and come away with your sanity intact. You are stronger and more sensible in many ways. Remember that you are the sum of *both* of your parents."

I nodded, trying not to start crying and looking ridiculously unbalanced in spite of his speech. It all sounded so obvious when he said it like that. Words spilled out of me along with the stupid tears I couldn't stop. "And Dad is so dull... And you're so magic and wonderful! I'm nothing like Mum was in university!"

"So you don't think that you're going to go crazy anymore?"

I reluctantly shook my head as he reached up and wiped a tear away with his thumb, the action making my heart flip. Truth be told, I hadn't really been looking forward to going insane very much. Perhaps I could let this part of my life plan go.

"I'm sorry I called you a rubbish boyfriend," I mumbled. "You're awesome."

"Were you really jealous of Rose?"

"A bit," I admitted. "You just seemed to know something about her that I didn't. Or... To know her in a way that you don't know me."

"I am afraid that it's an occupational hazard that I know a lot of people that you don't. And I would rather not go into the way that I might know her."

"Wait, you were just saying she *reminded* you of someone."

He smiled, not meeting my eye. "I'd rather she only *did* remind me of someone."

"What's the deal then? Who is she?"

"Can I please beg official business? I don't want you freaking out any more tonight."

"Freaking out?" I paused. "Wait, so. Something about Rose is... Oh! You can't tell me to calm down then say something like that! Now I'm just going to go crazy wondering who she is and what she did! I mean, um, not go crazy... I have got to cut that sort of language out of my vocabulary."

"Ally, you *know* I'm off the clock when I'm with you. If I started telling you everything about my work... if I started sharing the things I knew about the places you go and the people you talk to, you would end up like another Alana. And I don't want that. You're special to me because you are somehow still so untainted by this world. No matter what you see, you look at it with innocent eyes. I couldn't begin to start tarnishing it all for you."

"I look at it innocently and then freak out," I grumbled.

"It's endearing," he said, leaning over to kiss me on the forehead.

I blinked stupidly for a second, then slid off the chair, somehow managing not to kick him anywhere as I landed on his lap. I looked down at him, taking in his face as long as I could. As much as I tried to see it, I could never fully bring back what he had looked like in my memory. That first time I'd seen him in the fairy world, when he had come to help us bring my friends home, I'd thought I would never forget. All I'd found of that weird unearthly beauty since then was the stark white eyes which had overridden my image when I looked at him of the admittedly still cold but at least *human* grey eyes I'd first known him to have. And of everything on his face, the white eyes were things of his magic side that I least wanted to see. Interesting as they were, they made him yet more unreadable, and that was saying something.

I just had to hope that they reflected deep inside the same care for me that that he eventually got around to showing on the surface.

I suddenly felt self-conscious, fearing that my attempted gaze into his eyes had opened me up while telling me nothing about him, and I dived in for a kiss before he thought that I was worried or regretting something. My lips smushed into his chin and split as my teeth followed.

"Fuff," I said, leaning back and pressing a hand against my mouth to stop the sudden blossoming of blood which was gushing (possibly) from my face.

He laughed awkwardly and produced a string of black and white handkerchiefs from his pocket. I grabbed a black one and began dabbing at my mouth.

"Try closing your eyes *after* you've navigated your way to my face," he suggested, rubbing his own chin.

"Mrff," I said snidely, finding it hard to be witty with a hanky shoved in my mouth. I looked away out of a desperation not to see how amused he was. My eye fell on a couple of sheets of music lying on the floor, about where Rose had been sitting. I'd have said anyone else would have accidentally dropped them, but I had a feeling she just hadn't been bothered enough to want to take them. She probably knew the songs already anyhow.

What interested me though was I'd worked that out myself (go me!), because the sheet of paper had a completely different name on, not one from anyone in our little orchestra. If I wasn't going crazy then the odd stuff that was happening had to have an external influence. And there was maybe a whole second group of people who hopefully would know all about it, having lived the experience of playing these songs once before.

I slid away from the Piper and grabbed the dropped paper.

"Tori Michaels… I need to find this person." I looked around hopefully, I suppose expecting an approving nod.

"You probably shouldn't have tried talking yet," he said, making a gesture at his own mouth.

I clamped the handkerchief back over my face. But the Piper's poker face actually told me more than any patronizingly encouraging one. I shoved the pages into my bag. "To the internet!" I declared in a muffled way.

"You do know that the internet doesn't have an actual physical location, right?"

"Shut up, I'd feel too embarrassed to start yelling 'back to my bedroom!' to you."

"You only had to ask," he laughed, suddenly grinning cheekily.

I scowled and stomped out of the room. Really, he wound me up.

# Field Trip

"Tea first, investigation second," I decided, repeatedly jabbing my card key into the slot on the front door of Sherrick Hall. The walk had calmed me a little bit, but I remained determined. The Piper was still following me for some reason. At least he gave me an excuse to vocalise my thoughts without feeling slightly mental for talking to myself. Not mental. I wasn't going crazy.

"I'd never even realised until now, but if there were other people who'd played this, maybe they did something, or something happened to them when they were playing it which is causing the weird things I can hear *now*," I explained, after nervously poking my lip and checking my fingertip for blood. Encouraged, I continued laying out my theory. "Therefore there has to be someone I can contact and ask about it! And everyone's online these days! I just need to go on Facebook and search up any of the people I can find from our old music sheets and ask *them* what happened."

"Try putting the key in and leaving it for a second," he said, leaning on the cold brick wall like he was skulking dramatically in the shadows, perhaps pretending he didn't know me. "I don't think you're meant to swipe it like that."

I considered telling him to shut up again, but I tried it and the door clicked open. "Yeah, but it doesn't always work like that," I mumbled.

"Uhuh."

We went halfway up the stairs and bumped into three of my floor buddies coming the other way (yes, they knew that I called them that, but they hadn't laughed at me for saying it as much as I thought they would have done).

"Hey Ally! We're going to the big Tescos. Wanna come?" Angie had her own car as well as her own TV, and it made the trip infinitely easier for me, since the other way to get out there involved two buses and fifteen minutes total walking time in between them. I'd been living out of the little student shop for the past three weeks.

I looked imploringly at the Piper. He gave me an unimpressed look which said, "You have half a bag of pasta and an onion left to your name. You need proper sustenance."

"Alright," I sighed. "Can you wait two minutes for me to drop off my mandolin and get my money and shopping bags?"

"It'll take her that long to open the door," the Piper commented. They giggled. I had a feeling that the people on my floor liked him more than me.

"Sure." Angie and co. instantly broke into casual lounging poses, leaning on any available surface the stairwell offered.

"Are you going to wait here, or..." I started to ask the Piper, thinking I must have stretched his patience an unbelievable amount already today.

Angie interrupted: "Your weird boyfriend can come too. There's room in the car." Her voice echoed after us as we rounded the stairs onto our landing, me taking them two at a time.

"They call you weird to your face," I grumbled once we were in the more muffled hall B.

"To be fair, neither of us know how they really see me... And she seems to mean it in a friendly way in any case."

"Well, at least she doesn't think you are some sort of stinky old homeless guy," I sighed.

Story of my life, that.

*

Being freakishly tall has several advantages, prime among them being that I rarely get crammed into the middle seat in the back of a car. But Angie, easily the most and, in fact, only petite one among us, was driving. Dave from B9, Mike, The Piper and I were all hanging on one side or the other of six foot, and the only reason I was the second shortest was because they were all lanky giants.

At least, as far as I was aware the Piper was taller than me. Technically he sort of came from the Middle Ages, and people *were* shorter back then. I was not going to dwell on it in case I woke up the next day and found myself looking down on him, my personal glamour ruined forever.

I bunched myself up as small as possible and cuddled up against the Piper. Even with a few of the awkward personal space barriers I'd have felt with anyone else broken down, I felt like I was going to be crushed every time

Angie cornered and Mike was propelled into me. Somehow despite this being the oldest car that could fart its way along the road she was getting it up to dangerously boy-racer-ish speeds on the ring road.

"Why are you still here?" I muttered to the Piper under cover of the awful cheesy music that Angie had permission to play as the only one with a driving licence. Anyone who complained could walk back, as she had already threatened Michael with.

When the Piper frowned at me, I added, "You know, you should go off repeatedly saving the world or something?"

"I rarely actually *save* it from anything. That's not even in my job description. But I can go out and protect it any time I like. In fact, I was just in New Orleans."

"What? When?"

"Right now, as we were talking."

"And you didn't take me? Wait... Have you been popping off to foreign countries any time we hang out? How long do you go for!?"

"Um... First you were worried that I *wasn't* doing my job, and now you're annoyed that I was?"

"No! I mean... Maybe a bit. Oh, I don't know. How do you even do it anyway? I never notice when you are gone."

"It's a Santa Claus thing. I couldn't take you—imperceptibly—because you humans insist on time moving with you wherever you go. You don't know the first thing about a truly endless moment."

I raised my head from his shoulder and met his eyes. After about an eternity I thought, "You have no idea what you're talking about."

Somewhere in the distance Angie said in rail-announcer perfect tones complete with robotic pause, "We will shortly be arriving at... Tescos."

*

We grabbed a trolley each and set off in a procession of hungry students. I paused to examine a two-for-one deal on doughnuts and looked up to see the others were vanishing over the horizon: Angie had veered off at once to look at the cheap clothes and the boys wandered off into the aisles of technology and DVDs and what have you. I kept a straight course for the affordable unhealthy food, though.

"Not like I was going to get them anyway," I muttered to myself, shooting one last longing look at the doughnuts before I turned into the first aisle. I rested my arms on the handle of the trolley and leaned into it, propelling it forwards. I squinted along it like I was piloting it through dangerous skies. Considering the very first thing that happened to me was that I had to swerve to avoid an old man on a mobility scooter wearing an RAF hat, I was clearly in a bit of trouble.

"Engage evasive manoeuvres," I said, in what I thought was a thick German accent, and steered towards canned produce, missing out the vegetable aisles completely.

"You don't come here often, do you?" the Piper asked, laughing as he strolled after me.

"Er, not really. I think this is the first time I've left campus properly in a month."

"I can tell. You're having way too much fun. And if you were here every week you'd have a life ban by now."

I stuck my tongue out at him. "Do you ever go shopping?" I asked. "I mean, do you even need to eat at all when I don't make you? Or do you save some of that extra time you make to buy a ham and cheese sandwich and just sit on a park bench and enjoy the view?" I slowed to a dawdle to take in the wall of Tescos Basics tins, rank after rank of spaghetti hoops and baked beans and combinations thereof with little sausages. The identical tins seemed to rise almost to the ceiling, and tall as I was I felt the highest reaches of Mt. Alphabet Soup were unscalable.

"I don't think I have ever been inside a Tescos," the Piper said, picking up a can of baked beans to examine. "And I've been everywhere. Not many world-changing events occur in them. Asda, on the other hand…"

"Shut up."

He grinned at me and I somehow almost rammed the trolley into a ten-year-old boy who was running around waving a huge stalk of Brussels sprouts as if it were a lightsaber.

I cleared my throat and decided the best approach was to treat the Piper as if he were the stupid one. "Well back there you have the expensive fresh produce that little brat was demonstrating for us. Students can't afford to eat it though. And here we have the canned goods that we live off of. For example, buying all the ingredients for sauce is about two pounds, and a jar of really good sauce can be three or more. Yet this insignificant can of tomatoes that costs almost nothing works just as well in their place. And might even have nutrients in it!"

The Piper frowned, lost for a response. After a moment he said, "Fascinating."

"You wait until you see the chalk-derivative called 'cheap bread'."

After a couple more aisles of watching me um and ah over canned food, the Piper said, "I think I understand now. The goal is to buy as much food for as little money as possible, and then you stockpile it in that little tiny room of yours because the lock on the cupboard in the kitchen is broken, and that's how I found you using a giant sack of pasta as a pillow last month."

"Heh, yes."

"You know, I mostly see that behaviour in survival-obsessed people who are convinced the end times are coming. You have the same sort of paranoia about the person eating your Crunch Corners as they do about the radio transmissions their fillings receive."

"Shut up! Someone I think is my friend is clearly taking my delicious desserts and eating them!"

"I'm just worried that I was wrong about you... That you are getting emotionally damaged by the things you've seen and are turning that into a feeling of constantly being under threat, and this is the hidden cost of your exposure to the unseen."

"I do not feel that way!" I stopped the trolley short in the middle of the cereal aisle, turning to look at him with the best expression of incredulous anger I could muster, hoping that it didn't look like I was having a stroke as I screwed up one side of my face. "And if I do it was because I was already slightly unhinged when you met me! Who's to say I wouldn't have been just like this when I went to uni if I'd never met you?!"

He raised his hands. "I didn't mean to make you angry. I just worry about you."

"I can cope!" I snapped. "Life is not as hard as everyone keeps making out like I'll find it!"

"You've clearly mastered the art of shopping on a budget," he said, I think trying to calm me down. But he always had that look like he thought that whatever I was doing or thinking was just adorable, like a puppy who had just identified a high threat level from that long fluffy thing that always seemed to be behind them, no matter how much they rotated on the spot barking angrily.

"It's not funny!" I complained, grabbing a giant box of muesli off the shelf. I pushed the shopping trolley into gear and stomped off.

"Look, it's just..." He jogged for a couple of paces to keep up with me. "Just that to me I can see the whole world is a terrifying thing with an infinite number of ways to harm you. But you're not supposed to know that. You're supposed to just trundle along with your little human life. But now you've been exposed, I feel a greater duty to protect you."

"Well I wasn't worried about these 'infinite ways' until you brought them up. Are you saying that I should be scared?"

"No! I am looking after you. It's just..."

"Just what?"

"Just sometimes I wish that I didn't have to. It's not like I've been going around advertising it, but with the shake-up Teb caused, and her being friends with Alana who's been notorious since I rescued her, and that in turn making everything sit up and wonder what Tanya was going to do next... Well, you're not the odd one out. There's a lot of interest in you as well, because of who your friends are as much as because of me."

"Interest from who... or what?"

"It is better that you don't know."

"Aw, come on. That's your 'I can't talk to you yet' voice. That means trouble and you're going to have to explain eventually."

"No, I don't think so."

"That was not a request. You know how things go. Something will happen eventually."

"And you know how it goes. It's my job to stop it from happening, and my goal is to stop you ever having one of these 'adventures' again."

"You know what, you're really not helping me in any way here. I can finish shopping on my own."

He didn't say anything so I turned around to tell him to shoo, but he had already vanished.

I caught up with Angie in the frozen food aisles, where she seemed to be having an intense moment of contemplation between fish fingers or chicken nuggets.

"Uurgh, boyfriends, am I right?" I sighed, leaning over the freezer to cool my face off from its angry blushing.

"Definitely," she said, not realising she wasn't participating in totally normal human conversation.

"If you get the chicken nuggets I'll get the fish fingers and we can borrow them from each other?" I suggested, feeling enlivened by casual social interaction where no one thought I was a freak.

"Sure!" She beamed at me.

I was probably not engaged in caring and sharing just to prove a point.

# Cheerio

It took forever to pay, wait for the others to do the same and get home. I loaded up the shelves and even dared to put some precious desserts in the fridge (there was *so* not room for a mini fridge in my room). I ate one of the yoghurts while I sat at my desk and waited for my laptop to load up, enjoying the rare moment of having luxury goods to eat. I had the sheet music I'd found on the floor next to me, and I cracked my knuckles, sipped my mug of tea and assumed a serious expression ready to start my investigations.

Finally everything loaded up, but the little icon for the wifi kept flashing red. I clicked it, reentered my password, and then it went grey while it thought. I sat back expectantly.

It went red again.

I got up and, propping open my door with a book, I knocked on Angie's door.

"Ange, do you have an ethernet cable?" I asked. "The wifi's sucking."

"Don't bother, the whole internet is down for Sherrick Hall."

"Probably ghosts. Ha ha."

"Ha," she agreed.

I went back to my room and sank back into my desk chair. Checked my phone data and pulled a face. Well, that investigation lasted a long time.

I decided that, as understanding as professors were of the university lifestyle, I really ought to sleep soon. It was coming up on midnight, and the library was closed even to the latest-working students by now.

Once I had got ready, though, I just lay there staring up at the ceiling. I was way too nervous to think about sleeping. Why had I even considered it?

There was a knock on my door.

"No thank you," I grumbled. "We don't want any more visitors, well-wishers or distant relations!" Since I had barely spoken above a mumble, I was unsurprised not to get a reply. I had to shuffle over and answer the door.

For some reason the Piper was standing there. Nice of him to remember how to knock, but his laissez-faire attitude to doors wasn't the only reason I was annoyed with him.

"Well m—"

"Bugger off."

"What's wrong?"

"Aside from you being a grumpy poohead who is ruining my university experience? Aren't you going to say something like "I can't talk to you until at least three different monsters have attempted to gnaw your head off"? I'm just saving you the trouble. I'm not talking to *you* until I've worked this out and campus internet is down *again*, so I can't make a start until morning unless you want to lend me a tenner to buy more data because I spent the rest of this term's loan on all that yoghurt!"

"So you're not even investigating right now!" he said brightly, pushing past me into my room. He flopped down onto my desk chair and instantly managed to take up every square inch of space in my cramped room.

"That's not even fair," I complained.

"Ally, my dear, my sweetie-pie, my honey nut Cheerios, at what point did you assume I played fair?"

"Shut up," I grumbled, but I blushed a little at that Cheerios thing.

"We don't even need to talk at all," he suggested.

"I... Wha-huh? What are you..."

"I was just going to say we could watch a film or something, but you've clearly thought of something better."

I stood by my door, refolding my arms a few times.

"Come on, Ally. What's the matter?"

"You're really nice—well, at least tolerable—to be around... But don't you find me too clumsy? And argumentative? And lanky? And... weird? Not even in the way you're used to. I'm messed up and I don't even have good reasons to be."

The Piper drew back his legs, sitting up straighter. I sidled past to sit on the very furthest part of the bed from him.

"If you rarely even touch me I'll never get a chance to prove I find you... tolerable, was the word you used?" He carried on grinning. I thought he'd realised I was having a dark and sulky moment, but he may have been incapable of finding the woes of a teenager important. I really had to hurry up and get some more life experience so I could stop feeling so much like this was a terrible idea every time he smirked at me. The only reason no one had staged an intervention was presumably because the one with Teb and the Green Man had gone so brilliantly and in comparison this only had my entire sense of self-worth and what relationships were supposed to be at stake.

"Don't smile like that. I'm trying to be serious" I complained.

"I'm completely serious about how much you make me laugh, you silly thing." He got up and moved to the foot of the bed, though leaned halfway across it, all but reaching for me.

"Come on, I tell you how rubbish you are all the time," I moaned. "You could at least have the decency to pretend it's true." I folded my arms again, but didn't make the mistake of turning my back on him like I'd done the night before.

"So… You're worried that you're too clumsy and you'll punch me in the face? Is that what it's about? Or is it something more doom and gloom than that?"

I grumbled something intentionally inaudible, because he had me there; despite my freak out about our relationship at its core level earlier, it had been mashing my face into his and then bleeding for ten straight minutes which had shaken me up more. I was clearly incompetent.

"Do you know what I think?" he asked.

"What?" I said sulkily.

He practically launched himself across the bed, scooped me up and silenced my shriek of horror with a kiss. It was a long kiss, lasting well beyond him lowering me gently to the bed, and clearly involved a great deal of witchcraft. Quite apart from my fuzzy head, when he raised his face away from mine, I realised I was twisted around him, lying stretched out on the bed. Somehow neither of us were bleeding or clutching vital parts in agony, although he'd completely moved me around.

"You're not half as clumsy as you think you are."

There came a frantic knocking on my door.

"Ally! Ally, are you okay?" Angie called.

The Piper let me up and I stumbled over to answer. "Uh, fine," I said, blushing hard as I leaned on the heavy fire door to stop it sealing itself again.

Angie looked past me and saw the Piper, still lying on his side, smirking. "Oh. Um, I heard a yell. I thought you'd fallen over and knocked yourself out."

"I'm fine."

"I won't let her concuss herself on my watch," the Piper added.

Blushing as much as I was at that point, Angie hastily made her excuses and left us alone.

The Piper took my hand and pulled me gently back to his side, taking care not to pull too hard on my arm and overbalance me. I lay awkwardly down, stiff as a plank, but he put a hand on the small of my back and half-tickled me until I squirmed into a more comfortable position for the both of us.

He shook his head, smiling to himself. "Okay, so maybe you are infamously klutzy, but the point of a relationship is that we look after each other. Nothing should hurt you while I'm here, like I said. And you certainly can't hurt me. I'm not planning to let you so much as graze a knee if I can help it, and I have no plans to abandon you, mistreat you or leave you because I'm worried about something such as the ridiculous age or magic gaps between us or because I think you're an unworthy idiot. I took my time debating if I could treat you properly if I asked you out, and I'm a lot more worried about you having a problem with me. If you do I hope we can always talk it through and work it out. Together. If you trust me and trust yourself."

"Oh dear. You're too perfect. I knew it. You're a serial killer."

"Ally, if you leave me because you think I'm a serial killer I will erase the last three minutes of your memory and start over. You'd never know." His cheeky look was back.

"See, I knew it. That's the catch: why you're only tolerable. You're bloomin' annoying."

He ran fingertips across my forehead and over my ear, pushing hair out of my face. "I can live with you thinking I'm merely tolerable if you let me stay this close."

I found my cheeks were hot again, my throat too tight, my heart thumping. "I wouldn't mind if you kissed me like that again. Only! Only... Not so suddenly, please?" I grinned helplessly.

"Do I have to fill in a permission form first?"

"It might give me time not to break my own face on yours."

"Then get me the necessary paperwork. Oh, not literally!" he complained as I tried to get out of bed. I found myself pinned as he rolled on top of me. "You are the *worst* for flirting with. This is why I just make fun of you."

With the Piper at such close proximity, I could just about make a squeaking sound in the back of my throat. He took advantage of my muteness and kissed me again.

This sort of thing continued for several minutes. After a while we were lying side by side, sort of staring into each other's eyes. Well, he was staring at me. I was bad at eye contact, especially with him, so I was examining the logo on his shirt; some sort of runic symbol done up in faded white paint in the same sort of spiky, heavily-outlined style as you might see a heavy metal band's name on a shirt. I had a feeling it wasn't anything to do with a band, though. Or if it was it was a band that only cool cosmic interdimensional travellers got to go to because their performances were never and the mosh pit was on the head of a pin.

"Ally..." he said, then seemed to forget what he was asking me.

"Yes?" I asked curiously, glancing up as far as his chin.

"No, never mind."

"Whaaat?" I pressed, giggling.

"I was thinking… But it doesn't matter, it can wait."

"You're making me nervous. What can wait?"

"It's only that I know we're getting so much closer at last, perhaps…" It seemed like the 'at last' was slipped in a bit accidentally, because he winced at his phrasing. "There are still some things you don't really know about me."

"Some things?" I butted in, unable to sit and listen once he got to that gem of a line.

He laughed nervously. "Many things, then. I want to change that, but there are a lot of things I *can't* tell you, or you wouldn't understand even if you really tried, not because I think you're stupid but because they're on another level of understanding that human brains just can't handle unless, well… other things that you can't understand. But this is something you would presumably find out in due course anyway, and I didn't want you to freak out again—any more than you have to."

I was scowling at him, but I was curious and now a little worried, so I didn't try to argue that I didn't freak out about things. Because come on, have you met me?

"So what is it?"

He sat up, and I propped myself on my elbow, feeling weirdly empty and light now he wasn't hugging me close, a heavy arm resting over my side. My heart was beginning to thud along quite quickly from nerves. It didn't improve when he slowly pulled up his shirt, revealing a flat, rather buff stomach. I was turning scarlet from the sheer awkwardness before I could even think to beg myself not to. I sat up straighter so I could hide as much of my face as possible behind my hands, this close to just screwing my eyes shut and waiting for him to notice so we could discuss appropriate boundaries again.

But it took like a second to realise that he wasn't just flashing me, and what he really wanted me to see: running clean across his stomach was a huge mess of scar tissue, still vividly red like it had barely begun to heal in places. The flesh was knotted and twisted, and the heart of the scar, a long red gash of shiny skin, seemed to go a whole inch deep to my horrified interpretation.

I buried my face in my hands even deeper so only my eyes were visible and blinked hard. "It looks like you were disembowelled," I mumbled.

"I was."

It was surprising to me just how hard the tears were burning the corners of my eyes. It wasn't like he was dying now. Get a grip, Ally. "What happened?" I croaked.

"I was a dumb kid who stumbled into the spirit world, and found out why most people don't come back to talk about it. To be honest, the wound wasn't that deep. I didn't spill my guts, but I was going to die, whether the blood loss or infection got me first. But the important thing was, I had a day after the wound was made; time enough that I was taken to the monastery at Severstrong. The monks patched me up and gave me my last rites… And then the Piper came and saved me."

"You *are* the Piper?" Gyuh?

"I wasn't then. It's how we—those like the Piper, like me—work: there are a lot of us, and we save people who deserve a second chance. I, the Piper, saw the worth in such a selfless act I, the man you know as Troute, did that led to this..." He gestured his stomach again. I didn't follow his gesture to dare look again: he'd shocked me into some genuine eye contact. "It looks horrific because we all carry the scars of how we could have died. To heal it back might make us forget that we *deserved* this job. We were happy to take it. To do our jobs we must be a little human, and to stay human we have to be relieved to be alive. If I forgot how it felt to be dying, I might not think to save others who feel the same. There is a very, very deep pact involved."

"Does it hurt?"

"A bit. More when you make me eat."

I winced. "I'll stop feeding you."

"Don't. I'm growing strangely fond of what I'm sure is terrible cooking to another's tongue."

"You do know that backhanded compliments don't count as nice things to say?"

He laughed, and started to pull his shirt down again to hide the gaping scar.

"Oh, don't," I protested. My hands were shaking almost too much to accomplish such a simple task, but I reached out and touched his stomach. The smooth skin was warm, hard with muscle like touching a brick wall that had been soaking up the sun. I tried not to squeak as my fingers ran over the knotted, torn flesh, my fingertips jumping clean over the deep trench of scar tissue. Then it was back to smooth chest, and I pulled his shirt up. He obligingly raised his arms and I managed to yank the stretchy fabric over his head without throttling him or anything else I briefly feared.

"O-Okay, that's about the limit of what I'm comfortable with," I said, crossing my trembling hands in my lap to try and stop them visibly shaking. Aside from the horrific scar, he was *chiselled*. I wasn't sure I was *allowed* to touch a man of that build: some cosmic force on the same scale as him but to keep weird nerdy girls with no magic powers or special destiny in their lane would intervene and say, "Ally, I'm sorry, you're too skinny and nerdy and odd. Perhaps a regular human who collects Amiibos might be more up your aisle."

"Is this part of the illusion?" I asked.

"What, the scar?"

"Your abs!"

"Oh. I was a farmhand. You can't be lanky and push a plough around. Learn your history, silly. I'm sure Tanya has written the novel by now."

I grumbled annoyed noises. He reached out and pulled me close again, and in slow motion toppled us sideways so we were lying down again. I concentrated on hyperventilating quietly to myself to be pressed up against him: he seemed twice as warm with only a thin layer of fabric removed, even while I was still wearing my own pyjama shirt and a cardigan as well. He could have burned through them if he wanted, I feared.

"Are you alright?" he asked, a little teasingly I thought.

"I think I might die," I announced through a tight throat.

"Die happy though?" he asked, stroking my cheek soothingly.

"No," I grumbled. "Your elbow is on my hair."

"Oh!" He shifted his weight and I tugged a lump of hair back to my side and rubbed my scalp, scowling.

"You're as clumsy as I am."

At least one illusion broken, though maybe not the one he intended, I felt suddenly more comfortable. There was the faintest soundtrack to this scene, I realised as I lay in the dark in that long moment before I could trick myself into sleeping. But held close to him, it didn't take long for me to nod off, no panic coming to me at the sound of the strange music that had followed me all week. One of his many magic powers seemed to be curing my insomnia.

# Newsprint

I didn't have a lecture until noon the next day, so I got a nice slow start. The Piper had stuck around for once instead of disappearing in the small hours: when I woke up he was sleeping on my arm. I tugged it out from under his shoulder and, picking the useless limb up in my other hand, used it as a club to smack him with. He didn't stir. He was probably off saving the world in his dreams.

The thump had brought horrible tingling sensation back to my hand, so I went off to get my morning cup of tea before I got too grouchy and finished him off while his guard was down.

Angie was sitting in the kitchen, reading a textbook that was almost as big as the microwave.

"Hey Ally. So you made up with your weird boyfriend, then?"

"Yep. Everything's great, if I overlook the fact he's a total moron with a worse sense of humour than my dad."

"You definitely could do worse," she said and went back to reading her— oh, right—psychology textbook.

I made cereal and shuffled back to my room. The Piper was gone. I took that as a sign I should get on with my Serious Investigating. The internet was still down, so I read a few pages of one of my set texts, got dressed and headed out of Sherrick Hall.

On campus I dithered for a moment. The fresh air and chilly wind shook all my indoor thoughts from my head. The air had that great autumnal smell.

Out in the countryside like the campus was we got a lot of the same disturbing farmyard aromas as Troutespond was treated to. Others seemed to hate it, but to me things only felt normal if you could smell wood smoke and animal waste on the breeze.

Then a chill of dread hit me that was completely different from the normal weather chill, which I didn't feel anyway. I was going to go talk to people in person, in lieu of being able to type into a magic box that would give me all the answers. I hated talking to people. I didn't have a problem doing it; it was stopping which was the problem, and then they looked at me like "What?" and then I would have to repeat myself, probably including *extra* information. Like they needed that.

I set off across the gravel paths, hopping the cycle lanes, looking for the Students' Union building.

It was in the complex with all the other bars, sitting atop a little bit of hill so, though it was tucked behind the others, it wasn't hard to point people in its direction. It had its own bar below: we'd had some initiation things there at the beginning of the year. I had promptly forgotten it existed unless someone was asking for directions to it. It was cheaper and apparently quite a nice place to sit, but my friends were still pretty casual: going to L Bar last night had been the most social thing I'd done out of scheduled meeting times for a couple of weeks. Mostly in my downtime I wandered around on my own or with the Piper, or just sat in my room chatting to absent friends.

So I felt a little nervous about going there alone. It only occurred to me when I was actually doing something that involved other people, but I was odd, and even doing something as inconspicuous as walking into a bar somehow advertised that I was not like everyone else. I felt their eyes on me. I felt like they were all wondering why I was alone. What I most felt was a conspicuous absence of three chattering friends as a buffer between me and everyone else. No Teb to shout for me, or Tanya to translate. No Alana to punch people if things didn't go my way. Yes, that's an oversimplification of their roles, but they were comforting to have about.

When I went through the double glass doors I found myself right in the bar, which seemed to have no other light source except the entrance. I squinted around it, but couldn't see a straight line I could take, scurrying through the building to my goal.

I stepped in and waited for my eyes to adjust, gagging a little on the sweet, slightly alcoholic smell in the room, a thousand spilled alcopops making a very unique aroma, different from pubs and their predominately yeasty beer smell.

The room had a huge bar that about fifty people could cram themselves along on a busy night. And the SU bar was responsible for some of the loudest nights on campus. Right now it was unnervingly quiet: a TV was playing chart music at a muted level, and a single bartender was leaning on the bar playing with her phone, paying no attention to me. The circles of sofas and armchairs were all over the place, not shoved to the side to make room for dancing as they had been the times I had visited and been so intimidated by this place before.

Creeping a bit further into the room, my desperately searching eyes located a tiny sign right below the one to the loos: "Students' Union Offices→"

I scurried over and pushed on the pull door before I glanced around and saw no one was paying any attention to me. Heartened, I slipped through and let the doors slide shut behind me. I was in a tiny smelly chamber which had the toilets and a set of stairs leading off it. Not encouraged at all by this work environment to run for public office any time soon, I headed up the stairs, since no university could be so dismissive of their Students' Union as to make them operate out of the men's loos in a bar.

The office did not offer much olfactory respite: the toilet smell was absent, but the presiding odour was one of alcoholic socks. Four computers were arranged around the edge of the room, one of them a huge state of the art Mac, the rest tiny boxy yellowed monitors on top of humming towers which were still running Windows 95, if the screensavers on two of them were an indication. The middle of the room was taken up with three tables pushed together, boxes of flyers and arts and crafts supplies littering the surface. A big Pride banner was rolled up, the end poking out with a rainbow half-coloured in marker pen.

Currently there were three people in the office. A tiny girl with huge glasses was sitting on the chair in front of the Mac with her knees up to her chin, typing furiously around them. She appeared to be on Facebook instead of actually working, though. The other two were guys in polo shirts, looking at something on one of the big cancer-causing monitors and laughing. I got the impression this organisation did not work particularly hard during mornings.

No one looked around when I came in and I briefly wondered if sheer social awkwardness had rendered me invisible. I cleared my throat. "Um… Hi?"

With the easy smiles of born politicians who had yet to lose an election, the two at the computer instantly looked around and beamed at me. "Hello!" they said together, and the one seated at the computer added, "Welcome to the Students' Union building! Can I help you with something?" His friend, leaning on the back of his chair, nodded enthusiastically. I almost backed right out of the room. Oh no. *People persons.*

"Um…" I said.

"Did you apply for your NUS card at the Freshers' Fair?" the leaning one prompted as I made goldfish faces instead of speaking.

"No! I mean, I did, but I'm not here for that!"

My blind panic sent them into an even more overfriendly setting, determined to counteract my fear. "Okay, well I'm Jared, the President," the sitting one said, "And this is Darren, my second-in-command. If you want to know anything about societies and stuff, ask him. I can deal with any other problems you have." They looked hopefully at me. They must have been bored.

"I'm Ally!" I squeaked, by now having completely forgotten why I was in the room in the face of their enthusiasm. "I joined one of the societies already, though."

"Just one?" Darren laughed, looking mock-offended. I instantly felt real-embarrassed.

"Yeah! Well I joined a bunch and never went after I decided I liked that one. It takes up a lot of time and I still need to study. This is a university, after all! Hahaha!"

"Which one was it?" he asked, a little more humanly and curious. "I haven't seen you at any of the meetings."

"We don't meet here," I said, managing to take and let out a whole breath without hiccuping from fear. "It's the Classical Music Society, except we call ourselves the orchestra anyway since that's what we do. We're performing at the end of this month in the big theatre and we use the practice rooms there for all our meetings so we don't annoy anyone by playing really badly. Well, they play pretty well, but…" I managed to stand on my own foot to shut myself up. I wobbled, caught a chair and lowered myself into it with as much dignity as I had left.

"Right." Darren said. "Do you have a problem with it?"

"Oh *no*, I love the orchestra!"

We sat there in silence for a moment.

Jared took presidential command. "So what is the reason for your visit, Ally?"

"Er, well, I just wanted to know a bit about the people who were in the society the year before us."

They assumed identical worried expressions, clearly showing they had no idea what I was talking about.

"Before?" Darren ventured at last.

"Not sure we know about 'before'," Jared said.

"But you *run* this place!"

"Yeah, I was the Sports Officer last year and this is Daz's first position in the Union."

"Hey, mate, I helped you all last year running around putting up posters and shit!" 'Daz' complained. "Basically the same amount of work you did!"

I sighed. These were just students who had an extra room to goof off in. "Well, thanks for the help," I mumbled, and dragged myself to my feet.

"Hold on, hold on, hold on!" Jared cried. "When I became president I *vowed* to help the students! Something is bothering you. Ally, was it?" Maybe he wasn't as awful as he seemed.

I nodded. Darren was rolling his eyes. Maybe Jared thought I was cute and that was how I was getting the extra help. I never would have thought *I* would be batting my eyelids to get what I wanted, considering girls who did that usually had a figure and glossy hair, but whatever floated his boat. I knew at least one other being out there who found me attractive, after all. Maybe I shouldn't have been surprised to find a second, even if this one was a dudebro sports guy.

Was the Piper a dudebro, on the cosmic scale of things?

"Look, to be honest, when I was Sports Officer, I did a lot of stuff with the other societies. We even got the Indie Music Society out and playing Frisbee. In all my outreaching to the other societies, I don't remember an orchestra one. Are you sure they were around last year?"

I shook my head.

"Oh!" Darren said. "The girl who runs your society? About this big —" He gestured practically waist high. "— always wears a frumpy cardigan?"

"Molly."

"Yeah, yeah. She came to me first day of term and asked to start the society. I remember doing the paperwork with her."

"You *remember* her tipping your drink in your lap after you asked her if she wanted to go to the bar later," Jared reminded him.

Oh Molly.

Darren frowned and batted Jared around the head with a meaty fist. "Point being, she made the group from scratch. Wasn't like she was taking over leader from someone else. Sometimes a society is all leaving third years, right, and they don't find someone to replace them. But I was poking around the computer to make her folder in the system, and I found an Orchestra Society already on the system. All the files were from a few years ago, but they were just music and stuff, so I gave her the password instead of making a new one."

"Um... Do you mind if I see it?" I asked.

"Yeah, dunno if she didn't just clear out the old stuff."

"Well let me have a look. I'm moderately computer savvy."

They gave each other edgy looks suddenly.

"Pfft, I'm a card-carrying member of this society," I said, a flurry of activity as I found my wallet in my coat pocket and pulled out my Student ID and a printed scrap of card with my name and membership number for the society. Also some adorable clip art of a musical note. Oh Molly, again.

"What if Molly decided to quit? Would these files be so secure I couldn't walk in and check if she had like a list of favourites saved on here to succeed her?" I giggled, despite my attempt to be dramatic.

"Well, we encourage students not to keep any personal data on the Union's Dropbox, so..."

"That's settled then. Move over, I want to see." All my shyness vanished as soon as I had something to do and I wasn't just here to be stared at by strange boys who might judge me.

Jared vacated the chair and gestured to the screen, where he seemed to have already opened the folder I wanted while we were talking.

It really was about as boring as a folder could be. Three different drafts of

Word files with designs for the flyers Molly was desperately handing out on campus to advertise our show to students who wisely guessed it might not be the music event of the century. Some subfolders of sheet music on a suspiciously Christmas theme. A rota and minutes from our one official meeting. I scanned the member list but everything looked very fresh and Molly-related.

"She's deleted all the old stuff," I said sadly. I sunk down in the chair, trying to work out what to do now I was back at square one. I couldn't see which direction square two was, if that hadn't been it.

"Uh," said a small voice.

We all looked around: Jared and Darren seemed as surprised as I was to remember the bespectacled girl sitting in the corner on the Mac.

"What is it?" I asked, but she clammed up, her lips squeezed together so tightly they almost vanished. She drew her knees up further.

"Come on. Spit it out," Darren joked.

I think it was a more kindly look from Jared than unsealed her lips. "Um, the Union newspaper has a lot of information about societies in it and it's thirty years old."

"Are there copies online?" I eagerly asked.

She blinked at me and then hesitantly replied, "W-Well, only from thirty years ago. I've been scanning them in and uploading them. I only started last month. I-I have the first year and a half up."

"Why did you start backwards?" I asked.

She shrugged one shoulder.

"History student," Jared muttered to me. "She's meant to be editing new issues, but…"

"Well, can you show me where the old copies are you're using to scan?"

"There's hundreds in that cupboard," she squeaked. Overwhelmed with too much social interaction, she looked back to the computer screen, glancing at me from the corner of her eye. I wanted to reach out to her and assure her that I was just as bad at this as she was, and I wasn't another society-obsessed jock, or even remotely well-adjusted. She may have mistaken my babbling for fluent conversation, considering how hard it was for her to get a line out. But I was too bad at social stuff to even try smiling at her for fear of distressing her more. So I got up and went over to the cupboard that she gestured.

I put my hand on the doorknob but a rare sense of self-preservation that was working overtime after the panic this room had brought on made me pause. I looked over my shoulder. Jared and Darren quickly looked back at their computer screen like they hadn't been watching me.

Extremely reassured, I pulled the door open.

It wasn't the waves of newspaper I'd been dreading, but I had been expecting a little supply cupboard, all the shelves slanted towards me from the weight of the paper. Instead of being attacked by old pages, a few drifts of newspapers slid down to stop by my feet. Perhaps the little editor had already been buried once. This room was more like a walk-in closet, and at that point I realised a fundamental fact: students were lazy, and if there was a big mess that was older than they were, they weren't in any more of a rush to clear it up than the last thirty student councils. A path had been beaten to the back of the room, and closer to the door the papers had been stacked at least in piles of the same issue. But what I was looking at was an overwhelming heap of mixed up papers, stacked floor to ceiling on shelves that lined the room.

My eyes began adjusting from the horror, and logic crept back. I wasn't here to sort or tidy, or to dig up the oldest copies. There was a girl with a haunted look on the other side of the wall who was doing that for me. I just needed a few back issues from recent years. The paper was fortnightly, but generally only ran to four pages unless it was an election, sport or other special event, in which case it didn't get more bulky than eight.

I could do this. It wouldn't kill me.

I ignored entirely the most recent papers, ones I recognised from the bins of them that sat outside the student shop or were left on the tables in the bars. I waded in and began picking up issues dated back to the previous summer.

While I had been running around after fairies and doing my A Levels, the university had had a rather tame Leaver's Ball with no giant monsters of any description, and a Fairtrade Week with no names on the market. This was mundane and safe. But somewhere in there might be a note about a performance from a certain society and in those words may have been just what I needed to hear: a name, a hint that something strange had happened to them. So I kept on collecting, grim determination in my movements.

I had gone three years into the past and had a towering stack of paper clutched in my arms when my phone began buzzing. I hastily shelved my stack and answered it.

"Ally, our lecture starts in two minutes. You didn't come to the discussion group we were going to have," Lucia tetchily informed me. "Or Rose. Which, you know, is the entire group aside from me sitting on my lonesome reading my notes out loud in the group study room."

"Oh my god! Really? What time is it?"

"*Lecture time.*"

I hung up in a panic, grabbed my stack of newspapers and legged it from the Students' Union building.

# Intrusions

Sneaking into a lecture hall late while carrying your own weight in unbound newspapers is not really a feat you should attempt to recreate. I made it through the push door, heading in backwards, and took one look at the yawning chasm the stairs made when I couldn't see my feet. Images of myself tumbling down them with a blizzard of loose newsprint drifting after me burst into my head.

I sidled in to the back row seat nearest the door and put my newspapers on the chair next to me. I could see Lucia down in the sixth row among the students craning around to look at me. It was a small class; for a two hundred seat lecture hall they filled just over a tenth of it and were mostly arranged in a blob in the middle. She didn't look well-pleased. We had a mini presentation in the seminar.

The lecturer just cleared his throat and picked up his thread of conversation from where he had left off. I stayed totally confused about what subject he was discussing for the rest of the lecture, and instead I glanced back and forth from him to the newspaper I had slid off the top of the pile and under my notebook, reading its slightly-less-dull headline story about the football team. His voice buzzed with an extra resonance in the back of my mind if I began to drift too much, but every time I started to hear notes from a song or mistake his words for coherent song lyrics from the set, I managed to jerk myself a bit more awake and the sound vanished, the little shock of fear it caused keeping me alert for some time afterwards.

When he dismissed us and shuffled off to drink the Irish coffee he was known to take about this time of day, leaving us in the hands of his Ph.D. student, I grudgingly began stacking the papers in my arms again. In the intervening forty-five minutes I'd forgotten the hassle, and my poor stretched arms had even begun to feel like normal again.

Thankfully the seminar rooms were beneath the lecture hall, and so all I had to do was stagger back down two flights of stairs with lots of sharp corners and a line of two hundred students queuing to use the room after us. I remembered how back in school boys would invariably stick out a foot and try and trip anyone walking past: almost no one fell for it (he he) because it was such a feature of the stairs, but even walking past these responsible adults in a totally different environment it had programmed my brain to be on a twitchy level of paranoia that they would do it to me anyway.

Lucia was waiting for me at the bottom: I think she had gone that far just so she wouldn't be given a stack of papers to share the awkward journey with me. "Can't believe Rose didn't even show up to the lecture. Did you see her arms last night? No wonder she's not here. I'm amazed she made it this far without flaking out. I hope you know what you're doing for your half of the presentation." Her eyes drifted down to the bundle of papers I was hoisting about to try and get a better grip on. "Uh, those aren't a part of it, are they? It's supposed to be about intertextuality and modernism."

"Oh! Yeah! It will be! I mean, it is... I wrote it already, sort of."

"So why *are* you carrying your weight in old student newspapers?"

"Uh... I have a hamster."

"What?! Here?"

"No, back in Troutespond, silly..."

Lucia didn't ask any more questions, perhaps scared about what I might say next, leaving me to enjoy the shiver that I got from saying the name of my town. It was like a spell. Tanya's theory was that saying the true name of a place brought it closer, which was how we had travelled to the fairy land. I might not have been able to step sideways and find myself standing by the old war memorial in the centre of town, eyes turning to the thousand year old church my boyfriend had built with his bare hands. But the name brought memories closer, a sense of belonging that I missed.

Despite everything else... I had never been made to feel like an outsider in the town. If anything, I had been scared of never being able to leave, like we would set off down the motorway and find ourselves a minute later at the junction that led back into the town from the other direction. Now that I had escaped and proved to myself it was possible, it was a lot like guilt for not writing that gripped me as I remembered home. Though the town wouldn't be able to read any letter I sent it, I still felt rude for not doing it.

I mumbled my way through my hastily scribbled notes in the seminar, and with Lucia rather peeved at me but at least *more* annoyed with no-show Rose, set off with the aim of dumping these newspapers at last before orchestra practice.

I toddled along, my vision largely obscured by back issues, finding my way by memory of what trees were where.

"Hey! Ally!"

I very nearly dropped the whole lot on the damp path. That voice sent a shock of familiarity through me: it was so clear, so unobstructed by phone static...

I looked over my shoulder, a genuine smile blooming on my face. Alana was sitting on a huge wheeled suitcase, almost completely blocking a side path. Her hair was a newly-dyed deep burgundy, wavy and loose to her shoulders. She looked sophisticated with a blouse and skinny jeans, much the same as she'd always worn, but on a university campus she looked grown up instead of hipster and trying too hard. I may have known her less than a year, but she was wedged firmly in my heart already.

"You're here!" I cried.

"I heard you had a little problem, so I decided an extra few days wouldn't hurt."

My smile wilted.

"You... did."

"Um, yeah."

"My boyfriend?"

She nodded, her own excited smile beginning to fade in the face of my waning enthusiasm.

"Hold these for one minute." I dumped the whole lot of the papers into her arms while she was too surprised to realise the burden I was about to pass to her.

I stomped off across the wet grass until I was out of earshot to her.

"Where are —" I started to snarl, but he was already leaning on a nearby tree.

"What happened?" He looked genuinely confused.

"Alana's here!"

"Your friend, who you've been so excited to see? Or did I find the wrong one?"

"You *told* her!"

"I sent her early."

"I didn't want her to know!" I shrieked. Birds took off from the tree above us. "You knew that! What if I was imagining things? What would she say? Or what if I wasn't? She might burn the whole place down! I wanted my *friend* Alana. Just like I want the normal, boring you. But you can't turn it off, can you? You're as interfering as ever and now I have your little helper monkey bouncing around after me instead of someone I can genuinely enjoy the company of!"

"I thought you *wanted* to work out what the ghostly music was?" He looked so hurt, but he didn't even understand. And I couldn't help but get angry with him for that. Except I *was* angry.

"Yeah, on my *own terms.* This is my life! I'm coping! I don't need a load of crutches and assistants! I can sort out my own problems in my own time!"

"I can't turn off caring about you," he protested. "If you don't want me to actively do it myself, I will find another way to look after you."

"You know what, if something strange is going on here, you're going to be a crappy boyfriend until it's sorted. You've broken my trust. Maybe you shouldn't drop by *at all* until I've worked it out myself. I don't need you sabotaging my attempts to be my own person."

He gave me the single most hurt look I've ever seen, his expressive features all twisted downwards, and he blinked out of sight.

"Aw, no, wait!" I said, instantly running out of anger now he wasn't standing in front of me looking like a great big unjust brick I couldn't move.

He didn't come back.

I trudged back to Alana: "Come on, let's go," I mumbled to my feet, setting off down the path.

She followed me with a great rumbling of her wheeled suitcase that made a great baseline to the violin part stuck in my head. It took me twenty paces to remember the newspapers, and I finally looked over my shoulder at her. "Where are the——"

Alana was beaming at me, a single rolled up paper under her arm. "I found the one you need!"

"What?!"

"Yeah, I was going to prop them up on the suitcase and use a belt to hold them in place, but then I knocked the stack over and I think I found exactly what you were looking for. Aren't you glad?"

I turned away and carried on mooching miserably along. "No."

*

I got Alana into my halls and to my room without further incident. It was a noisy day: peak time after most people were out of lectures, when the kitchen was crowded, the TV was on, and those who had retired to their rooms were playing music or their own films to try and drown out the noise of the rest.

I shut the door, somewhat muting the racket outside, and turned to Alana while giving a huge sigh. Her suitcase was almost too wide to fit between my bed and desk, and that was the only free space in the room.

"We'll be clambering over that a lot, then," I said.

Alana grinned sheepishly. "It's not even full. I just realised while I was getting ready that I only took two suitcases with me, and the other one had no wheels. Ask me to carry a suitcase through the London Underground, go on, I dare you."

"Carry a suitcase through the London Underground?"

"No. Fuck off." She giggled, but then saw that my expression was still stony. "Aw, come on, Ally. Lighten up. I came here to have fun!"

"Well, I didn't."

"You *live* here."

We shared an awkward silence, much like the first we had ever shared, where we sullenly crossed our arms and glared.

"So…" Alana said.

"What?"

"Are you going to tell me what you've experienced, so I can start to make sense of this?"

"You already seem to know more about it than me and you've been here five minutes," I grumbled.

"Seriously?!" she cried, confusing me for a moment until she carried on ranting. "I came *all* this way on like, five different trains, one of which got stuck at Milton Keynes for an *hour*, and after all that time and money, the only thought keeping me going was how much fun you are to be around, and you're just sitting here sulking. What on *earth* is wrong?"

"Aside from the fact I'm hearing voices and nonstop flute music in the back of my brain? I told my boyfriend to get stuffed, and in a week I am *performing live in front of gods know how many other people*. AND I CAN'T PLAY MY INSTRUMENT."

"Oh, yeah, about the Piper… You do know that every time you stick your nose up in the air and ignore him, he comes to me all 'Waaah, why isn't Ally talking to me?' If you two could stop fighting and just be all Disney happy ending with each other, that would be lovely."

"Alana! Focus! I've been trying to learn the mandolin for three months and I still can't even remember which string is which note! I have bigger problems here than stupid ghosts or boyfriends!"

"Why don't you just write tiny stickers with the notes on and put them under each string on the fret board? We could do different coloured ones for different chords you use a lot as well where you're supposed to put your fingers."

I stared at her, my mouth falling open. "Or," I suggested, "I could just smash the thing, quit the choir and be rid of two problems at once."

"Calm down, stage fright is totally normal. Take a deep breath. We'll sort this out for you. I'm here now."

I shook my head miserably and flopped onto my bed, curling up so I could hug my knees.

Alana went and picked up my mandolin. "Has its face changed since Hester gave it to you?"

"If it's the source of the curse I am firing my boyfriend for good."

"Dumping?" she asked, alarmed.

"No, he can still be my boyfriend, but I'm revoking his Piper credentials."

Alana turned the instrument around in her hands and shrugged. "I was just saying that to scare you... *Unless* the spell is so strong that I just *think* it hasn't changed, and I'm messing with you..."

"Out, now," I ordered.

"Anyway," Alana said, like I hadn't just strictly informed her to get the next train home. "Are you calmed down enough to look at this newspaper yet?"

"Give it here," I grumbled.

She produced a folded paper from her handbag. It struck me just how thin the student rag was: if this was, as Alana thought, the only information I might find, and half of it would be sports results and a comic strip about a drunk fish, then there was not going to be a great deal to read, when I needed a whole novel.

I unfolded it, but it took me a moment to realise what I had read as the huge headline. My eyes passed over the titles five times before I could read on, my stomach suddenly filled with a block of ice.

**Candlelit Vigil for Tragic Orchestra Society Deaths.**
Three hundred students past and present filled the theatre on Halloween to remember the members of Orch. Soc. who passed two weeks ago in a tragic series of accidents. The Evlyne Hall had been booked months previously for the society's performance of a variety of Halloween-themed classical music, but this was not to be.
On the thirteenth of October the society visited London to see ancient instruments on display in the British Museum. On the return journey the coach suffered a fatal collision with an out-of-control lorry, which killed seven members of the society instantly. Over the next week the remainder of the orchestra then sadly succumbed to their injuries and the stress of the accident, with two more tragically dying in hospital, another slipping in a freak snow storm on her discharge from hospital. The horrific week ended with a girl toppling from the balcony in the theatre, still closed off as the mourners began to arrive. The president of the Orchestra Society was later tragically found dead in his room. Coroners still have yet to determine the cause, but rumour swirls...

I had read enough. "It's cursed!" I cried, throwing down the newspaper.

"Cursed?"

"It's not ghosts I'm hearing! It's a-a banshee call! We're using their sheet music, their practice space. We'll die just like them as well!"

"Or you are hearing their ghosts," Alana said far more calmly than she should have.

All I could hear after that was a whooshing noise, which I suppose was the blood running out of my head. I managed to sit down as my vision was blurring to white and got my head between my knees. But as soon as the threat of fainting had passed I was up on my feet, clumsily blundering around my room, knocking stuff off the shelves.

"I might still have time before it gets me. If we leave now we can make the next train to Heathrow before tomorrow. We can decide where to go from there on the way, and I will get my bursary at half-term: that will cover it! No time to get another suitcase. I can share yours…"

"Ally!" Alana finally managed to stumble past her suitcase and grab me by the shoulders. "You're being ridiculous!" She gave me a little shake for good measure.

"Ridiculous?! If you hear about thirteen people dying all at once, in ways you're deeply connected to and were pre-haunted by, what would you think was going to happen to you next? This time last year, they were already dead! It could happen any time now!"

"Three years ago."

"What?"

"That newspaper is dated from three years ago. Let's sit down and get some facts here before we emigrate, okay?"

I reluctantly sat down and took another look at the date on the newspaper.

"There's no mention of it happening before or after, is there? You can't have missed a dozen separate headlines about orchestra deaths, not to mention the university would probably quietly advise against anyone trying to start the society up after the third time. And I reckon people would still be talking about it. You have second and third year students in the group, don't you?"

"I-I guess."

"And they never talk about how glad they are to have a flood of first years to replace all their dead friends from last year?"

"No," I had to admit.

"Think about the life of stories at a university. It has a two or three year turnover for most students, except for those who take a Masters in the same place as their BA. There must be only a tiny fraction of the university who even still remember the events in question, tutors aside. This accident is ancient history."

"Molly would know!" I blurted.

"Fact gathering. Good." Alana nodded approvingly. I was already scrabbling around for my mobile, scrolling through my contacts with shaking hands. Why hadn't I done this sooner?

Molly's phone rang once and then she answered.

"Helloo-o?" she trilled cheerfully.

"Uh… Hi Molly."

"Are you going to be late to practice this evening?" Molly asked, a little resignedly.

"Oh no! Am I late?!"

"Calm down, it's an hour and a half until practice. What's up?"

"Oh. Um." I glanced at Alana. She nodded encouragingly. "I was just wondering about Orchestra Society, actually. I mean. Was it your idea to start it?"

"Yes, Ally. It was. Why?" She sounded very matter-of-fact. Her voice got more and more like that as she recognised that anyone else would be losing their patience, but wasn't she wonderful for politely sitting through this time wasting?

"Er, well... I found out..." Alana was furiously nodding at me. "Did you know that three years ago that the whole Orchestra Society died?!"

"Oh dear. How did I know that it would be you who asked me about this first? Yes, I did."

"And you started the society back up anyway!?" I shrieked.

"Calm down!" Alana and Molly chorused into either ear, unaware of each other's synchronisation. Molly continued: "It was a coach accident. You're not worried a phantom coach will come rattling into the theatre and plough us down as we play, are you?"

"No, but, but... Doesn't it seem unlucky?"

"I made a third year friend when I started here who was in the original society when she was a first year," Molly said. "Anna always said that she wanted to start it up again, in memory of her friends, and continue their legacy."

"Why didn't she..."

"She had a pop quiz the day after the accident, so she stayed on campus to study instead of going to London with them. You're really reminding me of her, though, because even though she was always talking about getting it going again, she was always way too scared to do it for some reason. I begged her and begged her, but she... She seemed to think something bad would happen to us, no matter how much she wanted to play again. I don't know if it was superstition or just PTSD and survivor's guilt, to be honest. The accident kept holding her back. This year she's graduated, so I thought I could finally try. She wasn't there any more to stop me and sabotage me, so I went and registered the group and found you lot. So far nothing's bad happened, has it?"

"But Halloween is when they were supposed to play!"

"Ally, look, I'm not superstitious, okay. I'll say a few words before we begin about the old Orchestra Society, and I'm sure they'd be delighted to have us playing their old track list exactly as they would have done."

"*Exactly?*"

"Well, when I made the group Jared—the SU President—gave me access to Kris Carter's old files on their Dropbox, and he had everything set out ready for the performance right down to the order he wanted it played. I thought it would be a mark of respect to perform his show for him."

"Kris being the one who from the sounds of things killed himself?" I asked flatly.

"Why are you blaming me for this?! Back when this happened I had only just started my A Levels! I didn't even know what university I was going to go to!"

"It's just…" I couldn't tell her. She'd woken the wrath of thirteen angry ghosts by stomping into their resting place, which in this case seemed to be the very music they'd been learning in the time leading up to their deaths. "It makes me feel weird. That's all."

"Look, Ally, if you want to back out of the show, I won't hold it against you. You're our most amateur player, and I understand how scary it must be to go from being a beginner to performing in a show in a matter of months. Why don't I give you the Christmas music and we can start you before the others, so you'll be more confident for that show?"

"No! I want to play! I just —"

"Well, if you're out of excuses, I expect to see you at practice, alright?"

"Alright," I mumbled.

"Later, Ally."

I nodded at the phone and hung up.

"So?" Alana prompted.

"We're going to practice, same as normal. If I end up dying from it, I will never forgive you."

"Understandable."

"So we have an hour or so to kill."

"Shall we get something to eat?" Alana asked hopefully.

"I was going to offer you a campus tour."

"How about a tour of places to eat? My treat!"

"Maybe just the cafeteria," I decided, seeing somewhat manic desperation in her face. "It's close."

Alana hopped to her feet and was standing at the door before I'd even begun to look around for my shoes, thrown somewhere in my earlier panic. My flip-flops were on top of a neat pile of my shower things, though, so I slid them on. I saw Alana's smile at that. I shouldered the mandolin and off we went.

# Wonderwall

We made it to the cafeteria without anything magical or mysterious jumping out on us, to my deep surprise. I suppose Alana sometimes managed to walk to the shop and back without having fairies getting under her feet, but the two of us together...?

The building was wedged into the side of the expensive snooty new halls that people like Molly could afford to live in: it literally looked like a wedge of glass and green-painted supporting beams had been crammed into the white concrete of the building, one end of the crashed cafeteria still poking out of the side of its victim.

Alana didn't wait around for my observations on the architecture here, though, but powered right through the automatic doors into the warm gravy-smelling room the other side. In this weather all the glass had steamed up: once we were inside I suddenly realised how dark it was getting outside as a wash of light dazzled me.

Alana homed in on the queue, and by the time I drifted after her she had a tray for the both of us and had already loaded hers up with a bottle of ice tea and a crusty roll: she was ordering soup from a student server.

I glanced around the hall while she was holding the line up. It was still before the main dinner rush: the catered students were on a strict schedule for their meals and we had about half an hour before they'd flood in here. There were mostly harassed research students in the corners, laptops and books spread across a table, desperately spooning Bolognese into their mouths one-handed while typing or turning pages. Some gossipy girls in the uniform yoga pants which showed they were the drama department were nibbling from a single shared plate of chips and making screechy giggling noises over something on one of their phones. Holding court by the door was the campus's resident kooky professor: we'd swapped stories, and my miniature Indiana Jones, one Professor Kingston from the archaeology department, had won hands down to Tanya's "looks like Professor Trelawny" and Alana's "Olde Timey Gentleman IT Technician". Professor Kingston was standing on his chair, getting away unnoticed by the cafeteria staff because that man could not be pushing 4'8" if he wore heeled shoes. His arms waved dramatically as he told of some adventure, narrowly missing knocking his hat from his head. The archaeology students, all in their branded hoodies like some sort of cult, were laughing hard at his tale.

In the middle of the room was a table with a stack of musical instruments on it, and sitting at the table was someone wildly waving at me: Lucia, apparently on a date with Sam, considering it was just them. She looked pretty eager to double the number of people at the table.

"I think I've found a table for us," I said as I scooted in to take my place in front of the servers.

Alana paused before heading to pay. "Should we butt in on them? That boy is scowling like you stomped on his sandcastle."

"Oh, Sam hates me. But Lucia's cool."

While I showed Alana where the forks were, she asked me in a low voice (despite the clattering babble of the cafeteria), "Have you asked your friends about the ghost noises in the orchestra?"

"Mhm," I said unhappily. She interpreted that noise correctly as saying my friends were as dense as a pile of bricks when it came to ghostly things.

"Well then, I suppose it is time to socialise!" With considerable enthusiasm, she set off across the room to get started on Part Two of why I really didn't want my past life friends joining me here.

She at least let me make the introduction before plonking her tray down on the table.

"This is Alana, a friend from home who's visiting me."

"Yo."

"Alana, this is Lucia, and Sam; they're part of the violin section. Lucia also stars in some of my Literature class anecdotes I may have told you."

"Hi," they chorused. I flopped into the seat next to Lucia out of force of habit, leaving Alana to seat herself beside Sam. He deserved it.

"So are you here for the performance?" Sam quickly followed up with.

"I'm staying until then, yes," Alana said. She shot a look at me and grinned. "Though I bet Ally is going to ban me from going to see it."

"I won't!" I complained. "But don't listen too closely for my part, okay?"

"What part?" Sam snorted, mostly to himself.

Alana rounded on him, her furious puffed up like a cat thing going on.

I swear her hair actually swelled up a bit. "What do you mean by that?" she demanded.

Sam actually looked freaked out. Well, you would be if you only just met someone and already they looked like they were going to kill you...

"It's just a joke we have," I said before my rush of pity for Sam ended and I went back to feeling something on a range of disgruntled to disgust with him. "I'm pretty new to music, so..." I gave my rather lame and unconvincing giggle.

"So she is terrible," Sam said.

I scowled at him to say, *don't push it*. I couldn't back up any threats I made all on my own, but with Alana here...

"*Anyway*," Lucia said, sweeping back her hair for the tenth time since we had sat down. I was buying the girl a scrunchie for Christmas. She better not sneeze through our performance and make it any worse than it would already be with me playing in it. "We were just saying we should get Molly something after the show. Flowers or something."

"A bottle of something," Sam said.

"Something *dignified*, like wine. We're not getting her Jack Daniels."

"She drinks it," Sam said with a shrug.

"She drinks it when she's on a date with you and wants to make the evening go faster."

Sam abruptly stood up. "You know what, Lucia, I'll see you in practice." He didn't even say anything to me as he grabbed Lucia's violin case by mistake, got two steps away, backtracked and switched instruments, then stormed off.

"Touchy, much?" Alana said.

Lucia groaned and flopped forwards to rest her head on her arms. "I swear Ally's the only one he's not hit on this year, and that's probably just because he's seen how huge and, like, metal her boyfriend is."

"You could get your own huge boyfriend?" I suggested, giggling. I did sometimes forget I was in a bad mood with the Piper when people complimented him.

"Meh," Lucia said.

"Or a girlfriend?" Alana asked hopefully.

Lucia scowled. "I had a pretty bad break up before I came away to uni. I'd rather just forget about all that stuff for a while. I *told* this to Sam last month already, but he clearly just heard 'oh, good, she's single!'" Lucia shook her head sadly.

"So what's wrong with Sam?" Alana asked curiously. Yeah, like she didn't have a huge crush on Lucia in ten seconds flat. I'd never seen Alana beam at someone else like she was now. Except for me.

"He's a total *jerk*," Lucia sighed. "What we need is someone as sweet as, like... Amir, to be as forward as Sam. Would fix the world if all the boys were like that. But no, the arsehole ones are the only ones bold enough to go talk to girls."

"Amir talks to girls," I said, a little confused. "We talk about stuff all the time."

"Yeah, but you have that terrifying boyfriend, so of course he doesn't see you as girlfriend material and can actually hang out with you without muttering terrified Arabic to himself and fleeing as soon as I say hi. You know he's the sensitive sort who would *fall in love* first, with one girl at a time, and spend months agonising, probably writing poetry, that stuff, before ever approaching someone. By that point she has a boyfriend!"

"Well... Ask this Amir out yourself?" Alana said, looking excited to be carrying on a proper conversation about boys despite her brief hopes over Lucia. As a rule, our group back home was not good at boy talk.

Lucia looked disdainful. "I only said boys *like* Amir."

Alana sat back in her chair and looked around for another topic of conversation, probably deciding it was easier to leave this to people who cared about boys.

"Say, would Amir be a tall, Arabic lad with a guitar that leers at people?" she asked suddenly.

"Why?" I asked, with all due dread.

"Someone of that description just legged it out the hall."

"Oh god," Lucia groaned. "He was sitting behind us, wasn't he?"

I turned and inspected the table behind us: a mostly untouched plate of pizza and chips was sitting there, mysteriously unguarded by a hungry student.

"Seems like."

"Well, I'm done alienating every boy in the orchestra now. I'd better get on. See you there." Lucia stood up abruptly and ran from the hall.

"She left her violin," Alana said.

"I think she was crying," I said. "We should really go after her."

"Poor Amir. Maybe we should go after *him*."

"What, and tell him that she felt bad for insulting him? We can't give him false hope..."

"Ally, he had a guitar with eyes on it. He's mad like us. Lucia and Sam are normal. For the most part. What do you bet he's been hearing ghosts this whole time as well? We're going after the lanky kid and that's final."

*

I was dragged along by the wrist, two instruments clutched under my other arm. Alana powered along without really knowing where she was going: she took us outside, then a sharp left.

"Are you sure you're following him? He's had quite a head start."

"I know where he went," she said.

"You can't! You don't know him, and you don't know campus!"

"I walked through it before meeting you and took in some sights. What's more, I am getting a lot better at reading people and places. Trust me."

She took me around the halls and towards the Admin block, where there were also a few tiny outposts of banks, nothing more than a single teller every other day and a row of cash points, the site most busy the first week of term when everyone realised they had to sort their room insurance still. There was an official university shop which sold just monogrammed pencils, the boring blue hoodie plus society and class ones on order, and Aaron Sherrick's biography. The medical centre. And the quiet contemplation room.

Alana slowed down as we drew close to the door. It was the same as all the other miniature shops in the row; a big glass front, probably sweltering in the summer. But it was mostly an empty space: a row of prayer mats, a rack of leaflets and a radio. A couple of bean bag chairs were up against the glass, and Amir was sunk down in one of them, staring blankly at the ceiling, his back to us. His guitar was in his lap, his hands resting on it but not playing.

"He looks so sad," I said. "Normally looks like the top of his head is going to fall off he's grinning so much."

"You're his friend. Go in first."

"What should I say?"

"Well, be nice to him! He just heard that a pretty girl he likes would apparently never dream of dating him. He's fragile."

"Yeah, but… Ghosts?"

"Weave it in to conversation. I don't know, you're the master at all that nonsense."

I did not understand what on earth she thought I was. But I put my hand on the glass door. Amir suddenly straightened up and picked up the guitar properly, right before I cracked it open. His long fingers began strumming slowly. The chord changes were hesitant, but I knew this wasn't something we played at the orchestra. Then he began picking out a tune and he hit enough notes for me to look at Alana, who rolled her eyes.

"*Wonderwall*, right?" I whispered.

She smirked. "I guess you have to settle when you want to play something in a moody moment and your repertoire is three songs deep."

He missed a few notes and managed to turn the chorus a little inside out.

"Enough of that," Alana said. She leaned past me and pushed on the door.

Amir bolted upright, dropping the guitar. "Sorry!" he squawked, but relaxed when he saw us. "Oh. Hello Ally."

"You probably shouldn't use a *quiet* contemplation room for guitar practice, if you don't want to feel guilty every time someone comes in the door," Alana said.

Amir looked at me. I shrugged. "Alana, Amir, Amir, Alana. I thought I was done collecting friends whose names began with A. Too many and it looks like I'm building a personality cult around myself, but…"

Alana waved. "So, poor love fool… have you been hearing strange music these past few days?"

Amir's mouth fell open. He looked from Alana to me and then back to Alana. Then back to me. "Is your friend... Ghostbusters?" he asked.

Okay, I would concede points to Alana for this round.

"Yes, Amir, she is," I said, patting Alana on the shoulder. "I've been hearing the playing and singing as well. She's come to sort it out."

"Can she?"

I nodded. "She's very skilled at this sort of thing. So, what *did* you hear?" If it didn't match up to mine and we were two different sorts of crazy in the same room...

"At first I just think it is an echo, but then I hear my part! Same song! But, of course, they play it better than me. I think, is it a guide to be a better player... I had prayed for help of course, and I thought it was this. So I follow along to the ghosts, and I mess up, Molly laughs at me. But still I am hearing it. And no one else can. I hear a singer, I hear a double bass, and I think, this isn't us playing, no one sings here. So one day I phone Molly, I say I am not feeling so good today. I go up to the practice rooms, I press my ear to the door. I hear you playing, I hear the other people playing too! I go all around that theatre and check the other practice rooms, but they are all empty. No one but the society playing up there!"

"Bah, you make my investigations seem halfhearted," I grumbled. "I went to the Students' Union building to ask about the last Orchestra Society and got the Sherrick Shout from three years ago with a ghastly story in it. Molly confirmed it after I confronted her: they all died horrific deaths just before Halloween, where they were about to perform the exact same songs as us in a show. We are legitimately being haunted by them."

He sunk his head into his hands. "I am never going to be able to explain this to my parents when I come home because of ghosts."

"Um, Amir, have you heard them elsewhere *aside* from in the theatre?"

He shook his head, eyes wide. "Have you?"

"Yeah. I guess so. Alana thinks there's a link with our instruments, with the eyes cursing us or something."

"No I don't," Alana interrupted, but then her mouth dropped open. "Oh! Oh! I get it! It is!"

"The instruments are *not* cursed, Alana," I found myself telling her, despite my earlier panic. "Amir drew the eyes on himself!"

"Pfft, you can't curse yourself. No. Those eyes are a *charm*. Wisdom, or farseeing or second sight! I guess they do basically nothing for the mundane, and that normally includes you two. But in a situation like this, those eyes have made the two of you *just* receptive enough to hear the music. After all, you're in a position roughly equivalent to stomping all over the haunted house on the anniversary of the murder-suicide."

"Helping?!" I complained, a chill running down my arms despite the stuffy room.

"Look, your instruments are uniquely tied to this case. They have the mark on them, and you've been using them to play the actual songs of the ghosts for months. They *know* you. I wouldn't be surprised if the haunting hadn't reached into both of them, but Amir's eyes are too… individual… to be strong enough to channel all these ghosts except in the presence of the whole choir. What I am saying is, I think we can use Ally's hoodoo banjo to talk to the ghosts!"

"Mandolin. Do we want to talk to the ghosts?" I asked. "We know how they died. We have a pretty good idea about why they are angry enough to haunt us. What more do we need to know?"

"Why they're angry, yes. But not why they are ghosts!"

"We know how they died!"

"We don't know why. When do thirteen people in a weirdly specific group die in a crash that left way more survivors as it killed outright? Some of them in 'just a scratch' condition!"

"I hadn't thought about that. I guess I was working on the assumption that they were killed by thirteen *more* ghosts from the Orchestra Society *six* years ago."

"Oh, Ally, you're a silly person."

"Ghosts and death aside, none of it matters if we don't go to Orchestra practice!" I cried, catching sight of the clock in the room.

Amir grimaced. "Molly will add to the number of ghosts herself if we are late."

"I am *so* looking forward to meeting her!" Alana enthused.

"She'll be nice to you," Amir pointed out. "You do not play for her."

# Gallows Hill

It was the most cramped I had ever seen the room. There were thirteen core members, Molly included.

Lucia refused to move her sweater off the chair next to her when I came in accompanied by Amir, and she was sitting next to Sam for some reason. Spite. That was the reason. It seemed like she'd already been giving Rose evil looks too and had just added me to that list on my arrival. Seeing as she was having about the worst week ever I was seriously going to have to figure out how to spend the next semester getting her and Amir to make up and get together as an apology. I passed her violin over and grimaced at her, and to my relief she gave me and only me a softer sort of weary look. I could work with this.

That left me crammed into a corner with all the extras that I had tricked into coming. Alana, Rose and... The Piper.

He had said nothing, and I had to glance at Alana and then jerk my head towards him to make sure I wasn't the only one who could even see him. He sat on the floor at the back of the room with his legs stretched out, impossibly finding the space to do so with one of his minor superpowers. He might have been asleep.

Alana had opted not to fight her way over to the one spare chair when she wasn't even participating: she leaned on the door, grinning apologetically at Molly. I bumped elbows with Rose, who had found a suitable acoustic replacement for her old electric guitar.

Amir kept looking sidelong at it, eventually turning in his chair and poking the guitar.

"No... Like Cobain? No!"

"Just like," Rose said, grinning and spraying a few cookie crumbs. She patted the dinged up guitar fondly.

I decided to ignore this, because clearly she could not have the money to buy two authentic rock star guitars and still need to do a Literature degree. Therefore... She knew the Piper? She must know some magic. She was messing with Amir's in-depth knowledge and hoodwinking him for a laugh. Had to be it.

Else I was going to spend the entire session having a piece of history crammed into my ribs every time Rose did a chord change or strummed too excitedly.

Once we had all settled down, Molly led us in with a rather longer speech than normal.

"Okay, gang." (Yes, she was exactly that uncool that she said 'gang'.) "It's really not long before the show now. I think we're getting to grips with these songs, and I just want to say thanks to everyone for giving up so much of your studying and social time to come here every night."

"I'm claiming course credits for this performance!" someone from the flute section butted in.

Her friend nodded enthusiastically. "I've written up a whole report!"

Molly cleared her throat. "Well, particular thanks, then, to those of you unfortunate enough not to be on music courses. Um..." Her eyes darted to me. I almost never heard her hesitate or er and ah. "Before the show, I think I'll lead it in with a little tribute. I don't know if the rumours have worked their way around the whole group yet, but *some* of you have found out already that the Orchestra Society has been on a three year hiatus after the tragic deaths of, er, the whole Orchestra."

There was a minor uproar, but mostly along the lines of shouted "What?!", so it quickly died down as they waited for answers.

"It was only a coach accident, but some of the more... superstitious of you have expressed concern about my decision to use their set listing and old sheet music. I thought a minute of silence would be appropriate before we begin playing. We owe a big thank you to them: we would be much further behind without all the groundwork they set for this show before they sadly passed."

"Does a minute of silence ever appease angry ghosts?" I mumbled to Rose.

"Not usually," she replied with a snigger.

Molly scowled at us. "Are there any more questions, or shall we try and work our way through these songs in a timely manner?"

With that she pointed us at the first song, waved her hands, counted us in, and we screeched and squeaked our way into it, my mandolin in particular weeping from the treatment it received. I'd been trying to tune it up without plucking the notes harder than a feather brushing across them while Molly was talking.

But for all the odd noises I produced, I didn't mess up that time. Well, I missed the start of a few bars and had to wait for the next to come along, and once I played D for three bars instead of switching chords in between, but it slipped Molly's notice. She was fuming, still annoyed, I realised, about the silly panic I had created.

I'd heard the fear in the Orchestra's voices after her announcement. *No one likes to hear about a matched group dying all at once.* No matter how unique the circumstances, sane people reach for their neck and say "What if it's me next!?" because it is normal to feel irrational panic for your own skin. Seriously: go tell a left-handed person that their average life expectancy is lower than a right-handed person's, and just for a moment their eyes will narrow at their sinister appendage like it might just twist around and come at them.

I think the haunting must have been getting to the whole group, whether they realised it or not. As I glanced furtively about while strumming quietly to myself, I saw a lot of extra-frowny faces. Lacklustre bowing on the violins. Eyes darting up from the sheet music and looking around.

My ears were confused though. It should have been the worst group effort we'd ever put in, but the ghostly noises were there, stronger than ever. They washed over us, a perfect rendition of the piece. And so it should be, if the ghosts had been practising it incessantly in the back of my head for a week.

I think everyone could hear it that time, but they didn't realise why or that it wasn't coming from the rest of the group. As their energy and skill was hampered, each note they missed, they glanced up. "Who is playing it so much better than me that we still sound this good?" was in their thoughts, and they checked and checked, but only saw more worried faces, and me, playing along with my tongue sticking out, determined not to flub it for once. But that was hardly more reassuring.

At the end of the first song, Molly flipped the page on her music stand, announced we were onto *Thriller*, and counted us in without another word. Off we went.

The only person playing *well*, I realised, finally managing to tune the ghosts out, was Rose. She had her eyes closed, her mouth no longer chewing but in a small smile. Her fingers danced over the fretboard, her strumming perfectly rhythmical. It took me a second with the crowded soundscape in the room, but she was only playing Amir's part. But she had totally nailed it, and brought it out of just being "chord change, rinse and repeat," and was wringing genuine music out of it.

I knew she was a good player, but few people in this room were abjectly bad. Rose just seemed immune to the ghosts.

And Molly, I realised. Whether it was her stubbornness, her scepticism or just despite being the instigator of all this, the last one of us to get haunted, she was standing at the keyboard, resolutely mashing keys, providing our piano accompaniment without a single hesitation, but scowling at us and clearly aware of how much of a torturous process this was today.

By the end of the session, forty-five minutes later, I was exhausted and my brain ached from staying focussed on one task for so long. My arms were shaking and my new calluses this month on my fingertips were livid red.

Even Molly looked dazed, though she might just have been in a state of shock that we played the whole set in one go without stopping, no matter how badly. "Uh, that was very good. Um. Very good," she said, shaking her head a little as if to clear her ears of a ghostly aftersound of the music. But from horror at how bad it had been, not the regular brand horror we were dealing with. "Let's wrap up there and see if we can go over some specific songs tomorrow. Thank you."

Rose casually shouldered the huge guitar, bumping it into the chairs behind her (definitely not a priceless rock artefact), and turned to grin at me. "I thought that was fun. Didn't you?"

I looked around to the very back of the room, but I had the sense she had just covered the Piper's escape: it was empty.

Alana opened the door and let in a blast of very welcome freezing air. The whole orchestra seemed to be sucked out of the door, we were so relieved to have a change of atmosphere. In the stampede down the stairs I misplaced Rose and just followed Amir's guitar. Upside down on his back, the eyes with their long lashes seemed somehow sad. I could see the wobble in the permanent marker where his hand had shaken and he'd done the eyeliner extra thick. Mundane. When we reached the bottom and I was glancing around for Alana, I realised Rose had already slipped away somewhere too.

"That girl is up to something," I muttered.

"The chunky girl with the guitar?" Alana asked at my side. I jumped a little. Look, she was a foot shorter than me, at least. She could have been at my elbow and I wouldn't have seen her.

"Rose, yeah."

"Let's get somewhere less public."

The orchestra was already dispersing. Despite the friendships we'd formed in it, everyone seemed to have an urgent reason to get away that evening. Already there were only two standing talking near the door, one checking her phone while she waited for hot chocolate at the café. Amir had slipped off. Lucia had left with Sam, I thought, but I was too dazed to have seen her go. For all I knew Rose could have waved goodbye to me.

"Back to Sherrick Hall?" I asked, thinking of getting comfy for the evening and not moving again. I disliked busy days.

"We'll just walk for now," Alana said.

I'd sort of been dreading it. And knew somehow she'd have an answer like that.

*

Alana stuck to the paths around campus at first. I dragged myself after her, the huge difference in the length of my legs only making them heavier to pick up and slide along the ground after the fast little toddle Alana managed. My flip-flops filled with dead, damp leaves and I began to see that this was definitely one of those days.

Once the theatre was safely behind us, hidden by the ubiquitous campus trees, Alana finally spoke again.

"Ally. You said there were thirteen people in Orchestra."

"There are."

"Did you mean thirteen *and Molly*?"

"No!"

"See, while I was standing there listening to you play, I was counting, and I definitely saw fourteen people playing instruments."

"Did you hear the ghosts?"

"No."

"No!? I thought you were all receptive and stuff now!"

"Well yeah, but I think that session confirmed my theory that you have to be playing along to hear them. I think that's what Rose is doing."

"What does Rose have to do with it?" I asked because I knew that Rose was clearly everything to do with it and I didn't want to know the answer so I was playing dumb.

"She's number fourteen. When thirteen people sit down together… She's not in the Orchestra."

"She paid the fee to the SU."

"She's not *in* the Orchestra. She's not haunted, not… a part of it. She might be able to hear the ghosts though. She's not like everyone else. I'd say she was, like, some sort of undercover investigator, but she's not like *me* either."

"The Piper said she was."

"You've talked about this?!"

"He said she reminded him of someone. And then he said she didn't, and he only wished she did. And then he begged official business and smashed my lip open."

"What?!"

I giggled, self-consciously licking the still-healing split. "I'm kidding. That was me being clumsy."

"Jesus, Ally. We don't have a contingency plan if he starts beating you. He's a freaking… I don't know. Not the sort you can go into protective custody to avoid."

"He's not beating me!"

"Good!"

We walked on in silence for a few paces before Alana regained her composure. "Anyway. Rose. She doesn't… remind you of anyone?"

"What do you mean?"

"She *knew* me. While you were playing, she looked right at me, and she… She knew. I mean, I'm not the sort of psychic who has conversations with people in their heads, but oh my gods, for a moment when our eyes met, I could feel her saying, *I know who you are.* No one should be able to project that sort of mental power."

"No one?"

"Ally, the only reason this world hasn't imploded into a great big ball of pixies and wizards is that *magic doesn't work.* You are phenomenally lucky to keep stumbling on the instances where it does. My power only works in those situations, and yes I get to do a lot of magic because the Piper sends me places where the veil is thinner or people know what's up, but… Day-to-day, I'm as dull as you. When I came on campus, I knew something was up because I could feel the tingle of power all over the place. It's not coming from the ghosts, and the Orchestra's music creates a tiny amount of disturbance. Rose is the spider in the middle of the web. All of it leads back to her, and she's just sitting there, watching things get caught in it. Do you know the only other time I've felt something like that?"

"Er, no?"

"Seeing the Piper wandering about in Troutespond. He *owns* the place, and everything he does affects everything else and everything you do comes back to him. I'm not pointing fingers, but…"

"She's *like* him like him?"

"She might be. What I want to know is why she's here. What the Piper is, is unusually helpful."

"Helpful!?"

"For what he is. He's not the only one of his ilk, but he's one of the few who plays a deeply active role in the world. The only one who seems to be on our side and *helps.* Most are just observers, I guess. Or do jobs that keep them out of the public eye. We don't *need* any more interference with the Piper on the case, everyone's case, all at the same time. His job is to be the one who interferes. And then we have Rose. Going to your classes, blending in, sleeping in halls, eating… Joining Orchestra Society."

"The Piper finds it hard to stay in the same place for more than ten minutes."

Alana nodded. "Whatever Rose is, she's fixated on you, and she's quite possibly the reason the ghosts are even able to haunt properly. Maybe even with that banjo, you wouldn't have heard them if she wasn't here."

"Mandolin. Fixated on me?"

"Well she sat next to you, whispered to you, and generally seemed all… *buddied* up to you. It's very, very suspicious."

"So the ghosts aren't the problem, Rose is? But if she's like the Piper…"

"No contingency plan. We just have to let her beat you."

I swallowed hard.

"So what do we do?"

"You keep being friends with her, and we deal with the ghosts. It might be a test. If this whole thing is about the Orchestra, then there is a very clear issue: there are ghosts, and a clear resolution: stop the haunting, or otherwise appease the ghosts. And for that we need to talk to them." She stopped and gestured the fence we'd been walking alongside.

I stopped too, staring blankly at it. "I fail to see how a fence helps with the ghosts."

"Climb over it, silly."

I did, and then offered a hand to Alana, since she actually had to scramble up and over instead of raising a leg one side and putting it down the other like I had.

The ground underfoot was squishy and muddy: we were at a brief break in the hedge, and though the fence continued obstinately over the gap, it was clear this might as well have had a "Public Footpath" sign next to it. The field on the other side had a beaten muddy track for ten meters into it, and even in the dark I could see a paler line of beaten down grass running over the rise in the hill and out of sight.

"We're going for a little country stroll."

"It's the *middle of the night*."

"It's like eight o'clock. People are still eating dinner. Some people are still in classes!"

"It's *dark enough and I'm haunted*."

"Come on, you big baby." Alana set off across the field, leaving me panicking by the fence. Despite how beaten in this path was I still felt like I was trespassing. I finally convinced myself to go after Alana by pointing out to myself that I was most likely to get caught if I stayed in sight of the uni, and, well, Alana was far enough ahead now that I'd hear the warning shot if there was a farmer fed up of students cutting across his land lurking around the corner.

I set off in a rush to warn Alana not to bump into him.

However the other side of this field there was another hedge, this with another gap in it, and a real footpath. It ran alongside the wild moorland that my university was nestled into and as it was free countryside, there was no fence to stop us wandering out onto it as we pleased. I guessed the path went to a nearby village one way and back to the university by a rather longer route that wasn't near any halls by the other. Alana didn't care about what was in the village: she led us out into the moor.

Now, I hadn't been *so* campus-bound that I hadn't gone out for a little exploratory walk, during the daytime, with a picnic and Lucia, Angie and two random friends of Angie's for company. With a group like that I was the one most suited to tromping through the wilderness just because of the various girly mannerisms I lacked, like caring about looking hot and sweaty, which got in the way of their hiking ability. We'd made it up one hill before we sat down on the assumption that going any further would take us out of phone signal and we didn't want to die out there. Still, that was enough of a foray into the wilderness to show me that we were surrounded by rolling hills, with only the odd clump of trees on them and a great deal of heather and bracken and low scrubby, prickly things that made finding a spot of wind-beaten grass to spread a picnic blanket on a challenge, especially as there might be things like wild sheep or highland cows (imported for land management reasons) out there too.

The campus was nestled into a bowl-like valley and filled up with unnatural tree plantations along all those endless pathways, making it a lush green spot in a brown-and-purple landscape, but at night it was the bright spot on a totally black-and-black landscape. I could see the lights of the farm we'd crossed the land of a little ways off, but aside from that, only a faint glow of some big Northern city I knew nothing about did anything to the night sky, and that was far off on the horizon. The hills were a little lighter than the sky, a dark-grey line in the distance. Around us my night vision had crept up on me. With a clear night and a waxing moon it wasn't so hard to see your way after all. True pitch darkness could only come when you sealed yourself away from the sky.

Alana seemed totally in her element: she found a path through the rugged ground and led me on with strides longer than my own steps as I stumbled after her, kicking stones and small spiky plants as I went.

Panting slightly, she broke her brief silence to tell me stuff I didn't even know. "There's an earthworks on the big hill to the north," she said. "I think a ruined church in the valley down there: a river runs right through it. And a cairn or... cross? On the hill above it. Look at the stars!"

I looked up. Now we had left the lit-up, tree-sheltered campus I realised how splattered the sky was with little points of light. Even at home there was a town, or a village, every three miles down the road. It was awfully *crowded*. And stargazing was less than optimal, what with the damp leftover Welsh weather that constantly came our way and overcast the sky.

"Shiny," I observed.

"Every one of these tumbled down stone walls follows the Milky Way," she said. "I don't think the farmers even knew they were doing it."

"What farmers?"

"Thousands of years ago," Alana said dismissively, like I was being weird for assuming they might sneak up on us with their shotguns. "Look, there's a wall there."

I looked down in the darkness and realised that what I had taken for more bumpy ground had sharp-angled black stones poking out of it very regularly, looking stacked up and somehow woven together.

"They made the walls without any cement: just stacked the stones together in a long line with such skill they never fell over and you could kick them without shaking it."

"How do you know all this?" I asked.

Alana shook her head. "I don't know. The land's telling me. I thought I knew all this stuff back home because, well, I had to pick it all up as a survival instinct, right? But when I got to my university, the Piper was like, "Right! There's stuff that needs doing!" And, well, I'm down on the coast, right? I set off to walk along the beach, and I can *feel* the tides before they're coming in. I know what caves are special and which were used by smugglers and which are just holes in the cliff face. I could see where the lighthouse once was, like the light was still beaming out to sea, but I had to climb right up onto the rocks to see where the ruin was. I walked through town, and I knew the house the famous coven had lived in before I came around the corner and saw the blue plaque on the wall. I even could taste the freaking pagan crystals-and-incense shop as soon as I got off the train. I could hear the dead sailors crying in the voices of the seagulls... And when we went to the nightclub on the pier, I saw the Victorians ballroom dancing alongside us for just a second. I think the Piper has taken my third eye and jammed it open with... like in the cartoons where they put matchsticks in their eyes to stop them from falling asleep?"

I nodded. "That's strange."

She shrugged. "He said I'd get more powerful, but I thought he meant more, *better* spells. I forgot that magic doesn't work like that. You can't just *do spells* and stuff. You can only do that if you understand everything in the first place, and write your own spells. Which I'm terrible at."

"That's a shame. That you've got such a useless tutor, that is."

"No, it's not. I've had all this... this *understanding* forced into my head. And I get it now. People who learn all the spells somehow but don't get why... They end up like the infamous witches I mentioned. They cursed the whole town with the mess they made. Even after the witchfinder got to them, the town was still suffering. You can't fling spells about. It doesn't work that way, and when it does, you break stuff. I bet they meant well sometimes, but it never did go their way. Your mum is the most powerful witch I've met, *still*, and all she does is random little rituals to ask what the weather will be on Friday, since she thinks the TV lies to her, stuff like that. But she *gets* it."

"So basically you're saying you're practically useless, but you could sit and write a book on the subject once I get bored of listening to this and you have no one else to talk to?"

"Nah, I brought you up here to do a spell."

"But you just said!"

"Yeah, well I said earlier that right here, right now, with Rose and the ghosts... We can do *proper* magic now."

*

She stopped at last on what she called "Gallows Hill."

"Oh, people were hanged here for centuries," she said casually as she plonked her bag down on a nearby rock. I immediately twisted myself around in my fear of touching anything, lest I get more ghost-germs on me. Last thing I needed was to be haunted *twice*, and one of those ghosts being a murderer. "The gallows were about where you're standing... *were* standing," (I leapt to the side) "But historically that was quite recent and they were in a bit of the wrong place. Criminals from the old Bronze Age clan that lived nearby used to be brought up here and staked down for the birds where you're standing now."

I shuffled away. "Do you have anything bad to say about this particular patch of earth?"

"No."

"Okay."

"We're up here because this is obviously a great place for communicating to the dead. If you'd be so kind as to lend me your banjo."

"Mandolin."

She took it from me, wrestled it from the case, and then there was the click of her lighter.

"Don't set it on——!" She lit a candle she had pulled from her handbag, and I relaxed. She used that candle to light six more, little stumpy things made of dark red wax, which she had arranged in a loose circle on the rock. It was big enough to place my mandolin in the centre, safe from the flames. It looked very cross at the treatment nonetheless, although it looked cross at everything.

"Okay, now you go stand that side of the rock."

I shrugged and, assuming that it must be at least a little safe since she did like me, shuffled over and stood the other side of it. We had a little pool of yellow light around us now, but it didn't stretch far at all. It was just enough to give Alana a ghoulishly happy shadowing to her face. My night vision was totally destroyed when I looked away, a circle of flames imprinted into my retinas.

"This rock is interesting," Alana said. "I think ritual magic has been done on it before, but it's not screaming out as part of the landscape. Must be local witches who don't really know how to use the country around them to make their spells."

"Is that bad?"

"Means it doesn't work when they try. Probably why there are only trace amounts of their magic here. They must have given up."

"It was probably bored students."

"Aha." She nodded like this explained everything, never mind that we were bored students too. "What sleeves are you wearing?"

"*What?*"

"Well I was going to ask you to put your hands on the banjo, but knowing your fashion choices and the number of candles..."

"Mandolin." I held up my arms to show sensible sleeves; a university hoodie that had elasticated cuffs and hem.

"Okay, pop them on."

I rested my hands on the mandolin, feeling like this was the weirdest Ouija board in the history of ridiculous attempts to contact the other side. At least the rock was too heavy for her to knock and tip about.

Alana was getting into her role as a professional medium. She too put her hands on the mandolin, tipping her head back to look at that clear, clear sky.

"Spirits of the orchestra!" she called into the night. "Dwellers in the music called forth from this instrument! Come speak with us, and tell us of your deaths! I call on the musicians of the past, trapped in these strings, to let themselves be known to us! I call to you, lost artists, to come forth so we may show you the way home!"

"Good, good," I mumbled, though I felt a little nervous about her shouting. Yes, we were basically alone in the world right now, but it was still super-embarrassing.

"Shh!" she hissed at me. "You can't spoil the mood!" She turned her face skyward again. "I call on you!" she called again, mostly to make up for me.

There followed one of the longest silences I've ever had to endure, longer even than awkward moments or that time when I dropped my phone and there was a huge cracking sound and the screen went off and I was holding down the power button to see if it would turn back on...

The C string gave a sudden twang all of its own volition.

I'd like to point out that Alana screamed too at that point.

We stood there with hands clamped over our mouths, shaking. Alana reached out first to put her hand back on the 'banjo' and recovered enough to give me a stern look. I started to reach out for it.

"This is it," Alana whispered, suddenly thrilled, her fear vanishing as quickly as the shock had hit us.

Well, my fear was still intact. I almost knocked a candle I was shaking so much, and spoiled the mood a little to myself by a quiet panic that my sleeve was on fire. It wasn't, so I tentatively poked the mandolin. We stared into its fearsome face, waiting for another string to twang. Perhaps the ghosts were waiting for us to get our shit together and ask them some questions.

Instead we heard a muffled cry: "It came from over there!"

Before we could react, a stunned voice called, from right beside us, "Found them!"

Stunned? I meant stoned. It was Bus Stop, of all people. "Mate, it's Ally, from your floor!"

"Ally? No way, right?" Mike came crashing through the shrub land and emerged onto the candlelit hilltop. "What are you doing out here?"

"They've been doing magic," Bus said, totally impressed. "Look, they summoned a demon banjo!"

"Mandolin."

"That's her weird banjo thing, right?" Mike informed Bus. "She actually owns it."

"Mandolin."

"Why do you keep saying that?" Alana asked me. "No, wait, more to the point," she turned to the boys, "What the fuck are you doing out here, and Ally, how do you always know the weirdest people in any given place?"

A grim realisation had hit me. "They're stoners, not weird, and we now feature in some rambling epic story that they will be telling all over campus. I bet this isn't the strangest thing to happen to them tonight."

"Nah, mate. Not even close," Bus said with a wide grin. "You're not hanging out with Rose, are you?"

"No?"

"Shame. She always has biscuits."

"Ally," Alana said, ignoring them completely though they stood a pace away from us, "They're blunderers."

"*What?*"

"The goblin economy runs on fools like this. I'm amazed your Mum didn't end up being one on her little jaunt. Ask the one in the stripy top what his name is."

"Er... It's Bus Stop..."

"Ask him."

"Hey, Bus? What's your name?"

He frowned, crinkling up his badly-shaven face. "Bus Stop, innit?"

"Is that what's on your birth certificate?"

"I dunno man, probably."

"Goblined," Alana said to me.

"Or so stoned he can't remember."

"Or so stoned he thinks he can't remember, but it was stolen by goblins."

"Normally being stoned makes you remember the goblins and not the boring answer."

"Well in this case if they actually bumped into goblins, then they'd want him not to remember." She turned back to the very bemused pair of stoners. "Hey, guys, you come out on the moors often?"

Bus was beginning to look really quite panicked by the interrogation. "Man, are you MI6?"

"No!" Alana said, a laugh bursting out before she could keep her strict composure. "I'm a paranormal investigator from an independent contractor."

"Stop telling my friends you're a ghostbuster!" I groaned with exasperated amusement. "None of them knew about this stuff before you were here!"

Our laughter was clearly contagious: Mike and Bus were giggling too. "Okay, okay," Bus said. "You're cool."

"So, the moors?" Alana prompted.

"Man, I dunno, we come out here a lot. Sort of feels important, right?"

"It's off-campus, so we won't get busted for smoking out here either," Mike said. He seemed a lot less baked *or* weird than Bus Stop. I could tell he was still nervous from the way he glanced over his shoulder, a mile away to campus. Like campus security had a telescope they scanned the moors with from atop the Arts building tower. Maybe he was just getting paranoid.

"You going to come to the party on Friday, Ally? Tomorrow, right?" Bus Stop said. "Hey, Friday Ally would be a great name. You should use it."

"Why?"

"Dunno, got a ring to it. You go with these things when you find a good name."

"Is that why they call you Bus Stop?"

He gave me this hugely affronted look. "Why do *you* think they call me Bus Stop?"

Alana nudged me. "So, this party? Yeah, we'll be there. Where is it again?"

"Aaaall over campus." Bus spread his hands wide, his big happy smile back again. "See you Friday, Ally. *There you go, it works.*"

"Friday Ally," Mike said.

"You can't just make a nickname up out of thin air!" I complained. "I'm not a nickname sort of person."

"Later, Friday Ally," Bus said, waved, and set off tromping down the hill in a clearly randomly picked direction.

Mike's eyes darted about; he gave us a curt nod and went crashing off after his silently moving friend.

"Shall we keep trying to communicate with the ghosts?" I asked nervously, once the noise died away.

"With the noise those two were making, they've probably scared off every beastie for ten miles. Come on, Friday Ally, grab your banjo and let's go get hot chocolate or something."

"*Mandolin.* I'm not sure I can count the number of other things wrong with that sentence."

"If you don't have any hot chocolate I'm going to be very upset."

Alana blew out the candles, plunging up back into darkness.

"You're not putting those back into your bag all full of hot wax still?"

"Nah. Next person to come by this way will have a very unsettled feeling when they notice them. It'll keep the magic in the land alive for another day."

She wasted no more time, setting off back the way we'd come.

# Hall of Fame

Once we were warming up in the cave I called my room, I finally found it appropriate to ask Alana some more urgent questions she'd thrown my way. "Why did you say yes to the party? You hate parties... Don't you?"

Alana frowned into her mug (handmade by my mum. I had the best mug collection in the Hall, and no one ever borrowed them without asking). "Bus Stop, poor lad, is a part of this. I can feel it. But I'm not sure how. Either he's wiped his own memory with all the weed, or the goblins took it from him. He's a fixture around here, isn't he?"

I nodded.

"Does he still have classes? I mean, he studies here, or is he just... like a vagrant student?"

"I assumed he had classes still. I think he's a chemistry student."

"Oh."

"Yeah, and there's a certain lecturer here who's known to write chemical formulas on the board and leave the class to it and, well, let's just say if some of the proceeds slip his way, the chemical cupboard is left unlocked for those students..."

"He's getting course credits for being Bus Stop. Marvellous."

"Well, it's graded by lab work, with not as much written assessment under that teacher, so he's putting in plenty of hours. Can't kick him out if he gets a solid 2:2 for participation."

Alana gave a long sigh that turned into a groan. "I missed this."

"What?"

"Sitting around hearing your barmy theories."

"It's not a barmy theory! It's the actual truth!"

"Mmhmm. Do you think Teb or Tanya are online?"

"I don't know about Tanya, but it's gone eleven. We should find a Teb easily. If the internet is working again." I pulled my phone out and turned airplane mode off, still enabled since practice. It searched around for a second and then I was connected to the clunky free wifi, like the weird internet outage had never happened. Was the Piper messing with me? I clicked on our chat and found one Tebster Magee online.

"Call her, call her, call her!" Alana said, bouncing beside me, her own phone clutched in her hand.

"Whyyy? We normally just type stuff. I never call her. I bet you never do!"

"Yeah, but there's two of us here. She should see by video just how much fun we're having without her."

"I'll ask her," I said, beginning to type a "Hi."

"Loser," Alana said, snatching my phone, inexplicably making the call from my account.

"She's not going to answer," I complained, as it got to the sixth annoying ring.

"She must be on the toilet or something..."

"Hey!" Teb's voice came out tinny but annoyed from my speakers. For a moment my phone's screen filled with a blank black image, and then it seared into a while halo and a black Teb-shaped blob of square pixels the size of a Post-it Note, and then her camera adjusted and in all her blurry, blue-from-the-screen glory was Teb.

"Hey!" I cried, a lot more happily.

"Oh for... Is that Alana? Tell her to stop moving! I can't tell how many pounds she's put on at uni." Teb sounded so... *rural*. I think Alana and I had both lost our accents immediately on being dropped into the mixing pot, or else we didn't hear our own when surrounded by all these foreigners from other parts of the country.

"I've *lost* weight," Alana said primly, freezing in place.

"From your boobs, maybe," Teb said. I obligingly took the phone and held it further away from us so she could get a better view. I did not understand this fight they were having, but I had to assume that this was something they had already had it out over and were now just ribbing each other. Else Teb was a complete monster.

"Yeah, well you look *glamorous*," Alana said. Teb was wearing a figure-distorting hoodie and her hair was limp and damp, making her face look gaunt as it hung flat around it. She must have just come from the shower, and obviously seen no reason to reapply make up until the morning: her eyes seemed pale and small without the thick line of kohl around them that she favoured recently, and her mouth a brown line instead of the defined pout she normally spent ten minutes on. Not like I should comment: I never bothered any of the time ever with things like making myself look pretty. But Teb painted her own face as a matter of course and it was strange to see the one underneath it.

"How's Troutespond?" I interrupted, deciding they really could keep insulting each other forever as part of this sick game and I would begin to doubt they were actually any sort of friend at all, which was depressing, if they kept it up.

"Warm and sunny," Teb said. "They're putting a new set of swings up in the Green, and all the village conservationists freaked out, you know, the nutters who still call it a village instead of a town, but apparently we're a 'booming commuter hub' because a new family moved here. So they want to make the place attractive to maybe a second young family who might decide to come live here."

"My god, the economy must be practically exploding with new business."

"Mm, the corner shop has renegotiated their contract with the farm for more milk, what with all the baby teeth that will soon be littering the streets from all the growing rugrats. The primary school is in a panic about the number of safety scissors they own. I heard Miss Silver wrote to the family personally to ask if any of their children, including the newborn, was left-handed."

"Teb, *why are you still at home?*" Alana demanded.

"I'm not *at home*," she said. "I mean, yeah, I'm in the bedroom I grew up in, but I'm not stagnating."

"You just told us a story about the town council."

"I'm basically here to eat breakfast and then take a shower at night! I'm in Severstrong all day doing *real history*!"

"I call her still living in the basement at thirty," Alana said to me.

"Just because I'm not getting a fancy education... Oh wait, I'm talking to a *Literature student* and a *Media Studies student*."

"Hey!" we protested in unison. "Literature is a real profession!" I added.

"I could be a *journalist*," Alana complained. "They don't let just anyone go to war-torn nations to ask obnoxiously insensitive questions of famine victims!"

"Do you make little paper hats with a Press sticker in your seminars?" Teb jibed.

Alana scowled. "No, we do theory and analysis and other stuff which you can't do because you're digging muddy little holes all day."

Teb stuck her tongue out.

She changed the subject: "Saw your Mum yesterday, Ally."

"Oh yeah?"

"She still looks barmy, don't worry. She said she's coming up for some sort of show you're doing at the end of the week?"

"Oh yeah."

"Eee! Your Mum's coming here?!" Alana squealed.

"Calm!"

"She's awesome!"

"She's not staying with us. It would be a bit crowded to cram my parents in this little room as well. They're staying one night in a B&B and they're taking me out for dinner before the show."

"Us."

"Okay, fine, they're taking us out to dinner."

"So," Teb said. "What are you two up to?"

"What do you mean? We're not up to anything!" I said at once, a little paranoid.

"Come on, you can tell me! It's you and Alana. How can you *not* be pursued by ogres or something?"

"It's only ghosts!"

Teb burst out laughing. "*Only* ghosts. What did you do?"

"Well we were doing a séance up on Gallows Hill behind the uni…"

"And you're wondering why you're haunted? *Don't do dumb shit like that.*"

"No!" Alana complained. "We were doing that *because* Ally is haunted. I was trying to contact the ghosts, but her crazy stoner friends interrupted us. Ally's haunted by her orchestra. They all died in a coach crash in mysterious circumstances."

"Oh well, then Ally will almost certainly be eaten by ghosts. Good luck!"

"*Thanks*," I said.

Teb glanced around, then grinned. "Yeah, I have to go now. It's getting late and I have to be up early. Nighty night, girls. Sweet dreams!"

"You can't just say that about me being eaten by ghosts and then go!"

"You're not going to be eaten by ghosts," Alana said.

"You don't know that!"

*

It took a lot of calming me down and a well-overdue cup of tea, but Alana, who was visibly wilting by that point, convinced me to go to bed.

Whether it was Teb's words, the tea I'd just drunk or my restlessness, I lay wide-awake, eyes jammed open.

Alana was top to tail with me in the bed, and I had the much easier deal since when she was scrunched up and snuggling her pillow she was so much smaller that all she could do was kick me in the arm. In a very deliberate way she was lying facing away from my feet, which poked out of the end of the duvet on the best of days, and were basically sharing her pillow. Sometimes she'd start to roll over and, even asleep, remember where my feet where, make a little groaning noise and roll right back again. She'd made me shower before turning in because of the amount of mud I'd caked onto my toes while gallivanting about in flip-flops. I'd like to point out I would have at least gone and hosed down my feet on a normal day with no guests around to see. It took six rotations to get sheets dried in the little laundrette on the ground floor, and that was a lot of money considering I never had much pocket change.

Most of all though, among the many horrible thoughts battling to keep me awake, the strongest was how much I missed the Piper. I hadn't realised just how many nights in a row I'd spent cuddled up to him, a radiator and teddy bear all in one, who'd mumble comforting things that made me go right back to sleep if I started to show signs of insomnia. I suppose even if I hadn't been a jerk and yelled at him I wouldn't have had him there that night, but it felt worse because I was in a strop with him. It wasn't like I was even ready to talk to him, but night had come sooner than me getting over him being disrespectful to my independence and I regretted it happening in that order.

And there was the music. It was persistently in the back of my mind now, a sort of extra humming in my ears along with the normal background noises when I wasn't paying attention. But as soon as it got dark it was like having *Thriller* stuck in my head, except that instead of little snippets that looped, the whole piece ran from start to finish and then the flute section picked up to run on into *The Addams Family* tune.

Eventually Alana began to snore gently, making up for the lack of percussion section. I got up and slipped my sandals back on, pulled my hoodie on and used a huge book of literary criticism to prop the door open. I went into the kitchen, quite surprised to find Corridor B mostly silent. I opened the fridge and stared blankly at the empty shelf that should have had all my food on it, then sighed, shut the fridge and looked around the room like a delicious cake might materialise on the counter in front of me. None did.

My feet moved pretty much of their own volition, dragging me through the hall to the perpetually open door onto the chilly stairwell. I headed up; Sherrick Hall was four floors that mostly ignored each other when they weren't thieving each other's appliances, since it was generally deemed that the worst smells and loudest music clearly weren't the fault of anyone on *your* floor. And we definitely weren't the ones who set off a fire alarm every night for three weeks in a row at the beginning of the semester.

But every floor had one thing in common: the smokers were their own clique, who instantly bonded and they had worked out right away that it was a lot less hassle to break onto the roof consistently than to huddle in the tiny shelter down behind the building, which was the only place they were allowed to smoke on ground level until the yards around various bars.

I wasn't going up there to smoke, and it was so late by that point I doubted I would be crashing their party. In better weather and daylight a lot of girls sunbathed up here. Most people had been dragged up there at one point or another, so I knew it was a good view and was somewhere I could sit and be alone and thoughtful and maybe find something to look at to distract me from hearing any more phantom music.

The stairs ran up one extra flight and ended abruptly in a single door with a foot of space for a landing. The heavy fire door was propped open with a metal bin, the kind with the ashtray on top. There was no bin bag in it: I reckoned it was brought up by students. And it reeked, full almost to the top with cigarette butts. This was the reason the hallway was always cold. If the smokers gave in and closed it, they'd have to wait who knows how long for another chance to prop it open… Or just set off the alarm each night when they sneaked up to reopen it until someone managed to trick the system into forgetting it was open once more.

I slipped past the bin and stepped out onto the roof. The stairs were bang in the middle of the building, the three wings of its T shape spreading out in each direction from the door. It was a flat roof, a sickly grey colour of roof felting with big puddles that never dried up in this autumn weather. Various small pipes and ventilation shafts jutted out, venting all our kitchens and showers, making the furniture and trip hazards the smokers knew and loved. Some areas smelled strongly of steam and soap at certain times of the day, others of grease and curry around dinner. The whole edge of the building had a waist-height brick wall, with a smooth finish in white stone to match the highlights under the windows and around the doors. It wasn't an ugly building from the front: just every other angle inside and out.

I wasn't alone up here.

And of course it was someone who I couldn't not talk to.

I had a feeling that I had been summoned up here all of a sudden.

Rose was wearing unusually smart clothes: a red top with a large collar, shell buttons up the front. Black trousers with a sharp crease. Shiny shoes. She was smoking, and looking up at the stars. Her hair tumbled down past her waist, curly and bouncy and a glossy chestnut that all mousy-haired girls like me hope people think of when they announce they're a brunette but few actually have.

"Hey Ally," she said. She sounded sad. Her eyes were dark voids. It was hard to see any sadness in them when they just went on forever like the cold depths of space.

"Rose."

"So Alana stomped in and ruined everything."

"A bit. But not *everything*." Friend loyalty had quickly been restored once my initial tiff with the Piper was out of the way. Who was Rose to talk about my friend that way?!

"She told you that I'm the villain here. And it's true. It's you and her, I guess, against me and mine."

"Y-you killed the last orchestra?"

Rose barked out a laugh with her last inhale of smoke. "Don't be ridiculous. I don't kill people."

"Then what's happening here?"

Rose shook her head. "It's part of the game: to work things out for yourself. I was just enjoying being your friend. I was enjoying a *normal* life for a while."

She looked distant, her gaze wandering out over the dark campus. Only fluorescent stairwell lights and lamps along the main paths cut through the night at this hour. For a campus with a thousand people living on it, the park was still, the buildings quiet.

I didn't want to interrupt Rose's thoughts, so I waited for her to speak again. She clearly wanted to, and I only had more questions anyway.

"He's forgotten that, you know," she eventually said.

"Who? What?"

"Your big dumb boyfriend. He's not been human in too long. Humans have a certain timeline set to their lives, a thread with a beginning and an end. It's how to be human—to live and die and never come unravelled from that pattern. Whereas we don't have beginnings or ends. I don't know what either of you are thinking, trying something like a relationship when you have that difference between you. I still don't understand it after watching you for these last couple of months. It didn't even occur to him to enrol with you. To get a name and a bed of his own! I have a toothbrush beside the sink, Ally! He doesn't. He probably wouldn't understand if you tried to explain to him why it's important to have one, when his teeth are never going to feel fluffy no matter how much he eats. And you're just..."

"You know I'm not talking to him right now?"

She laughed, a bit less harshly than before. "You love him. He's found enough of his old self in there somewhere to fall in love with you. Silly tiffs about ghosts won't stop you in the long run. And that fact is why I am still watching the two of you."

"Are you trying to find his weaknesses or something?"

"Nah. Couldn't kill him if I wanted to, which I don't. I'm interested in you. It's a human in… Hm, three in a billion, by my current count, who learns about us how you did, naturally, and comes unravelled and sees the bigger picture. As far as I know, hang-ups from our old lives aside, we don't *do* attachment to you lot, whether you know what we are or not. It's all a bit pointless when most of you are so utterly boring."

"So why are you watching me?"

"Curiosity! There's no harm in collecting a few humans here and there to take out your dirty laundry. You aren't doing any laundry but your own, and I can guess your response if he asked you to work for him."

I snorted dismissively.

She nodded. "There you go. I know he warned you about things taking an interest. I am one of those things. Interest is as far as it goes. I just want to know how *you* are so compelling that he will go collect your laundry for you. I've seen him do it. It's cosmically baffling."

"So you're just, like, evaluating me as girlfriend potential?"

"It's not for me to say what he does with his spare time, I just want to keep tabs so if this all goes tits up one day, I know where it started and why. And working out who the weird little human is in all this can be the secret to understanding disturbances on a universal level. Atoms are resonating differently across the whole void of space because he's distracted thinking about making you a cup of tea. So who are you that this is happening on your account?"

"F-from the sounds of things, less than an ant."

"That's the thing, Ally. You're not. No one is, and anyone can end up making change on an enormous scale. It was just chance that anyone famous and influential you've heard of went one way rather than the other and wrought the changes they did, as much as someone like your boyfriend tries to keep it all going safely on the rails. What I see is that you're a smart cookie and not shy to speak up with an off-the-wall comment in your classes, you're determined beyond belief to have not quit on that damn mandolin after the first week under Molly's care. You have all the hallmarks of someone who might just accidentally change the course of human history, whether you're recognised for it or not. I'm well within my right to scout this whole situation out, as a semi-impartial observer."

"That doesn't sound like a reason to throw a whole bunch of ghosts at me."

"I needed a pretext to be here, and a test to see you in action. They were convenient."

"You *did* kill them!"

"It was ready-made. They were already dead. I just needed to wake their spirits."

"*Thanks.*"

Rose smirked.

"And I don't suppose I can just ask you to call them off."

"They're not causing anyone any harm."

"They're unhappy!"

"Well make them happy. You like pleasing people, don't you? Socially anxious people usually do."

I shrugged. "Who *are* you?" I asked, since I didn't want her analysing me.

"Your friend, Ally."

"Really. Who are you *really?*"

"In the same way Justice-pants there used to be Troute-face? I was Melanie. Just some groupie." She turned her arms to me: her sleeves were short, I guess a deliberate choice for this meeting. She'd probably wanted me to ask at some point, if we'd had the extra time. That spilled drink seemed more deliberate somehow, despite it seemingly being Lucia's fault. "Just some junkie groupie."

I stared for a moment at her arm, the fragile skin over the vein pockmarked with little holes, bruised and discoloured. "We can't hide the scars of how we died, because we can't ever forget. Our deaths are what made us what we are now. Troute died being a heroic moron, and so they made him everyone's hero, free to pass judgement and maintain order as his supposedly flawless sense of wrong and right told him to. Melanie—I—was sad, empty, utterly destroyed as a person. When I came and spoke to Melanie in her dying moments, dumped in the alley behind the theatre because she was being a buzzkill with her sickness... When I touched her hand, that's the only memory I really have from her last months.

"I won't name names, since you will probably know who he was, but he was... Legend. In all the rock star halls of fame. I can't remember how Melanie got to go to his afterparties, but she was always there. She's some disowned child of rich parents who never missed her when she was gone, just were glad her personal credit card stopped drawing transactions out of their savings. This rocker... He had no idea who she was. I mean, they had sex more than once, but he still literally had no idea she existed, no concept of her as a person. She was a brunette in the crowd, heavier than the waify blondes he liked but not so ugly and without a certain appeal he'd turn her away. And so..." she shrugged. "I don't think it was a deliberate overdose, but she was unhappy enough. And that's who I am. A walking cautionary tale."

"So now you collect guitars from dead rock stars?"

She shrugged and flicked away her now smoked-out cigarette end. "It's a hobby. *They* knew who I am. I have *his* guitar as well."

Like it had always been leaning on the wall beside her, she reached down and picked up a battered electric guitar. Amir probably would have known instantly who had indirectly killed Melanie.

"I'm not happy when people's threads come to their ends, but him..." She plucked one of the strings. The note reverberated across the rooftop like she had it plugged into an amplifier. "Does he play to you?"

"Who?" I asked, bedazzled by the note still; it was humming around my head, the first sound in a week to clear the ghostly orchestra music out entirely.

She rolled her eyes. "Your boyfriend."

I shook my head. "Not really. Mostly I hear him on the job, or... If he's showing off." I still felt bitter about that scene in the bar.

Rose grinned wickedly, all her gloom about her past life disappearing suddenly. "Then let me show off for you."

"Can anyone else hear —"

She had the guitar's strap over her neck, her hands at rock o'clock positions over it, and her fingers were dancing over the strings, picking out a fast tune. It hit me like I was stood in the front row of a huge audience, a full band backing Rose's song.

I'm not a live music sort of person, mostly because it involves a degree of social life and being around a lot of screaming drunk people (if I went to see some of the sort of bands I liked—others might be more mellow hippie drum circles when drawing from what I got from Mum's collection). I'm not even great at playing anything other than chart radio loudly, out of some misguided belief that because everyone heard it all the time anyway they were more accepting of hearing it, and somehow it was more offensive to hear good but unusual music loudly.

Anyway, what I am trying to convey is just how unqualified I was to have the blare of a well-played guitar thrown my way at maximum volume, never mind a magical one played by some sort of god. All the words I could use to describe the sounds of the instrument feel flat and boring: she made it screech and wail and roar, but right then I had a moment of pure clarity about why we even describe the instrument like it's an angry caged wolf or someone on their knees screaming out some last plea, why people had been turning to the guitar to play the most raw, emotive songs that made rock such an important form of music to so many people in a way that in that instant completely changed my perception of music.

Rose used the guitar of the man who had let Melanie die to produce the fastest sad song I've ever heard: it was the wordless, wracking sobs, like when you're too sad to even talk, the scream that was held back inside. All the anger that she'd never been able to express out loud.

I understood just for one song how awful and lonely it was to be one of them. Not just Rose, but the Piper too, and a hundred more I'd never met. How loosely they were tied to this world, their dread of the pain when the time came to save another human and to step into their skin: the knowledge of how much turmoil we carried around in ourselves, how much they feared touching that even when their duty told them they had to. I understood why Rose had sounded so upset about the Piper forgetting. Maybe she thought he was clinging to me because it was an alternative to dying again. But in the reprise of the song, there was just a bit of a sense of how they needed us too. How blessed they felt to walk among us.

And then the last note from the tortured guitar was ringing out into silence, the echoes slowly fading each time they bounced off the nearby residences. With them all my insight slipped away as fast as you can forget a dream, and I was dumb old Ally again.

"W-wow," I stammered.

"We all have a song like that," she said.

"All of us?"

"Well, yours might not be very long, but maybe there's a reason he's never played for you."

"How would I learn to play mine?" I asked, thinking it might help me master the mandolin.

"Do you really want to know?"

Her ghastly smile convinced me that I didn't.

"Well, what about tomorrow?"

"We'll go to classes, same as normal. We're still friends, aren't we?"

She suddenly sounded so needy I had to say "Yes." As soon as I said it I remembered how she had opened this conversation—"I'm the bad guy." But I couldn't believe she meant it in a cartoonish villain way. For one thing, she lacked a secret lair.

She nodded. "See you tomorrow then."

I backed away, almost tripped over the big metal bin and fled back down the stairs, thinking of how warm my room was.

*

In the dark hall my eyes went right to my door: still propped open, I could see that someone had turned my lamp on in there. By "someone" I meant "probably Alana", but I remembered the sort of person she was and the sort of creatures she attracted, so I crept up to the door with my heart beating faster somehow than when I had sneaked up on Rose on the roof. Alana could be doing anything, from meeting with the Piper (who I still didn't want to see) and catching him up on the day's news to having a run in with some scary beastie that had stalked her here.

When I pushed my door open and peered around it like I was a snooper in my own sanctum, I found Alana alone, busy fumbling a dropped phone as she looked up in surprise.

"Where did you go?" she asked.

"Just to the roof." I shrugged and kicked aside the book so I could close the door. "I couldn't sleep."

She nodded, though she looked really unhappy at that explanation. Or maybe it was more than that: I thought I saw an abnormal shininess to her eyes.

I plonked myself back down on what I thought of as my end of the bed and stared blankly at her, wondering why she was so sad.

She picked up her phone and fiddled with it, unlocking it and then putting it back on sleep. "Ally..."

"Hmm?"

"Are you comfortable with me being here?"

"What? Yes! I mean, I was annoyed with the Piper, but that's nothing personal to you at all!"

"Well, I'm not. Comfortable, I mean. When I woke up and you were gone, I thought... I thought it was too much for you as well."

"Too much what?"

"Eurgh, you're making me say it, aren't you?"

"Say what?" I asked, totally baffled. "This is your conversation."

"You really don't care... didn't care... about me and-and you." She was suddenly quite sniffly.

"Oh. Um. I'm going out with the Piper," I said, waving vaguely at his coat, still hanging on the curtain rail where he had left it for me quite some time ago.

"I know you are!" It came out a bit screechy for two a.m. in a building with so many neighbours packed in like sardines. She continued at a much lower volume, looking tormented. I wished she hadn't been keeping all this bottled up for so long. It might have been a quieter conversation. "You weren't when we first met. It's a pretty recent development, all things considered. And all that time... were you never curious? You knew almost from the start that I liked you thanks to our blabbermouth friends and you never..."

"Um. Not really."

"Never even had a thought like 'Isn't it strange that my new best friend has extra feelings for me, wouldn't it be weird to go out with her?' and pictured yourself holding hands with me? Even if you shivered away in horror from the image? You can tell me! I need to know!"

"Er... No. To be fair, I never really thought those things about the Piper either."

"So why are you going out with him?!"

"I don't know!" I realised how that sounded and cringed. He probably didn't listen in on my private conversations, but just the thought of it... "I spent all that time just wondering where he was and wearing his coat and it just made me feel really, I dunno. Warm."

"It's a *coat*. Jesus! I could have bought you a coat, if that's all it took! I'd have thrown in a hot water bottle and mittens too!"

This conversation was making me feel awful—we'd never talked about this before, but the fact it came up right when I was actually angry with the Piper... Having to explain and justify being with him... All it made me think was how consistently stupid I had been in pretty much every significant aspect of both relationships. It was more than a coat. It was the feeling of having someone who would give me their coat like that, without even thinking about it. Everything he did was giving me his coat, in one way or another.

Alana had sunk in on herself, hugging my spare pillow. I was feeling my eyes burn as well.

"Gah, I'm sorry, Ally. Tanya even told me before the end of summer that she played on my feelings for you. I told her I forgave her, but I guess it was so easy because I took away from that conversation a stupid idea that she had been messing with your feelings for *me* too, even though she was right in the middle of her grand plan to get you and the Piper to finally go out. She said she was sorry, but... For a while I actually thought I had a shot with you. I should have actually read the signs myself. Or not been such a coward in the first place."

"Is that why you and her had that fight?"

Alana shook her head miserably. "Too many reasons."

"It's not your fault," I said, still wondering where in my blundering progression through life I had managed to almost end up with Alana. I hadn't seen it at the time. Hadn't seen the Piper thing coming either, though. "Ever since I first clapped eyes on him I think the Piper had dibs on me. I mean, neither of us realised it at the time, and he tried to sacrifice me to the old gods before he realised there might be more to me, but by the end of that first week all we could think about was each other. I'd daydream about meeting him again. Just, like, bumping into him in the One Stop shop or something. I mean, we're a really, really boring couple. Maybe he knew I thought these things about him: he took me to Nando's for our first dinner out together. *Nando's.*"

Alana sighed, wiping at her eyes. "Your standards are pathetically low. If you're that easy to win over and I never made it."

"So you're over me?" I asked a little too hopefully. It wasn't like she freaked me out, but it hurt to see her so upset over something I had zero control over. Well, unless I tried to blow my nose on her or something, but frankly I did value our friendship so I wasn't going to gross her away.

She shrugged one shoulder, still dabbing at her eyes, rightly suspecting that she hadn't cleaned her eye makeup off very well before bed and had made a bit of a mess with the deep clean she'd just given her eyelashes. "I don't know. I think you've made it easier. I should have talked to you long ago, but I put it off. I knew you and the Piper had a bit of a thing. I didn't want to trample in there. I just didn't realise he was *still* your thing until too late. I thought he was avoiding you and you were getting over him. I didn't know it would end up this way."

I laughed, still without my normal mirth but it was nice to make a "Heh" towards getting it back. "Neither did I. Right up until he pulled me off that altar and went berserk on the cultists I figured I was going to grow into an old cat lady with a ton of black and white cats all called Piper."

"You didn't think the cultists would kill you?"

I made one of my varied range of grumpy noises and changed the subject back to something less awkward. "So we're okay now, you and me?"

"Yeah, yeah. I think so. I mean, if you think about it I talked you *out* of eloping with me to Barbados when you were having your banshee panic attack earlier, so you know I'm putting common sense before attempts to seduce you. As long as I'm not the one messing up your sleep pattern, I feel better too."

"No, that's the orchestra in my head which is on its fifth round of *Little Ghost* by the White Stripes this conversation."

Alana laughed at that, although I didn't mean it to be a funny line. I'd take it if she was smiling again and not weeping all over my pillow. I didn't have any other pillowcases: I tended to use just one pillow and alternate washing the cases. It looked like the mascara-streaked one was making another round through the campus laundrette's clanking machines once Alana was gone. I hoped the Piper would be back on my side by then.

"We trying to go back to sleep, or do you want to talk to the Piper?" she asked.

I shook my head. "Nah, he can wait. Friends are top priority, after all."

Alana rolled her eyes and flopped back down. "Whatever, you big loser. Get the light."

She was clearly as happy as me to get out of the other end of that conversation.

# Bradley Hall

When I woke up the next morning I had a dim sense of dread about the coming day. It wasn't Halloween yet: the performance was still two nights away. I couldn't recall what it might be at all until I rolled over and fetched up against Alana's legs. Then I remembered that I'd exiled my boyfriend, found out that one of the very few good friends I'd managed to make at university was a terrifying agent of some higher order who had sought me out, deliberately thus invalidating all the hard work I put into making friends and not being lame and rubbish at socialising, and even more deliberately thrown a literal bus full of ghosts at me… And to top it all off Alana was here, and with all of the above my dream of a calm, normal social life had disappeared entirely.

I got up and went to make toast, because nothing on earth is more normal than toast.

I felt a lot calmer when I returned to my room with a stack of scorched bread. Alana had woken up, probably because I'd thrown back the duvet, and she was blinking blearily at me with her hair an unruly mess of tangles and black smears around her eyes.

"Mornin'," she mumbled, gratefully accepting a slice of toast. "What are we up to today?"

I glanced over at my giant wall calendar. "History of the written word at ten, then a lecture about… Building Romans?" I squinted at my handwriting.

"Why do you still have classes?" Alana grumbled.

"Because I go to a proper university that offers real degrees?"

"*I'm doing a real degree.* It's bildungsroman, by the way. Story of a hero growin' up and finding himself and all that. How did I know that? *Oh right, a lecture at my university.*"

"You wanna sit around here or come to classes? I don't think they'll mind if you sit in."

"Wow, great choices."

"I said to come down the day before the show! I kind of figured there wouldn't be any classes for you to worry about while you were here."

She pouted at me, then caught her own eye in the mirror on my little wardrobe. "What's the shower situation like here?"

"Awful. You can borrow my flip-flops."

She looked horrified.

*

I got to my first class a little early: a huddle of our class were sitting around dramatically reading *Beowulf* at each other in various ridiculous accents. Rose leaned on the wall a short distance from them, biting back a smile. Lucia was at the other side of the hall, intently watching the *Beowulf* nerds and not looking at Rose.

"Hey guys," I said. They both looked around, at least. I stood in the middle of the hall between them, kind of in the way of any oncoming traffic, but I'd rather have breached the awkwardness between them and not visibly picked sides.

Lucia gave me a pretty convincing smile, but Rose just stared at me, like she was somehow unable to believe I'd show up to my own classes when I was the one who needed to be there far more than she ever would. How old was she? She probably predated the world entirely, never mind the Olde English speaking part of it. I got why she never did the reading now.

"So is Alana a new student?" Lucia joked.

"Yeah, why not," Alana said cheerfully, settling against the wall beside Lucia. "Hey, so Ally knows a guy who's having a party at, er, Bradley Halls tonight. Are you going?"

Lucia's face split into a grin. "Oh! I think Sam mentioned something about that. That's his hall, after all. Yeah, I'll be there."

"Are we just giving you an excuse to see Sam again?" Rose said, rolling her eyes. I noticed the we. Apparently she'd judged my 'Hello' as enough evidence I was going to try being friends anyway (hey, I was already dating one of these weirdoes, if anyone was able to give them the time of day it was apparently me). Now we were back to her creepily inserting herself into my life again like she was an extra limb I hadn't noticed I had until I got to uni.

"We should invite Amir as well," I mused.

Lucia recoiled. "Why?" she demanded.

The hockey team took that moment to come barging through the narrow corridor on the way to one of their practices, and I was flattened to the wall next to Rose while they came whooping past in a herd. When they were gone I was astounded to find I'd been given time to come up with a completely natural, honest answer. "We were all hanging out the other night at L Bar… He's part of the group and my friend." I shrugged one shoulder like it was the most natural thing and I wasn't trying to set up my friends, or at least drive a wedge between Sam and happiness.

She couldn't argue with my apparent wide-eyed naivety, and then the *Beowulf* lot began excitedly crowding into the lecture hall, and I took that as our cue to start moving and leave this conversation behind.

*

The day passed in a haze of deep regret that certain songs had become spooky standards for Halloween listening. Going to practice was a bad idea: unlike normal songs stuck in your head that might clear if you just listened to them and scratched the itch, this just seemed to hammer them deeper into my inner ear. By the time Alana was walking me back to my residence I was actually having trouble catching what she was saying the tunes were getting so overwhelmingly loud in my brain.

We'd had another strange, draining session where we played from start to finish, each of us apparently only able to hear our own screw-ups in the song, yet each of us looking around convinced the others had heard us mess up. Rose kept playing with a small smile on her face, and the Piper didn't make a show.

"Hey, going to the party will flush the songs out of your brain!" Alana said, when I had thrown my mandolin into the corner and flopped onto the bed, hoping I didn't have to move again until tomorrow.

"I am not going to the party," I mumbled into my pillow.

"Excuse *me*, I came all the way to this rural farmer's school you call an institute of higher learning for more than sitting around browsing the internet from your laptop like I could have done back in my own room. There's fuck all else to do here, so we're going to the party."

"There's like *one* agriculture class," I grumbled.

Alana clambered over her suitcase and began rooting around in my wardrobe. "Hey, you have some not-terrible clothes," she said.

"Stop going through my things."

"Let's doll you up and work off your ghost-based anxiety with a good old-fashioned student party."

"No."

Alana threw an armful of fabric at me. "Get dressed." She rooted around in her suitcase, I thought to find her own best party clothes, but a moment later I heard a clunk of something heavy on my desk and that finally inspired me to sit up and open my eyes.

"Is that *rum?*"

"Never go to a party without a few pre-drinks," Alana said, picking up the collection of mugs littering my desk. "I have been learning a lot at *my* school." She clambered around the room to get to my small sink in a nook of the wardrobe, where she began very domestically doing the washing up, like she wasn't coughing up the most insane ideas of a very insane week.

"Did you sneak rum in here deliberately?" I demanded. There was a prickle of discomfort deep inside me remembering her awkward conversation last night.

"Well, I had a bottle open in my room and I didn't want to just *leave* it. I'm going to America for a couple of weeks after this as well, so I thought, you know, bring it along, you'd help me finish it off." She climbed back over to the desk and poured us both a generous helping into the reused tea mugs.

"My mum's coming up tomorrow. I have my performance! I can't be hung over."

"It's not a mythical illness that disables you for the whole day, whatever you've seen on TV. You'll be *fine*. I'll look after you and make sure you don't drink so much you puke." She offered me the mug, and I foolishly took it.

"Promise?"

"Cross my heart."

*

We located Bradley Hall easily: I knew my way around campus reasonably well by now, but I think Alana could have found it all on her own just by the noise coming from it. There were groups of people standing outside, smoking, goofing around, though not openly drinking because it was still only nine o'clock and kind of early; campus security didn't get truly lazy until past one. The door was wedged open with a chair stolen from one of the lecture halls, if the little table attached to it was any indication, and I wondered who was mad enough to have dragged one all the way from the classrooms to the accommodation. Then again, I'd heard enough student stories already to know that stealing small furniture was basically nothing. People wouldn't stop to listen until mattresses were being hefted around.

"So what do we do, just go inside?" I asked, staring at a paper jack-o-lantern that had been pasted up in the window. I was feeling a little buzzed from the mug and a half of rum Alana had eventually managed to convince me to drink while we were getting ready, but that was nowhere near enough to overcome the fear of walking into a crowded building full of people I didn't know with the full expectation that I'd have to socialise with some of them.

"Well yeah, unless any of the smokers are your friends?"

I had to concede that aside from Rose, I appeared to have chosen rather clean-living friends and was unlikely to see any out here, though I had, of course, seen Sam vape so Lucia may or may not have been still following him around.

"Let's get inside and take the measure of this party. Wherever the greatest concentration of alcohol and music is, eventually people you know will end up there. So." Alana put her hand on my elbow and started pushing me towards the door. I was just tipsy enough to not dig my heels in (I was wearing proper shoes, my best jeans, and a shirt with no visual jokes printed on the front—it was something).

Once we were in Bradley's stairwell it was obvious the most music was coming from upstairs and Alana led the way by ear. There were people sitting on the steps having conversations which were equal parts drunken hooting and closely-whispered confessions: we wove between them, wary of getting accidentally hit by flailing gestures or trampling through a tender moment.

Bradley was one of the more modern halls: once we were off the stairwell and through a conspicuously open door I felt a groan of envy go right through me. Our communal area was tiny: the theoretical minimum ten occupants of Sherrick's floor B didn't all fit on all the chairs in the room at the same time. Bradley seemed to be shaped around a vast living area, with a TV like the one from the SU bar mounted on the wall, and though the furniture had been pushed to the sides of the room and therefore seemed cluttered, I had a feeling the actual occupants of floor B and their additions would all comfortably have been able to settle in here.

Of course right now rather than use it for spacious lounging it was packed with at least thirty people, all of whom were clutching disposable cups or cans of beer and being very noisy.

The next thing I noticed was that the music wasn't just a blurry beat that was barely coherent under all the shouting. It was *Thriller*, playing at top volume, the sound coming equal parts from inside my skull as outside of it.

"I need another drink," I said weakly.

Alana grinned at me and tugged me towards the starkly lit kitchen off in the corner.

*

Three songs in I had to stop telling myself that this was a vaguely Halloween themed party (costumes tended to be nonexistent or the kind of "sexy version of—" that I saw so much of around campus anyway what with each bar running competing theme nights). The set list from our recital tomorrow night was blasting at top volume, the original songs sounding weirdly unfamiliar after months of learning their instrumental versions, but it was inescapable all the same. This was not, I had to conclude, the natural order.

"What's playing now?" I demanded.

"Arctic Monkeys, I think," Alana replied.

I scrunched up my nose. "That's *wrong*. At least in my stupid head."

"Well sorry, I'll find the person responsible for this playlist and tell them to inflict your mind worm on everyone else just so you can share reality again?" she shot back. We were crunched up on one of the sofas, having located Lucia, along with three housemates of hers who were much more into whooping and shrieking than us. Boys kept coming over to talk to them, and Lucia shuffled closer and closer to us, clearly seeing that this wasn't going to end with the group all still together and she needed to abandon ship to friends who seemed a bit more stable. I loved that she thought that was us, while not overhearing me having a breakdown about the music.

I hauled her over further and grinned at her with what I hoped was a knowing smile. "So are you here with Sam or Amir?" I asked, then realised belatedly that that was a really stupid question and now that I was four drinks down I really ought not to have been asking such things.

She narrowed her eyes at me. "Neither, at the moment. Are you going to keep asking about it?"

I shrugged. "Seems you're all pretty unhappy about *something*."

Lucia looked around over her shoulder. "Is that song from *The Rocky Horror Picture Show* playing *again*?"

"It's Lady Gaga," Alana put in helpfully.

"Don't worry about it," I said, patting Lucia on the arm. "We're suffering the most obnoxious curse in the world right now."

"Curse?"

Right, like the rest of the world didn't know magic actually happened. I shrugged. "So would you rather be here with Sam or Amir? I really can't figure it out, but I feel like Amir is —"

This time she didn't just blow the topic off, and I knew I really didn't have much control left over what was coming out of my mouth, so perhaps I deserved this. "Ally, I said I wasn't in the mood to go out with anyone right now. Would you quit asking? I'm allowed to have male friends."

"Yeah, like they ever see it that way," Alana grumbled.

Flushing hot and beating myself up inside I latched onto that comment, clinging to Alana as a way to dodge past the awkwardness of my unstoppable mouth. "Since when do you have guys who are your friends?" I was not particularly worried that the Piper was the only male-bodied entity I'd known her to befriend in pretty much ever. Not that she spoke about her mysterious past much.

"Well, I don't, but I thought I might at uni until it turned out 'gay' is just 'extreme difficulty setting'."

"Is it weird that I'm still ranking Teb as 'impossible'?"

Alana snorted.

"Who's Teb?" Lucia asked. "One of your other friends from home?"

Her comment prompted me to look around—yeah, her housemates had totally ditched her. Apparently, as annoying as I was, me and my conversation about friends she'd never met was the only option. "Yeah," I said. "She's married and expecting her first kid soon."

Lucia's eyebrows raised. "I thought you said she was difficult to win over?"

"She just had very high standards," Alana said, giving me an awful grin. I rolled my eyes. Yeah, I saw what she did there. I wasn't going to laugh and she wasn't going to make me. That wasn't even a functional joke without alcohol.

It wasn't long after that when Sam and a couple of the other violinists showed up and joined us. Lucia grabbed one of the other musicians to put between them on the sofa, and we carried on making the kind of awkward small talk about general subjects you make when tipsy and in a strange group of mixed friends.

Alana was doing her thing where she inserts herself into a group, and I recognised it as just what she had done when she joined with the original group back home. It made me uncomfortable to be the less talkative one when I was the only mutual friend of everyone present. Call me jealous that Alana was bonding with the other girls. I was just thinking about her getting to her own university and *inserting* herself into another random group of friends, replicating what she had done with us and making us only a random holding pattern to tide her over until she went from Troutespond to fresher pastures, newer, better forever friends. All the magic and fairies and the interesting bonding experience that had offered aside, she had basically known us half a year, so what exactly was there bonding her any more permanently to our old school group? By summer any new friends of hers from university would have had way more face-to-face time with her than me and my lot ever had. Seeing how easily she had Lucia laughing at her dumb stories about some awful class she took, I could *see* her slipping away to these hypothetical new friends of hers, ones who wouldn't make things so hard for her.

After a half hour or so of this I had to excuse myself and get up to go fetch Alana and I some more drinks, grabbing her plastic cup and seeing that mine, left empty beside the sofa, had filled up with bottle caps that someone nearby had clearly been flicking at it. I went to go see what I could do about getting a new one.

The whole thing about kitchens being where the awkward people went to hide was clearly a lie. A steady stream of people were coming through and helping themselves, all still loud and chatty and enjoying the party. The sink was full of ice and beer bottles, the counter at least fifty bottles deep, most of them sticky alcopop looking things and spirits all labelled with the price stickers from the campus Co-op shop.

The kitchens in Bradley Hall seemed to be in just as bad a shape as ours, at least, even if the appliances were newer and cleaner. Even tidied for the party, there were dirty dishes stacked in the corner beside the microwave, which had been hastily moved out of the way to make room for a keg, and behind that an overflow of things that didn't fit in the cupboard: tins and jars of Marmite and Nutella in ranks beside the fridge, the windowsill absolutely filled with half-empty jars of herbs and spices, most of them looking gummy and sticky and considerably older than anything else in the room.

A second queue for certain consumables had formed, smaller but more purposeful: Bus Stop sat on the kitchen counter in the one clear space beside the cooker, and though nothing seemed to be happening as he talked to his latest client, business definitely seemed to be happening. As soon as I looked away to find myself another cup, I saw money change hands from the corner of my eye.

I filled Alana's maroon-lipstick-marked cup with Malibu and coke, poured myself something weird and blue just for the fact I could tell people I'd drunk it (life experiences!) and found Bus Stop alone again when I turned to head back.

Sort of still in a sulk with Alana for daring to be social where I had not, I dawdled by, drifting over to say hi, since the queue had dissipated and Bus Stop was uncommonly alone.

"Friday Ally! You actually came to the party! Howzit going?"

"Do people still say that?" I asked, trying to be cool by leaning an elbow on the flat surface of the hob. *Hearing* how sticky it was, I pried myself off it and took a sip of Malibu instead.

"Are you having fun?" Bus asked, not paying attention to my attempt to shut down his confusing slang.

"Yeah, of course." Like I was going to tell him I wasn't after he'd been so excited about this party all week. It would be like kicking a puppy.

"You look like you could be having more fun," he said, leaning down a bit, concerned.

"I'm not going to buy your drugs."

"I wasn't selling. You're not very outgoing, right?"

"I have my moments."

"Man, if you aren't happy here I won't judge you. You can go back to Sherrick Hall and I won't tell anyone."

"Nah, I've got friends here." I took another drink, as if that somehow demonstrated the fact. Belatedly, I realised that holding two glasses and sipping indiscriminately from them was not a way to show they were for two different people, but rather that I had a problem.

"Okay, yeah. I remember freshers being tough, that's all. It's about *all* I remember of it. You gotta keep your head above water, right. Keep on swimming, no matter what..."

"Is that what you do?"

"Man, I don't know what I do. Week goes by, I'm still here, no one's telling me to leave. I'm good."

"That doesn't seem particularly healthy."

He gave me this *look* and I took the point. I remembered our last encounter with him, how Alana had seemed certain that he'd had his own encounters with goblins. I had zero tact on a good day and now I was drunk and curious. "Is there a lot of stuff you don't remember?" I asked.

He shifted uncomfortably. "Well, yeah, but it's not the drugs, right? They don't... *No one* was right after the accident. I started smoking weed to *help*."

"There was an accident?" I squawked. This university seemed worryingly prone to them.

"Yeah... Back when I was a fresher. It was around this time of year, I think..." He looked around in a rather nervous way, then leaned in. "You're a Literature student, right?"

"Uh...huh?"

"Right, well you probably wouldn't know this then, but there used to be a History Society, when I first came here..."

"I thought you were a Chemistry student?"

"Right, right, but they just played documentaries and talked about them—you didn't need to be a history student to join..." He frowned, suddenly doubting this truth. I wondered if he *had* been a history student, but this had been taken away from him like everything else, and now he was getting some wires crossed to rationalise how he had memories of doing something vaguely history-lecture-y.

"Okay... So you were in the History Society?" I prompted.

"Right. 'Bout this time of year, they put together a trip with a couple of other societies—like, some art students and music kids or something to pay for a coach to go to London to visit the British Museum."

"Oh no."

"Sorry?"

"Um, nothing. Carry on." I was leaning in to catch his conspiratorial whisper now, sipping my drinks with incredible stress for where this was going, the plastic cups crackling in my too-tight grip.

"Yeah, so, uh, we looked at all the old stuff, got McDonalds, ate by the river..." He stopped and stared around the bleak, fluorescently lit kitchen with a look of wonder in his eyes. "I remember *so much* about that day. It's so clear and bright. But then when I got on the bus, it just... stops."

"What does?"

"I dunno, everything. I remember it was hot. And then I remember sitting on the barrier thing in the middle of the motorway, like, with a blanket, and everyone was around me and... I dunno. I was going out with this girl, Tori, from the music group, and I'd been sitting right next to her. They said our whole side of the bus was crushed but I was fine, not a scratch, right? And so were all the history club, and the artists, but everyone from the music group..."

"I get the picture." I was feeling rather lightheaded in horror at the picture, but oh did I get it.

He shook his head emphatically. I decided not to argue, in case he actually tried describing the scene.

"Did, uh, you stick together with Tori the whole time you were in London? Or did they go somewhere else?"

"T-they wanted to go look at an old instrument display. They had a—a private tour where they could touch stuff. Just the Music Society paid to do it and I hadn't even heard about it until we got there, so I went somewhere else to look at Greek vases with the History Society while I waited for Tori to come back. I remember waiting outside the display, and it was all so... I was annoyed with her for taking so long, but I just wanted to see her again, right?"

I bit my lip, trying not to intrude as he looked sadly into the dirt-caked hob like the cooked grease on it could be read like a scrying bowl to his remaining memories of happier times. But I wasn't known for my bedside manner on the best of days and my panic about my predecessors getting *crushed* was overwhelming. "I thought you were in third year? This happened four years ago, right?" (He was presumably in no state to realise that I probably shouldn't have had access to that information.)

"I—I retook first year, after this."

"Um, right. Of course." Timeline issues and continuity errors sorted out to explain why I had a genuine witness to my investigation who had been in front of my nose the entire time, I forced myself back on track. "Did she—she say anything strange after? Or tell you anything interesting about what they had touched?"

He shook his head. "They were all really quiet about it. I thought it must've been boring, right?"

I helplessly downed the rest of the remaining drink in one of the plastic cups, then considered the other, which had only dregs left too, and drank that as well.

"Bus Stop..."

"Hmm?"

"I don't know if you'll remember this conversation tomorrow—it wasn't very legendary—but thank you. And I'm sorry."

He shrugged. "Right." He seemed to get it anyway. I backed off with the intent of finding Alana again. We *needed* to do that seance again, and successfully. We were almost completely out of time. We couldn't get to London and back in time for the show, and that was if we *knew* what to look for and what to do about it.

Somehow it felt a lot more personal when I wanted to avenge the sadness inflicted on the casual acquaintance of the uni's local cheerful weed guy than when it was the abstract threat of ghosts potentially about to murder me and all my new musician friends.

I left Bus Stop to his moping but also profitable doping, and turned to go back to the main room. I ran smack into Alana, like she had been hovering in the doorway.

"I need to talk to you," I blurted.

"Mm. Same. Can we go somewhere quiet?"

"I think so. Fire escape? If no one else has the same idea."

She took my arm and wobbled heavily into me as I turned her to face the fire door. In Bradley Hall it seemed each kitchen had a door and I knew from viewing the building from outside that there was a zigzag fire escape down each side. Logically it seemed these two facts should connect, yet I was practically delighted with my detective skills when I opened the door and found rickety metal steps up to the roof or down to safety on the ground. Bradley Hall also only had fire alarms that went off when there was an actual fire, which meant that people in our classes from here who hadn't gone through fifteen hour ringing marathons could be very smug about that fact, when all the Sherrick Hall students were identified by their weary looks of death the next day after an all-night ringing bell.

"Ally?" Alana's voice tugged me from my musing as I stared up at the fire alarm in the kitchen ceiling, and I stepped over the threshold into the cool damp night in a daze, moving on instinct towards the sound of her voice. The party hadn't spilled out of the building so much, no matter how Bus Stop had been advertising it, and so even just through the door the world suddenly felt quieter and calmer, the party music/cursed ghost playlist thankfully muffled to its normal ringing in the back of my mind.

The crack of yellow light from the door fell across the third row of steps up to the roof and Alana gestured to the highlighted step. "Shall we sit?"

"Uh." They looked damp and manky and even though I was buzzed, I remained way too self-aware still to *want* a damp bum. But Alana seemed to have been knocking it back with my friends, despite my terrible attempt to bring her a refill thwarted by Bus Stop's tragic backstory.

I plonked myself down for the sake of politeness and Alana perched a step up from me, which, without eleven inch height difference, put her on eye level.

"Ally..."

"I think it's a curse," I blurted as she swayed my way.

"Curse?"

"I talked to Bus Stop and he was there and then the goblins took his name and called him *Bus Stop*, which is the worst, but it got them, and now we can hear them calling us—the curse has latched onto this group. We're just repeating the pattern, and now we'll be crushed to death and —"

"Ally, shush."

"I'm not panicking—this is real, Alana!"

Her hand landed on my mouth, shushing my complaining for real and I found, in the long silence that followed, Alana looking imploringly at me, her eyes bronze in the yellow light from the kitchen as she leaned into its beam.

"I'm sorry, Ally, I..."

Sorry for what, I wondered, as she couldn't finish the sentence. Shushing me? Not knowing what to do? Sorry for my inevitable demise tomorrow?

Her hand dropped away and before I could open my mouth to demand which of the above it was, her lips bumped into its place. I stared in alarm at her closed eyes, caught out in the moment, stunned that she'd drunkenly crashed into me with exactly enough poise to turn it into just a soft press of lips against my mouth instead of taking out two sets of front teeth in one go.

Her eyes flicked open and this close I could see where the flecks of red were that patterned the fibres in her iris. She pulled away and I breathed again.

"I'm sorry, Alana. I picked the Piper. I can't do this."

"That's it?!"

I looked away, examining my stubby nails, desperate not to look at her face any more. "That's how it is."

"Ally, do you not *get* how you… How you've led me on? Over the summer, I thought—we –" She stopped abruptly and frowned, reaching up to touch her own lips.

"I said I picked. He—I… He gets me."

"And I don't?! You tell me every dumb thought in your head, and I'm understanding of it all. We talk so much, and… You can't say that, Ally. How much did you ever talk to him before?"

"It's not like that. Uh… I—I'm not what you want."

"How do you *know*? I felt pretty sure of that –"

I buried my face in my hands, rubbed my eyes hard and looked back up to see how pained and frustrated her expression was. Same.

"I don't want what you want. I don't want what anyone wants. And I feel safe with the Piper. He doesn't need me to be anything I'm not."

"You—you don't feel *safe* with me?"

"You just kissed me out of the blue when you know I have a boyfriend!"

"So what, you think just because I did that I'm some sort of a gross rapist who wouldn't be able to keep her hands off of you?"

"No, that's not what I mean. I'm a bad investment, Alana…"

She got up with a violent clang from the stairs where I think she hit her shoulder on the railing. "Fuck you for thinking that of me, Ally. And fuck you for thinking so shittily of yourself you wouldn't even try." She stomped back into the kitchen and slammed the fire door behind her.

# All-nighter

I didn't even bother trying the door to get back into the party, fairly sure that if it hadn't automatically locked itself, Alana would have turned the lock on me just out of spite. I climbed back down to ground level on the fire escape and stormed back in the direction of Sherrick Hall, dialling Teb with a shaking hand.

Her phone rang out and went to voicemail, and I immediately hung up before I had to figure out what on earth the sort of message was I had to leave in this situation.

I was stumped. I had no one to turn to here—no neutral party to mediate. I knew I had to talk to the Piper eventually—I figured he already knew or guessed a lot of it, but we had to air it because it had been choking our relationship all summer. And I didn't want to talk to him now. Not when I was so angry with Alana.

"Ally?"

It was like my distress had summoned someone. I knew it wasn't Alana—the voice was too unlike her—but I didn't recognise it until I'd already turned to look back towards Bradley Hall. Molly was wandering along the path, looking almost rumpled, her Alice band sliding too far forwards and rucking her hair up into a lump at the front, her shirt untucked from her jeans, her cardigan hanging back on her shoulders. She was holding a bottle. Maybe this wasn't someone to talk to.

"Are you okay?" I asked.

She blinked at me. "You're crying," she finally observed.

"Yeah."

"Oh."

"Is it the performance? Are you scared?"

"I… Hadn't thought about it much today," I admitted.

She swayed past me. "I'm scared."

"You've put a lot of work into it. It's like your child or something. Your haunted, spooky child."

She gave me a very weird look. "We have a show tomorrow, Ally. You should go home and rest."

"You too," I told her. "You okay to get home?"

"I'm fine. I'm staying with a friend in Heathley Hall." She pointed at a shadowy building which to the best of my present understanding was indeed that Hall. "Good night, Ally." She drifted off down a side path that would take her there. I watched her go, feeling one point of human contact fade away, leaving me with my confused misery.

Maybe I should have gone after her, tried to talk to her some more. She and I may not have seen eye-to-eye on the existence of ghosts, but there was plenty that I could have poked out of her about her fear in a more sober mind.

I consulted my phone again, like if I scrolled through my contacts again I might spawn a new friend, and my finger froze over one. It couldn't *hurt*, right?

I dialled.

"Hey, Ally?"

"A-Are you at the party in Bradley Hall, or…?"

*

We broke into the library. I honestly didn't know why we were doing it, but I think Rose wanted to distract me first before I was ready to talk about it, seeing as I'd just phoned her up and made whimpering noises while trying to coordinate meeting her on the footpath outside a lecture theatre roughly halfway between our respective halls.

She casually touched the library door and, I guess, killed the alarm system, because nothing happened when she pulled the handle like we were just strolling in to get a book out in the middle of the day. She took me to the patch of comfy chairs on the first floor that our Literature group had sporadically used as a study area when I could corral Lucia and Rose both at the same time.

Weirdly, once we were sitting together on a sofa, Rose didn't offer me any cookies, which I had figured was her default sympathy response.

Kinda felt miffed about that even among every other bit of turmoil going on with me.

"Can we just… talk, without it being about whatever's going on with the ghosts?" I asked.

She nodded and put her hand on my shoulder and I didn't flinch away, though I saw her hand coming up in my peripheral vision and had the thought that she was kind of... Death. Right then it was a gesture of her being my friend, though. I leaned into her touch and took a long deep breath before I tried explaining an entire long, confusing year of all our nonsense in one go.

When I was done outlining what amounted to more like a summary of our adventures rather than an emotional history, Rose was still looking kindly at me and in a way that suggested she had actually followed the major plot beats. She had one question: "So you loved Alana?"

I buried my head in my hands, almost surprised to find my cheeks were soaked. "I don't know. Maybe. She was so interested in me. She made me feel special when she paid attention and singled me out. I liked getting her attention... I know I played up to it. She didn't have to tell me that part. But I didn't feel... You know, anything like..." I gestured vaguely. "I dunno, I just thought I wasn't into girls in that way and I just really liked having a new friend and it couldn't be a crush if I didn't want to..."

Rose gave me a minute before realising I had no idea how to end that sentence. "And it was only after you and the Piper..."

"Yeah. I don't know; he makes me feel special too. In much the same way. When he's not being a total dingus."

Rose snorted, "I did try to warn you that he was going to be a terrible boyfriend."

"But I feel like a terrible girlfriend too!" I squeaked, feeling it was too loud in the crypt-like library but still unable to stop myself.

"You're probably not, as long as you are actually happy together."

"Yeah, we are. Honestly. Mostly. It's nothing about our actual... dynamic... that was why I yelled at him. I think."

"Okay, take a few deep breaths and try and tell me what you actually think the problem is then."

"I dunno, it's just... I'm angry because it's the same thing as how I felt hanging out with Alana, except I thought because he was a guy and all, it would be different, more... Something better that was what I was supposed to want, but that's not how it's ended up once I was with him. Now I feel like I missed out on Alana because... I just didn't know what it was. But... I'm with the Piper? I can't just go back on that because I had a summer love for someone else that never worked out because I didn't even know what it was at the time."

"It's not wrong or bad to love two or more people at once, you know. It just means you have a lot of heart to share."

Now I was the one laughing dismissively. "In this case, sharing isn't going to happen. You *know* that's not a dynamic I should be caught between for those specific people."

She shrugged, her look saying that anything could be possible.

I pushed the point more insistently: "For Alana's sake. Not because I'm being all self-sacrificing because I'm defective. For her relationship with the Piper. I can see that's too important and I've broken it enough as it is…"

"Ally, you know you're not defective?"

"All that gossiping about your boss and that's what you care about?"

"Well I *can't* comment on who he chooses to help, but I would say that first anyway. If there's anything I learned in my life it's that if you think there's something wrong with you and you let it fester, you're never going to be happy. You're scared of your relationship with him for the same reason you were scared of Alana—even if you think at the front of your brain he gets you there's the scared voice at the back of your head saying that it will all turn bad anyway."

"The little voice in the back of my head is humming *Rocky Horror*."

She snorted. "Sorry about that."

"Can you… do anything? Just about that?"

She hastily held up her hands. "Not my doing. That's all down to the ghosts."

I let out a long sigh.

Rose put her hand on my shoulder again, trying hard to recapture my full attention. "As much as I am so not the one to give you the talk… You don't seem to have done much research on this."

"On what?"

"Um. Aw, Jesus, this is totally out of my job description. And as a friend, I'm… Look, there's a word for what you're struggling with understanding about yourself. You're probably asexual."

"Like a plant?"

Rose groaned. "You're your own worst enemy, kid. You're just not attracted to people."

"But I love —"

"Not the same thing. Trust me."

Her grimace reminded me of the last time we'd sat alone in the dark together. I didn't poke at that comment.

"So that's it? What can I do about it?"

"I dunno. Keep being you. He's not gonna care once you tell him. He went a thousand years without getting any. He can outlast you. I have to say, my head's been much harder to turn since I've been possessed by an eons old force of spiritual guidance." She clapped me on the back, grinning like that had been the punchline.

"Does that make me more like you guys?"

"I'd hope not. It's still a normal human thing to be. Like I said before—you're special like you are as a person. I'm feeling revolting for being so endlessly affirming, but… eons old force of spiritual guidance, etc. It really puts the human condition in context."

I hummed uncertainly instead of agreeing because that was an extremely hard comment to relate to.

After a while she ventured to say, "I suppose that's why you made him so unattractive?"

"What?"

"Well, we all see what we want with the Piper—I don't think he even knows how ugly he's got since he started dating you. He's not actually half-bad looking."

"I don't need to know that."

She shrugged. "True, though."

"I'm not... making him deliberately unattractive to prove a point that I love him anyway or something like that."

"Maybe not intentionally. I get it, though. Alana's really cute, pays a load of attention to how she looks. You think it's for something external—a signpost to say what she wants. But not all masks are feathers and gold like Teb's. Alana's every bit the same—scared and putting on a face so she can fight."

"What does she have to be scared of?"

"I'm not going to pretend to know her by more than reputation, but that would be enough to make me say she's scared of her own destiny."

I grimaced. "Maybe the way I yelled at her wasn't the best call."

"You think?"

I groaned, sliding down on the couch until my head thunked on the cushions. "I should find her."

Rose closed her eyes and inclined her head. I was about to push her for an answer, but she said, "She's with the Piper. She'll be okay."

"Is he going to give her the same basic class on how to deal with me?"

"Probably briefing Alana on how to bring me down in order to take her mind off things."

I looked up sharply. She raised her hands in defence. "I said I was the bad guy. I'm causing serious waves here, and if there's anything that he hates it's waves. And they're waves that are upsetting you."

"Remind me never to take him to the seaside."

She laughed. "You feeling better, then?"

"I feel like crap for treating them that way. I *said* I'd never get in a dumb love triangle and I didn't even notice I was in the middle of one."

"You weren't to know."

"I could have tried to be more aware of how Alana might have felt. Everyone wasn't exactly subtle about hiding that they knew she had a crush on me. I just thought it was something... I dunno, mild."

"In my nearly unrivalled experience of hearing people talk about bitter hindsight, harping on these sort of things is a source of an incredible amount of regretted wasted time."

I pulled a face. "Not harping enough got me into this mess."

She laughed kindly.

I shook my head to myself. I was quietly reconciling my own non-sex life with everything that had come before—from my bafflement at Teb's elopement or the seemingly overbearing pressure to be paired up for the prom, to everything about my ridiculous love triangle with Alana and the Piper. In hindsight I'd got too close to her—close enough I'd caught Teb looking askance at how comfortably Alana fitted against me when we were next to each other. I sort of wouldn't have minded carrying that on forever, except for the crushing weight of knowing how much more she'd expect, which had always lead me to dismiss it as a friend crush since I hadn't wanted more. I was feeling less a sense of personal revelation and more like suddenly my choice of the Piper as the break up with Alana that she had probably taken it as at the time—all in this moment of painful hindsight.

"Well I'm out of advice. If you are going to sit here and sulk, go ahead. I'll just kind of… exist. Reassuringly. Inevitably."

There was nothing like existential dread to help with a situation, to be honest. Rose was… probably better at this than she thought she was. "You really don't do this often, do you?"

"Strange times." Rose picked up a discarded book left on the table between the sofas overnight and buried her nose in it pointedly.

I decided to take her advice and picked up a book as well, and then accidentally spent five hours researching a non-exhaustive account of famous historical curses, which made me wonder much later if she had left it there on the table for me.

# Petty Theft

The library opened at seven, so Rose knocked me on the head with a heavy book at six fifty five to wake me up and I allowed myself to be smuggled out of the library, bleary and confused.

I went back to Sherrick Hall meaning to shower, still trying to work out if I'd slept for two or three hours, but I got no further than a cup of tea to gather my thoughts in my room when I realised I had six missed calls from Mum. I called back and got a long progress report on their drive, but to my relief they were, at the end of that, still a little way away. I was feeling nervy and strapped for time once I was let go. It was nearly seven thirty and other people would be waking up soon, despite it being a weekend, and after a relatively heavy night. Early risers weren't completely unheard of, even if this culture was against them except around deadlines or lecture days.

I wandered back into the common area and dumped the dregs of my cold tea in the sink. I stood for a long time in the centre of the kitchen just processing stuff, thinking and letting my brain tick over. I wasn't hungover in the way that I'd dreaded, but I certainly felt oddly disassociated from the world, like the alcohol hadn't quiet let me go even if I'd stopped wobbling. Finally I made up my mind: Rose's presence was comforting as a friend, but disquieting as a death omen or at the very least *memento mori*. I had a day to sort everything out, and I was starting it from the lowest of the low: no Alana, no Piper, Rose only helping me in the barest way... It was down to me and my own resourcefulness not to die now because, oh, right, I'd still managed to accomplish nothing about the ghosts, even though I'd had a week to—oh no. Oh no, this was a metaphor about not procrastinating on my projects and getting everything done in time. Here I was, having to write it all at the last minute after scant research. Hooray.

Still I hesitated, frozen on the spot for a minute, feeling like a decision that had settled into my mind after all that late-night reading had immediately lit up a neon sign above my head that read "THIEF"—I only just managed not to look up before going over to start opening all the different cupboards in the kitchen, nosing through all my supposed friends' food.

Mike, predictably, just had tins of beans and a loaf of bread, nothing fancy. Angie's cupboard was much better stocked, but still very basic pantry ingredients of someone uncertainly feeding themselves alone for the first time: onions, tins of fruit and soup, for some reason brioche rolls instead of bread... I worked my way along, feeling a faint glimmer of hope when I opened Xuilang's cupboard and had my heart sink just as quickly when I realised all her herbs and sauces were labelled in Chinese.

I took a deep breath and backed out of the kitchen, not letting the breath go until I was already on the stairs up to Hall C. They stole enough of our stuff. I knew for a fact that the student shop never had heard of a spice rack unless the display of Pot Noodle counted, so this was the only way to get anything on short notice unless I cashed in every friendship card I had with Angie to wake her up first thing in the morning on the weekend to take me to Tesco.

The door to Hall C predictably was open, just like ours. The hall beyond was sleepy and silent, just like ours. All the doors may have been closed, but I paused for a long time to listen. Somehow early morning theft felt wrong in a way that midnight raids didn't, like I was being unsporting by taking advantage of an hour when no one would catch me. The blurry refrain from something to do with the Friday the 13th franchise was getting in the way of me sleuthing out if anyone was stirring beyond their closed doors.

I was being ridiculous—how many times had I opened my door or wandered into the kitchen to find a near stranger there, and thought nothing of it, because of the semi-public life living in close quarters with all these people and their myriad lives... I almost laughed to think that so many of them were probably hook-ups and partners—that anyone clapping eyes on me would think that my hungover expression and normally rumpled appearance just from being me was a symptom of a walk of shame, me sneaking around still wearing traces of yesterday's make up and hair. Right when Rose had just opened my third eye on not having a sexuality also being an option.

That gave me a push to move on into the hall at last. If my calling was going to be investigating supernatural mysteries instead, I couldn't well be too scared to do even that. I scurried past all the closed doors with my heart hammering, but a faint sense of success when I made it to the other end.

Their kitchen was identical-ish to ours, but yellow instead of red on all the accents and some of the peeling plastic letters. Somehow, they had our old fridge. At this point I was probably going to die by the end of the day when I got ridiculously Drag Me To Hell'd in the middle of the performance, and should have been beyond caring, but my brain made a pedantic note of it anyway.

I was just reaching for the first cupboard along—the doppelgänger of my own—when I heard rustling that made me yelp and draw back.

In the open plan seating area adjacent to this sticky linoleum corner, someone was rousing on the sofa the back of which formed the 'wall' between these sections of the room.

"Ally?" a bleary voice mumbled.

"Mike?" I hissed, as my floormate emerged, grey faced, to squint at me.

"You 'bout to put the kettle on, right?"

"This is floor C," I replied stupidly, blowing my perfect alibi of his morning after confusion about where he had woken up.

"Whatcha doing on floor C?" he mumbled, getting out of the sofa on his second attempt. While I made a goldfish face he shuffled over and put the kettle on anyway, even though this wasn't our kettle and it *certainly* wouldn't be our tea, milk and mugs. Unless this was the explanation for where our various instances of disappearing tea, milk and mugs went. I was fighting theft with theft, to be honest.

"I'm looking for herbs. For a cleansing spell."

"What do you need one of them for?" He paused and, while I made more awkward non-attempts to answer the question, he tried for me. "Is this about when me and Bus saw you and your friend out on the hill talking to ghosts?"

"Yee-ah. How did you know we were talking to ghosts?" I mean it was fifty-fifty that or Satan worship.

"I saw 'em with you. S'Halloween, right? You see this stuff around then."

"Uh… 'you' as the general human population doesn't. Are you psychic?"

He shrugged one shoulder and raided the fridge for milk.

"Well, tell me what you saw, at least?"

"You had them all standing around you—all with their instruments. They were… reaching for you."

I swallowed hard.

He pushed a grimy mug into my hands and grimaced as he sipped his own without waiting for it to cool. "So you need herbs and shit?"

"Uh… Yeah."

"The kitchen at Bradley Hall had tons of spices and stuff on the counter. My mate there says most of it was there when they moved in. No one will notice if you nick some."

"I…" really didn't want to go back to Bradley Hall. It was remembering that pile of spices from last night that had inspired me to go try finding something similar in *our* hall.

"C'mon, it will still be unlocked." Mike gestured to me to follow and left, still clutching his purloined mug.

I decided to live a little and followed him out.

*

"So you and Bus Stop... You see a lot of strange things?"

"Right?" Mike said in agreement.

"I mean, you never said anything, in all those stories..."

"Well who'd believe us, you know? You see a lot of strange stuff when you're out at three a.m. You don't think it makes any sense the next moment so it's better not to say anything... Uh."

"Uh?" I mirrored.

"If you know about the ghosts... I don't want you to freak out..." He left a very long, weighty pause, filled only with the chattering of a magpie sitting in one of the trees that lined the path between Sherrick and Bradley Halls. It was still early enough and weekend enough that there were very few people out and about on campus. The air was cold and the grass touched with frost, making me glad of the contraband tea I was clutching. Reflecting on the turn of the season made my stomach sink with sick dread about it being Halloween and the day of our performance.

"It's about your weird boyfriend," Mike finally blurted. "He's... really strange to look at."

"Pfft, tell me about it."

"Yeah but, I mean, he always feels like the same guy, you know? Don't get me wrong, I never thought you had a ton of blokes—but some days he's this tall black guy with all the dreadlocks like you said, and once he was Chinese and all in red, then sometimes he's white and really tall and thin and ugly? And when we all went in Angie's car to the supermarket, he was so fat I had no idea how we were all fitting into the backseat together, let alone how the car managed to move anywhere? Like... Do you see him as the same guy every time, or..." He trailed off in horror at what he had admitted to seeing. "You must think I'm totally crazy," he muttered.

"Not at all. He's, uh, special. I don't know what he's really meant to look like. Not completely. He says I have it wrong too. Mostly the hair. But at least I mostly see the same thing every time. What do his eyes look like to you?"

"Um... I don't go around staring into other people's boyfriend's eyes."

"But they seem normal? They're not..." I didn't want to influence him, so I just waved vaguely at an imaginary projection of the Piper in front of us that neither of us could see.

"He just has normal eyes, so far as I saw."

I let out a breath, somehow feeling a sense of possessive happiness that Mike couldn't see through him like I could. I wondered if he'd ever met Rose, but I couldn't think of a time she had hung out in the kitchen of our halls, or how to describe her to him if he might not even be seeing what I was.

"What does he look like to you?" Mike asked.

"Why?"

He shrugged.

I gave it a moment, trying to work out why he was asking without him saying anything. "I think… you were projecting your own insecurities about Angie's car on him that time. Apparently we can do that. Not that I'd care if he was fat," I hastily concluded. "I, um, don't really care so much about how people look."

"Must be handy, when he changes all the time."

"… Yeah."

We reached Bradley Hall and at that point I was glad we could drop the conversation, which was becoming unintentionally extremely probing and leading me to wonder about someone using the Piper's glamour to their advantage because they wanted an aesthetically pleasing trophy wife. Apparently I was just borderline gay enough to worry about accidentally giving myself a trophy wife now. The things you learn at university.

Sure enough, the door was still woefully unsecured and Mike held it open for me after putting down his empty tea mug on the steps beside the door. I put my own next to his, commending them to whatever god may take them, and we headed up the grim stairwell together, probably officially partners in crime at this point. I could feel my heart picking up speed as we ascended, my spidey sense for confrontation growing. There was noise coming from the floor the party had been on—whether because it was later in the day or because it was impossible to sleep in those circumstances or just because they'd never really stopped partying. Mike had no idea what was going on with me, and just pushed open the door like it was no big deal and I could do nothing but timidly follow behind him or risk having to unload my entire argument with Alana on him.

The main room still had a handful of people in it, the TV playing some American comedy at low volume, and a few dedicated groups were slumped together in close circles, talking and laughing in murmurs, still clutching drinks, cans of Red Bull clustered around them to explain their all-nighter endurance.

The sofa was occupied by two people curled together in a tangle of easily identifiable limbs. The back of Lucia's head, the huge mass of dark curls, was turned to me as she nuzzled into the crook of Alana's neck. They both seemed to be fast asleep, and I felt a ridiculous pang of jealousy to the both of them for completely different reasons. I had to shove that away for thoughts of poor Amir, missing out on Lucia once again. "Oh my god, I'm a homewrecker," I groaned.

I turned to see Mike was paying no attention to my drama and was already standing in the door to the kitchen, making a hurry up gesture at me. With a long look over my shoulder at the surprising and uncertainly welcome crossover of my social circles, I followed.

The bottles of alcohol that cluttered the surface had been mostly emptied, though left out in place like an offering. There was no one there, at least, so I let Mike beckon me over to the ranks of manky old herbs and spices with a minimal amount of further stress, probably to everyone's relief. After that it was a frenzy of clattering through the glass jars, holding each up in turn to read the stained labels until I recognised the ones from the spell that I had read about in the night.

The one good thing about being haunted by restless spirits was that pretty much every culture believed in ghosts and allowed for a space in their beliefs to figure out what to do if the souls of the restless dead got a little over-friendly when they should have disengaged from their old social lives already. And so there were many, many different ways to handle it, some of which were easy enough to cobble together on the student budget.

I had a fairly basic plan in place, but at least it was simple enough that it couldn't really go wrong. The ghosts were drawn to our performance, or were going to try to stop it by killing us all... Either way, they would want us to all be in one place to make it easier for them to achieve their goals, so they'd either kill us at our last rehearsal (if they were trying to stop the performance) or at the performance itself, if they liked that sort of drama. We had the main theatre under the practice rooms for both events, so I just had to go set up all my purifying herbs somewhere within distance of the stage, burn them, then tell our noisy friends to be at peace when I knew that they'd all be listening,

And if that didn't work before the main performance then Alana had a plane ticket to California in her suitcase that was locked in my room and I wasn't ashamed to flee the country to save twelve other lives. Everyone already knew that I was unreliable and flighty anyway. In the long run, what was a story about me getting cold feet and leaving the continent to avoid playing to a small crowd of family, friends and really bored students compared to me knowing that I had saved the lives of some people who were tolerable to genuinely nice?

Yeah, I thought so too.

# Luncheon

I spent the rest of the morning in my kitchen—correct halls, correct floor—mixing herbs in one of Mum's unstealable mugs (maybe I'd take a couple upstairs as an apology—sneakily since they'd never take them). There was a fair amount of double-checking the book I'd smuggled out (it wasn't *my* fault that the loans desk hadn't opened yet when Rose and I were leaving) and chopping and grinding with the end of a fork and crushing herbs between two spoons, some deliberating if greasy table salt was theologically the same as chunky rock salt... But I ended up with a mug of stuff I would just have to drop a match in and I'd be done. If I could work out where to find matches. Everything was an uphill struggle, honestly.

I was ambling back to my room clutching the mug that would save my life when I met Alana coming the other way. She stopped short when she saw me, her mouth making an O.

"Yep, I still live here, and I'm still holding your stuff hostage," I said. "Not sure how you were planning to do this without seeing me again."

"I can't believe you're just shuffling around making tea like nothing happened."

I glanced down at the mug and not sure what else to say, tipped it towards her.

She blinked at it. "Did you forget to add water?"

"I'm dealing with the ghosts by myself."

"Oh."

"Uh, my Mum is coming for lunch. She'll expect you to be there, since I told her you would be, weeks ago. I mean, you don't have to. I understand."

Alana nodded, although it wasn't exactly clear to what. I took a chance and let us into my room, where she clambered over to sit on the desk chair.

"So, um…"

"I went back to Bradley Hall this morning. For the herbs. But, I, uh… saw you and Lucia…"

"Yee-eah, that's probably not going to last. She's nice though, don't get me wrong. She's just, you know, far away. Messed up as I am. Mostly just working some things out. She didn't know what to say to me this morning."

I struggled with mastery of my face to just look sympathetic rather than relieved. God, I was as much responsible for this as Alana had said. "Are we still friends then?"

"Of course." Alana breathed in such a rush of relief that I felt myself immediately forgive her all the stupid grudges that I'd been holding just for how lovely it was to hear someone so *earnestly* wanting to be my friend.

"And lunch with Mum?" I prodded.

She groaned. "Yeah, okay. Is she going to expect whatsisface to be there too?"

I burst out laughing at how that wonderfully vague phrase described him perfectly. "Did you know that Mike—weird stoner Mike from my floor—is a little bit psychic too, and has been seeing all sorts of different faces on him?"

Alana laughed too at that. "Oh my god, how many boyfriends did he think you had?!"

"Just the one. But he was so confused!"

We lapsed into a more comfortable silence after that laughter, and I looked into the mug that I was still clutching.

"I suppose I've managed to deal with the ghost problem all by myself on my terms just like I said he should let me… Without even *you* raising a finger, like I wanted."

"Uh, séance?!"

"So I guess it's okay for me to call him up and, I dunno, broker a peace deal?"

"You are so catastrophically bad at people, Ally. He'd be delighted to hear from you. He's been moodily pining this whole time. Last night he looked so grim I swear it made the room darker around him. I had to shoo him away so I could enjoy the party. Also: he came uninvited to a student party you weren't even at any more."

"You're so horrible to him."

She grinned.

I dug out my phone and, feeling weird to see an old smoopy conversation on the screen when I found his name, texted him about lunch.

I'd make up with him, sure, but first he would have to suffer through my parents for me to feel he'd really earned it. Like for like, him inflicting Alana on me. It was a fair trade, by his weird cosmic rules. He'd resentfully approve.

*

It was a complex operation to draw my parents from the guest parking somewhere a mile across campus to the little car park next to the halls, when arguably we could have spent the time walking to the administrative buildings rather than going through the stress of me trying to guide my dad blind off of memories of road I, as a perpetual pedestrian, had never had cause to learn since cutting through the park was always easier. On the other hand... No walking.

And then we were on the road again, heading into town— not just along the modern ring road that would take us to Tescos but into town proper. I guess Alana had seen it all from the bus the day before, since the train station lay between this and the university, but I found myself pressed up against the car window.

"It's so steep and medieval!" I exclaimed as we made an awkward turn around a clock tower that had never been intended to have city traffic crawling around it as a roundabout.

"You said that when we were looking at the university for the first time," Mum reminded me, looking up from the map. (The GPS was plugged in and working fine, but she didn't trust it, so kept an outdated AA map on her lap all the time on any long trips.) "In fact, that was what sold you on the place. You said that you'd like to come into town sometimes to explore."

I huffed and sank lower until the seatbelt was digging into my neck. "I've been busy with classes and stuff. And the bus costs a fiver for a return into town."

"We could explore a little after lunch, while we're here, if you'd like! I'd love to have a proper look around as well."

"I have to get back for practice."

"Pfft, you've been practicing all month. You know what to do by now, surely!"

"It's a matter of life or death," I groaned, instead of something more sensible if dishonest about our one practice on the actual stage itself.

Mum turned in her seat and gave me a weird long gaze that danced back and forth to Alana as well. "I see," she said, settling back into her seat to resume map-reading.

Great. Mum had probably spotted the ghosts lurking over my shoulder or something. I hated those moments I had to explain supernatural goings on to my parents. Or parent. Dad was hearing all this too with complete obliviousness, and therefore looked placidly unstressed. Hopefully Mum would lay off asking about it until after the performance. Maybe I'd die and avoid the conversation about how I had gotten myself into yet another scrape as soon as I was left unsupervised.

We finally parked and wove our way back to the town centre on foot.

"We were going to ask you for a recommendation, but if you haven't been to town…" Dad was saying as we reached a pedestrian square well-known enough as a meeting place that we could find our way there easily by signs. The square was lined with cafés, restaurants and boutiques all waaay out of a student price range.

"Oh! I think we must be eating there," Alana said, gesturing past my shoulder as I tried to remember the taste of something other than pasta.

I had the weirdest stomach jump of looking right at the Piper and recognising him without recognising him at all. Like I had blinked my vision clear without anything actually happening, the jolt of alarm somehow reasserted him back into the familiar visage of my boyfriend, and I didn't have to explain to myself what I'd seen—or have a clear picture of what it had been, just that for a moment I'd been looking right at a stranger and somehow known it was him. My stupid boyfriend. The fact that all this had made the glamour slip for a moment from looking like that fascinating first impression I'd had of him terrified me. I hadn't meant to let him slip away like that. I hadn't wanted to alienate anyone that I cared about.

I led the scurry over to him, and squeezed him on instinct when we collided. I nearly backtracked, looking up at his face for confirmation that this was okay, but he just bruisingly squished me right back against him like he hadn't seen me for months. I guess he had to be committed to come to lunch with my parents while we were still technically fighting. That or he was painfully aware after telling me that he could Santa Claus his way around time and space that he had negative amounts of wiggle room to excuse himself for being busy or late.

"I already made reservations," he said, letting go of me finally as family and friends caught up.

"Reservations for lunch?" Dad asked, sounding warily impressed. Lord knows what he saw in the Piper, but he'd come into our house and politely asked Dad if it was okay to date me so I sometimes imagined he saw a sort of 1940s polite teenage gentleman with combed down hair and a blazer, and that made me giggle a lot.

"It's an exclusive sort of place—don't worry, I'll pay."

Dad *bristled* at that. I suppose life wasn't complete without some posturing here and there, even between the laid-back Piper and my mild-mannered Dad. He didn't say anything, though, his glance at Mum going completely unheeded as she sparkled happily at the Piper. He held the door open for us all so we had to shuffle through at that point.

The café didn't feel oppressively fancy in its grungy hipster décor, but a coffee was seven quid and sandwiches ten. I figured I may be dead soon anyway and ordered an extremely expensive panini that boiled down to a ham and cheese sandwich if you ignored how every single ingredient was some fancy extreme of the base ingredients. Alana went for a thin soup and a scowl like she didn't trust the Piper to include her lunch on the company credit card.

"Have you seen Teb lately?" I asked Mum, once we were settled in a bit and relaxing enough for proper chit-chat.

"Not much. She's out of town before anyone wakes up in the morning and back late. I see Sarika at the corner shop sometimes, though. She says Teb is looking thin. I said, well, of course, she's digging all day, not sitting around studying and eating biscuits like you lot used to do. But she's been worried about her since she went on that crash diet for the prom. Always tells me if Teb looks too skinny or too ill."

"She's fine," Alana grumbled, being aware of the mysterious reasons behind Teb's weight loss, which is to say, three months in the fairy realm not eating anything, and Alana was none too subtle or patient with Teb when it came to coddling her behind her back. I sort of figured by now that they didn't really like each other, but there was a lot of respect for how they might have to one day fight a terrifying magical duel and they still couldn't call who would win that one.

"Did she say anything about how the dig is going?" I asked, rather more interested in the work since Teb had been so tight-lipped towards us when we had called her up, not to mention every time I had asked before.

"No... Sarika just talked about how she keeps tracking mud into the house and how her nails are wrecked and she never wears nice clothes anymore and so on. I'm glad you were never so concerned with that sort of thing."

"I'm glad you weren't!" I cried, since it was rather more obvious from my end where the motivation was for Teb looking so neat and perfect all the time.

"Well, like I said to Sarika, girls will be girls. When you and Teb and Tanya used to come in from digging tunnels in the garden... You always did love having adventures together."

I froze violently as I stopped myself yelling something about Tanya and adventures and nearly getting me murdered by Alana's dad, nearly upsetting my lemonade, and Alana glanced sharply over at me. I could see her begging me not to start, while the Piper put a warning hand on my knee.

Let it never be said that Dads are useless, because he cleared his throat at that moment and asked me how my studies were going, and, bless his boring soul, he was actually genuinely interested in my essays and lecture schedule and all sorts of dull things that I could talk at him and get curious questions in response. Alana looked grumpy at the change, but it was fine by me.

Our sandwiches and soup came, the Piper grinned and picked at a basket of rosemary and sea salt chips he had chosen to share with me, perhaps in reminder of the spell I had to cast later in the day or perhaps just because they were delicious—either way the lunch hours slipped away and I started clock-watching on the Piper's wristwatch. Which was clearly something he wore just for my benefit since I perpetually forgot my phone or let its battery run dry.

"Are you okay?" Mum asked, after the millionth time I tapped on the Piper's arm to make him turn it towards me.

"I just… Rehearsal is at three and we took an hour just to get here and park. We really need to make a start back to campus. I have to get a ton of stuff out of my room." Like the spell that could save my life—the mandolin was optional.

The Piper got up to either pay or Jedi mind-trick our expensive lunch (something I wasn't sure he could do or not for real, but wouldn't put past him if he could). Dad let out a sigh. "He's not even studying here with you? He really just moved all the way up north for you?"

"He travels for work anyway," I tried to explain for the millionth time. It never stuck—he could tell that we were lying—Mum too—but he could never work out how or why, just the same as people struggled with the Piper's glamour sometimes. Like I had just done. Dad looked over my shoulder to glare at the Piper talking to the waitress to settle the bill. I busied myself struggling back into my coat before I gave in and sneaked another glance.

He still looked like my Piper.

It had been altogether a less awkward lunch than I had expected, those few moments aside, and it had left me wondering what the catch was.

*

The Piper rode back with us, with not much happening of note, except that he admitted he played a musical instrument of his own, then I had to yell at him not to start playing in the car, because I was terrified about what would happen if he randomly bespelled all the traffic around us. Or sent Dad into a frenzy behind the wheel, tap dancing his feet on the pedals.

When we fetched up back in the correct car park it was, by the Piper's watch, ten to three.

"Tell you what," I said, scrambling out of the car, "You guys wander around campus and explore the park while I'm in rehearsal. There are bars around that are open in the day, and they won't think it's weird for you to be there—there are a lot of mature students on campus, after all, and only the Students' Union bar ever does anything where they want your student ID for entry. I'll go to rehearsal and nothing about the show will be spoiled for you."

"I've already heard all your songs," the Piper said.

"Same," Alana agreed at once.

"Shush, you guys don't matter. Keep the folks entertained."

"Gee, it's a good thing we like your parents," Alana said in blatant, favour-currying earshot.

"Thank you, dear," Mum said. "I'm sure we'll have a great time together while Ally is busy." I was expecting mockery, but she actually beamed proudly at me. Of course, she'd bought me the stupid cursed mandolin in the first place. This was all her fault, I thought, as I cheerfully waved  goodbye like I wasn't walking to my possible doom.

Well.

Rose had implied that she had orchestrated—ha—the ghosts, so perhaps in an alternate version of this story it would have been the spirits of everyone who had taken out one of my literary theory books and consequentially died of intertextuality instead, if I hadn't done something more attention-grabbing. Though there was always a flair for the dramatic with these weird entities so who knew—the tale of how I had to exorcise my essays before handing them in would perhaps have given me an edge in arguing about which of us had the toughest academic challenges between my friends in our varied post-college adventures.

When I finally let myself into my room it was five to three by my alarm clock. I reckoned not everyone would be at practice bang on three o'clock anyway. I could mess around pretending to be in my bag getting music out or turning my phone off until all thirteen of us were present. And then I could do the purification.

I grabbed my mandolin and sheet music, spotting my phone on the desk by the mug of herbs and Alana's gorgeous rose-patterned lighter. When I picked up my phone it bleeped miserably at me about its battery, and I unlocked it to see seven percent life left, twelve text messages and fifteen missed calls from Molly. My stomach dropped as I remembered how weird she'd been when I bumped into her in the night, so I called her back immediately from the notification panel without bothering to look for my charger, saving power by not dawdling through the texts.

"Are you okay? Is everyone okay?!" I demanded as soon as she had picked up.

"What? Yes, of course! Where were *you*?"

"What do you mean, where am I?"

"Practice was at one, Ally."

My stomach dropped. "What!?"

"We changed it two weeks ago. If you didn't keep rushing off after practice… I thought Lucia told you!"

"No! Oh my god, oh my god…"

"It's okay, Ally. Breathe. No one's going to die. Just come early for a sound check because I know you like to play quietly and hope no one can hear you. You know all the songs. You just—"

My phone made one miserable soggy bleep and expired.

"Dammit!"

I stared up at the ceiling and concentrated very hard on not crying from fear. Of course it had been too good to be true. It wasn't just Death testing me. I was sure Fate was out to get me too (and probably had been for some time). No way would she let me off easy with a carefully executed and in-control plan.

Looked like I was going to have to exorcise myself (and everyone else) minutes before the performance.

So much for California.

# Performance Anxiety

I had time, but not time enough to research an entirely new plan of action, mostly because I had literally no idea where to start and still make it on time. In truth I didn't really *know* anything for certain except that there were ghosts and that I could hear them. And presumably, if they cared about the Halloween playlist so much, if anything were to happen it would be at the performance.

Also the last orchestra had been cursed to death. There was that.

I felt *hideously* underprepared.

I couldn't stay in here any longer, trying to magically get *more* prepared.

I packed up, changed into a slightly nicer shirt and looked around my room with the wistfulness that comes from really disliking a room but still feeling like you may never see it again.

Finally I put on the Piper's coat, shouldered my scowling mandolin, scooped up the mug of spell ingredients and Alana's lighter and headed out the door.

(Then went back and put my phone on to charge.)

My feet took me across campus, and I didn't pay much attention, lost in a huge array of sickening thoughts. I stopped only when I realised where I'd walked myself: trying to keep away from where my friends and family would go, I'd arrived at the admin part of the school. I strolled along the row slowly, half-hoping but not expecting until I saw a familiar lanky figure sitting in one of the beanbag chairs in the quiet contemplation room.

*Technically* it was completely non-denominational, and he was slouching and on his laptop rather than praying. He also wasn't playing Wonderwall, thank goodness, because the ghosts were the *only* reason it hadn't been stuck in my head for two days, so I pushed open the glass door and went in.

"Hey Amir. Nervous?"

"*Terrified*," he told me, grinning. "I can still hear the ghosts, everywhere I go! Your friend is not very good at busting ghosts."

"Tell me about it," I said, rolling my eyes. I dropped into the beanbag next to him. "Are you doing homework in here?"

"It's quieter than halls, and people are scared to come in here if they are not religious. It makes a nice space to think."

"I don't wanna think," I said petulantly, putting my mandolin and mug of spell ingredients down, and leaning back against the window.

"You always have a lot on your mind. You worry too much."

"I... I dunno. You have a best friend?"

"Yeah, we talk every day on Skype. I tell her about the silly things you do."

I rolled my eyes. "I haven't talked to my best friend—there's two of them, but one I always felt so much closer to emotionally? The other one I looked up to like..." I snorted because he'd never know the truth if I could help it. "Like she was a goddess. Anyway, the other one, the one I told all my secrets first even if I told to the other friend later the same day... I haven't talked to her for months. I haven't told her any secrets or how I feel for so long. And now we're at university I'm out of contact completely. And now thanks to stuff that happened at lunch and how this is... I dunno, similar to situations she was in, I can't stop thinking about Tanya."

It was not that we'd fallen out exactly... Certainly there had been a few fights towards the end of the summer, but we had at least tried to part civilly. I'd just let myself not think about her for several months, and found that until now my life had been much calmer and less frequently endangered by monsters... Until now. I'd been walking into a trap from the moment I signed up for Orchestra Society, not even a week after I had last seen Tanya. In hindsight, our passive-aggressive fallout was utterly pointless. I'd been angry at lunch, but this realisation was gnawing at me and making me feel sick and hollow about the fighting. And by this point it was all I could think about.

"Is it that bad?"

"If I die today, I'm gonna come back as a ghost and she's going to be my unfinished business. She's been such a huge part of my life and now if it's all going to end, how terrible and weak that ending will be for us."

"If it makes you feel that bad, why don't you say something to her?"

"I can't just —"

"Ally, my best friend is halfway around the planet from me. I have to tell her everything that upsets me because if I don't, that is a long distance for bad thoughts to travel back and forth and they get stronger the further they go. Your friend is closer, but you haven't talked to her so long these thoughts they go back and forth between you anyway, getting just as bad, and she seems far away like she is on the moon. Because all those bad thoughts have got between you and made it all much longer. But she doesn't have to be. It is like my friend is right with me even when we are not talking, if we are happy."

I pulled a face, but Amir was looking levelly at me with such a meaningful expression I couldn't blow it off. He was probably really lonely if he latched onto people like Sam to be friends with, and quickly accepted strange invites to bars when he didn't drink with people he barely talked to outside of orchestra practice. I was blessed compared to him, and considering I actually liked him I probably owed him months of my time if we survived this. I hadn't even had a chance to be sympathetic about whatever drama llama stuff Lucia had managed to spin between them. I definitely had to rewrite my entire plan about setting them up and maybe spend just as much time with Lucia to help her through her apparent sexuality crisis, now I'd had one too and also figured it out and resolved the entire thing in one night with absolutely no more issues connected to it to deal with. I could be a voice of wisdom to her.

"Fine. What do I do?"

"Write to her. Call her?"

"My phone's charging in my room."

He lifted up his laptop and just dropped it on me. "Sign into Facebook, Skype, whatever you use. Pretend you *are* going to die today. What would you say to make it better?"

I shuddered, because he thought I was just being melodramatic about the whole impending death thing. Even knowing about the ghosts, he had this innocence of having never messed with all this so much that he could calmly trust that no one in the real, modern world *actually* got murdered by ghosts. Sometimes thirteen at a time.

I headed over to social media to snoop on how Tanya was doing, because it was safer than calling her. There was no mention of the supernatural in the first few posts she'd made on Facebook, just pictures of her with blue hair, laughing with various group selfies at clubs or outside in her new town, her baby face thinner, her eyes outlined nicely even when her hair was in a messy bun, still an adult upgrade to the braids she used to sport. She was blending in with the students so only the ache of familiarity when I looked at her face and missed it distinguished it from the others around her. It was like looking through her glamour too, and even harder to make my eyes uncross and see the Tanya I used to know.

I glanced over at Amir, but he was holding his guitar, silently practicing chords, so I knew he was giving me space. I should probably not start crying, but I could otherwise get some privacy. And he trusted me not to be snooping through his files.

I opened messenger and suppressed a groan at the three-month-old communication that had last passed between us. We'd been in *Troutespond* when it had been sent. She hadn't written to me either, and really I could have complained that this was going both ways, or said that she might not have even wanted to hear from me, not if she was still sulking about how I'd misunderstood her or whatever.

But I was the one who was sulking and she was the one who had tried to be upbeat and cheerful, so we all knew it was my fault.

I sighed and tried to work out what this argument even looked like. I had been worn thin with worrying about Tanya and, thanks to the first time she ran off, emotionally I found it almost impossible not to blame her in some part any time anything happened to us—this was the first incident of mortal terror from the Other side that I could not pin directly on her, though, no matter how many hoops I could have tried to jump through.

How about if I started with "So I'm about to be murdered by ghosts and it's not even your fault, so sorry." That would work.

When the thing with the cultists had happened, never mind that I had researched my way into the mess and the Piper never would have let anything happen to me once I put myself there, I had been so angry because Tanya had been bossing the cultists around trying to manipulate the situation in her (or… our) favour. The fact explained patiently to me by Teb (and ignored) that there was no time to tell me the plan, so she'd just offered me up to the cultists and taken a faith leap that I would be chill with it because I was always getting into weird scrapes anyway had been a trust fall too far. My fear got the better of me.

And Tanya had refused to come down to my level and see how genuinely frightened I'd been (as opposed to all the habitual fretting I did) and how this was following a long pattern that might lead my trust in her to break. How sometimes she really did seem like she was running off forever or throwing herself into danger with no care for her life, and that scared and upset me. And that Teb did the same thing, and she'd really committed to running away to the fairy world at one point. She'd been changed forever. In a matter of weeks my childhood best friend had become unrecognisable. How was I supposed to have faith in them as a bedrock like we'd once been to each other?

Was I really just supposed to believe in BFFs forever as a mantra that proved that we really did love each other so much we could never intentionally hurt each other? Like this was some fairy rule that was inviolable to the point of death before dishonour?

Maybe it was more important that Tanya believed this.

I looked at where I'd typed and deleted her name a few times. I had to sort this out before the performance. This was the one thing I couldn't just leave raw and open (now I had come to some sort of understanding with Alana again— for once Teb was the uncomplicated one because stuff with her didn't get sorted in an afternoon). There was no time to mince words here, though.

I deleted her name and typed it fresh for luck, and began my new attempt at a letter.

"Tanya, this is HILARIOUS, because I am haunted by 13 MISERABLE GHOSTS that won't stop singing in my ear, and they will probably KILL me today. Even though this is BLATANTLY not my fault (or yours), it makes it pretty hard to judge you, 'cos this happened to me ANYWAY despite me trying to steer clear of the weird stuff. In short, you are one of my BESTEST FRIENDS IN THE UNIVERSE, and I'm sorry I got weird about everything when you did the thing with the cultists. If this thing with the ghosts has taught me anything it's that death is a CRUSHING INEVITABILITY and that life is TOO SHORT to have fallings out when you love someone.
Wish me luck with the performance tonight! I need some of your CRAZY LUCK. If I survive I might have Thriller stuck in my head forever, but played badly on a flute, so I may have to reevaluate this apology as I suffer a FATE WORSE THAN DEATH.
Lots of love, ALLY x x x x x x x x x x x x"

I read it over, hoping she didn't think there was a secret message in the random capslock, and looked at the time.

"Good enough," I said.

"You sent it?" Amir asked.

I looked hard at the little icon that confirmed that yes, indeed, I had sent it.

"Oh God, can I delete it from the Internet?" I asked.

He yoinked the laptop off my lap. "No. You've done your best. Now leave it for her to do her best."

"How do you know she will?"

"You said she was your best friend?" He made it sound like that should explain everything.

I groaned, slumping down in the beanbag further. "What time is it?"

"Nearly four o'clock."

"We have an hour before we need to be there," I said, picking up my mandolin.

"You're going now?!"

"Better safe than sorry to get to the theatre."

Even if I might not get a chance to purify everyone until much closer to the performance, it wouldn't hurt being there and seeing how things were unfolding.

Amir just nodded like he totally understood, and got up to leave when I did.

*

The theatre somehow seemed smaller and diminished to my eyes as we approached it: while normally it was a place of awe, oversized as a learning environment, the thought that I was potentially meeting my doom there shrank it down and made me look at it as dull and inglorious, my eyes taking in the rainwater stains in the brickwork, the dull gaze of the darkened glass unwelcoming and grim.

Once inside I could hear music, the sound of a single piano, and saw, pushed to the fore, posters on easels about a dance recital that clearly was the reason our own practice had been rescheduled—this looked like something from an actual class rather than a society, so I guessed a professor throwing their weight around could easily bump us from the top slot.

It seemed to be free to enter if you were wandering around with a student lanyard hanging from your neck, but it did mean that our group was going to be literally last minute. Of course this was how it happened.

Not sure what else to do and with time to kill, Amir and I shrugged at each other and we slunk into the hall and sat at the back, watching the modern dance group act out Hamlet wordlessly but with a great deal of controlled flailing.

The bodies really began dropping around quarter to five, and an embarrassed creaking from the door as someone tried to sidle in silently drew my attention. Molly edged in, her clothes and hair looking as neat and perfect as ever, no sign of the state I'd seen her in last night. She'd probably never admit to having been scared. Molly scanned the scant audience (aside from us at the back, there was mostly just a line of other dance students and their professor, all in their leggings and hoodies, up front, as well as two of our violin section seated in the middle) and she gave me a significant look. I nudged Amir, grabbed my mandolin and we hurried to join her, heading out into the atrium.

"Backstage is closed until they're done, so we're going to have ten minutes before we start. Are you ready?"

"Yeah, I got in some extra practice while I waited since I missed rehearsal," I lied. "Sorry about that. Parents in town. Phone dead. The usual."

Molly nodded distractedly, texting. The rather more enraptured violin players jumped at the buzzing which was audible from their pockets across the room and over the lull in piano as Hamlet croaked, and they shamefacedly waded through the aisles to us, clapping as they went.

Right, that was five of us, skipping the encore to get ready for our own show.

We went backstage, finding Sam loitering by the door with a couple more violinists—nine of us present as we headed through the awkwardly curving narrow corridor to a small green room.

"Tune up," Molly ordered me, and I sat next to the girl who had lugged an entire harp to university for some godforsaken overachieving reason and had presumably been sitting in the green room since morning practice, defending her precious but heavy instrument from the dancers. Ten down, three to go. I suppose I could have just purified us and let the other three die, but that would be extremely unsporting.

I started messing around with the pegs at the top of my mandolin under

Molly's watchful glare, taking the notes clattering around in my head from the ghosts as my guide. The others did likewise, all of them scowling at their instruments, shaking their heads as if to rattle the tunes free. They all looked unrested and on edge. I wondered if we'd all had a sleepless night—up close Molly's normally rosy cheeks looked grey, her eyes shadowed. I was accidentally much better at student life than some, with my fast metabolism and habit of staying up right through the night just by accident. Whether the rest of the orchestra had been all out enjoying the three day Halloween drinking holiday as we had, or they'd just been kept up by the ghosts yelling spooky music in their ears, they looked shattered. Even Amir's guitar looked happier than him for once.

A bunch of dancers came in, grabbed bags or coats they'd left in here even though there was a sign for them on the door to absolutely not do that on account of the next performers using the green room after them. When they were gone, another member of our group had arrived in the rush.

All these last stragglers to show up definitely were ones I recognised as partygoers from Bradley Hall. Soon twelve of us were sitting around and only one of our number was missing –

"Ally. Have you heard from Lucia today?" Molly was suddenly looming into my personal space, fire in her eyes. "She's not answering her phone and she didn't show up to practice either."

"I, um… not since first thing this morning."

Molly scowled at me. "I expected you to be the one to flake out first, not her."

"S-she'll be here," I whispered.

Molly gave me a look that clearly said that I should keep better track of my friends, and stalked off to harass our sole trumpeter. Yeah, she either didn't remember last night or was holding the admission against me.

I sort of agreed with her—keeping tabs on everyone properly would have removed about ninety percent of my past problems. But there was nothing I could do about Lucia now. We at least hadn't fallen out, and if Alana's guilty grin had been anything to go by I might have some apologetic overtures from her with the feeling of having made off with my friend without my 'permission' for what power I actually had to tell her or Alana what to do with their own lives. But I also didn't exactly plant GPS trackers on my friends, so if she was off in a weird mood having some alone time to sort her thoughts out, say, wandering deep into the moors to think, then I was not going to be able to drag her back in time.

Because there were five minutes to go before we'd be heading out onto the stage.

I couldn't do the ritual without everyone here.

Well, I could, but exclude Lucia, and leave one of my only new friends who was not the personification of Death Incarnate at the mercy of potentially murderous ghosts fulfilling an ancient curse…

At three minutes to the performance I had sweated through my nice shirt, but also decided that the honourable thing wasn't just saving my own skin, but that I had a duty of care as the one person here who actually knew what was going on to save as many of us as I could, even at Lucia's expense. I hated how unheroic that was—that there was nothing special I knew how to do to stretch the purification to her… Could I have phoned up the Piper and made him teleport to Lucia's location and bring her back here for me in the blink of an eye? Or was that violating his terms and conditions? Could I have delayed the performance by fainting or would Molly force her way on through, even if I came to propped up in a chair on stage with the mandolin in my lap? Probably.

I had actually started looking for a secret way to light the herbs and get started when the door thumped open and Lucia came in, drawing all eyes to her and causing a handy distraction.

I flicked Alana's lighter and dropped it into the bowl of herbs: they implausibly caught alight at once and gave off spirals of a pungently green-smelling smoke.

Lucia, who by habit had been walking right for me, took one look, leaped back and yelled, "Fucking hell Ally, how do you cock up making tea *that* badly?!"

I looked down at the mug, where little flames were blatantly flickering below the rim. "It's, uh, a candle. For luck." I said, wondering how she had found it quite plausible that I'd be able to make a mug of tea in such an inhospitable place as a green room empty of everything but folding chairs and how I was truly incompetent enough to set it on fire once I'd done the first round of the impossible. I suppose I did have a reputation for acquiring cups of tea, but I also made so many you'd think people would expect that to be the one thing that I was actually reliably competent at.

And then the music in my ears abruptly stopped. For the first time in a week my head was quiet. The entire room reacted like kids on a train going into a tunnel and learning something fun about their ears all reacting to the sudden pressure change, jerking their heads around and touching their ears, some instinctively trying to pop them as if they'd been struck by momentary deafness, mouths opening in confusion without knowing what to ask the others.

I met Amir's eye and shook my head a little, warning him not to ask me about the ghosts out loud, since he was the only one who'd sort of ended up knowing what was going on.

"What's up with you all?" Molly asked incredulously, proving for once and for all my suspicions that she was the least Force-sensitive person in the room.

"Uh, my ears popped," I said. "Did that happen to you guys as well?"

Everyone looked around at each other and slowly came to the consensus that, yes, that made the most sense for what they had just experienced.

"It must have been some change in the atmospheric pressure," Sam said, always happy to try and sound like the smartest person in the room while I was being a confused ditz about it. Was it too late to explain to him all about ghosts and how I was right?

I couldn't work up my frustration with him—I was elated to have warded the ghosts off at the cost of crippling social humiliation about lucky candles that would no doubt haunt me just as intensely as the real ghosts. There was no way Lucia wouldn't bring this up the first time we sat an exam together. But for now—joy that my head was all my own. And that we may not die that day.

Molly cleared her throat.

"When you're all ready—we have a performance to do! Lucia? Get tuned up."

Lucia plonked herself down next to me finally and eyed the smouldering mug suspiciously. I tipped it away from her a little so she couldn't see the lack of wax at the bottom. I'd have to tell my mum the exact herbs and salts so she could start making some of these as actual candles. I had a feeling it would definitely save time if I ended up throwing away my Literature degree to become an actual exorcist.

"What's up with her?" Lucia hissed, nodding at Molly as she wrestled her violin out. "She's been twice as bitchy as usual?"

I shrugged, blowing on the embers to waft the last of the purifying smoke into the room. I felt so chill and calm as I smiled smug and happy. "Performance anxiety."

# Set up

We stepped onto the stage to thunderous applause from my mum and Alana egging her on with wolf whistles. The rest of the gathered audience— surprisingly far more than for the interpretive dance Hamlet I'd witnessed a short time before—clapped a little more politely as we filed onstage to where there was just a ring of twelve chairs, with one more in front of them for Molly.

It suddenly, very belatedly, hit me that I was performing in front of like fifty people. My knees went to jelly and I nearly dropped my mandolin and sank to the floor. There was a hand at my elbow at once, guiding me to a chair at the end.

"Eeeasy," Rose murmured, dragging an extra chair in from the wings to sit beside me. "You're doing great."

"When did you get here?" I hissed.

"I'm always around," she replied. Again: as a friend, reassuring. As Death… not so much.

"The ghosts are gone," I told her out the corner of my mouth as I propped music in the stand in front of me. Rose didn't have a stand. She adjusted an extremely fragile looking instrument that seemed to just be made of curved sticks, with string between them. "Is that —"

"Shh," she hissed, gently plucking the lyre to make the smallest noise to check the tuning. Even the near-mute *"plink"* had an otherworldly sound to it. Underworldly sound to it.

Molly cleared her throat, seeing that we were mostly set up, and she turned to the audience, introducing us as the lucky offerings for the sacrifice from the

Orchestra Society (my words not hers) and she moved on to explain the tragic, gory circumstances behind the macabre playlist with rather more glee than I had expected. She could have been holding a torch below her face around a campfire as she got to her dedication to Orchestra Societies past.

I scanned the audience during the scattered, uncertain pause. I could see Bus Stop and Mike, a couple more people from our Literature classes… Angie had showed up, to my surprise, as I hadn't been advertising so much and spent a lot of time apologising to her in case she heard me practicing in my room, so I was hardly the best marketing.

With my parents, Alana and the Piper I could claim nearly a quarter of the audience as people who were at least partially invested in specifically seeing me play. Was I really that obliviously good at making friends? If I survived this I was going to have to write a lot of cards at Christmas time.

Molly turned to us and raised her violin to her chin without any more preamble. She nodded to us. "Staring on one, two…" I could *hear* the echo in her voice, and the panic came as suddenly as being stabbed in the gut with an icicle as the voice that said "three" was not Molly's prim voice at all. For a moment I saw and heard someone else – another music geek from a time before memory (except Bus Stop's). It could only be Kris Carter, Molly's counterpart from three years before.

I wanted to yell—to get up and run around the stage, throw my mandolin aside, start grabbing and smashing violins. I could have vomited right across the stage…

Instead my hands jumped into position without my conscious say-so as everyone flawlessly hit their mark to start playing, and the music poured out of us like it had been spilled, three years of nonstop practice in the void was finally paying off.

The sound that came out of us didn't remotely sound like the instruments we played. The cello was back—and I had the most disconcerting feeling that I was the cellist. The sound of the violins was multiplied into the dozens. That voice that had haunted my dreams for days began to sing. If I half-closed my eyes I could see strange people in our chairs, people blurring wrong between my eyelashes to make a different face.

Beside me Rose had gone into a tune of her own, complementary to the main music, simple and pure and following along, yet alien and distant, filling in the gaps in the music with an awful melancholy sound I wasn't sure anyone else could even hear, a song dragged from the forgotten past, a song that could have last been heard echoing around the Underworld for all I knew.

She alone was not a vessel hopelessly along for the ride as the ghosts fell into their long-awaited performance. She looked peaceful, almost joyful, as she smiled down at her lyre. The looks on the other's faces were of panic and confusion—they knew they weren't playing their parts. I could see Amir at the far end of the row, the only person approaching as a co-conspirator in all this, making frantic eyebrow gestures at me to ask what was wrong—perhaps trying to see if I had a plan for this. I looked helplessly back. Just because I knew about it didn't mean that I knew what to *do* about it.

The lights had changed and I couldn't see into the audience any more—we were in a sea of light in a darkened room and nothing else seemed to exist beyond the circle of the spotlight that fell on us.

Molly, though, was not scared or confused. She was playing violently hard, a few broken hairs already curling around the ends of her bow, and she was rapturously lost in the music; her eyes were closed, but when her head tipped back her eyes opened a little to reveal them rolled right back into her head.

I looked urgently to Rose and nodded at Molly.

Rose raised an eyebrow, seeming to indicate that I was guessing rightly that something was extra wrong with her. Maybe that was why the ghosts hadn't left: their hold was too strong on the person who had gone nosing around into their affairs. If only she hadn't rebuffed me when I first asked her if she'd gotten us all haunted… If only I hadn't been so caught up in all my nonsense last night.

Our set was to play two songs back-to-back then to take a quick break for Molly to offer the names of what we were playing next (I suppose so if we mangled it too badly, the audience wouldn't be left trying to guess the song) while some tuning adjustments were made and then we'd be off again.

I kept my eyes fixed on Molly as we drew close to the end of the first set. (Who had decided we needed thirteen songs—*really*?) She looked as frantic as she had to start with as we made it to the final notes without anyone dying yet and I was terrified she'd keep going, swept up in possession and dragging us all along after her into the next song. I was going to try to protest, but as we hit the final note Molly slumped like someone had cut her strings and she staggered forwards. Sam knocked over his chair and all the music stands in the violin section dashing to catch her before she could topple into the empty orchestra pit at the foot of the stage.

I sunk sluggishly down in my chair as the ghostly good posture left me, watching the drama happen to someone else for a change. Rose muttered into my ear, "Of course he would snap out of it first. The simpleminded are much less easily captivated by a good song."

I was far too worried to laugh at that, struggling to get up to join the panic.

Meanwhile, enough people had roused that there was a crowd around Molly and Lucia was calling for the curtain. Someone gave up a chair for Molly to sink into.

"Don't crowd her," Sam complained, flapping at the fretting flutist who could see her extra credit assignment going down the drain. "She just needs some air."

"I need *Ally*," Molly gasped.

Everyone turned to look at me.

"*Busteeed*," Rose giggled.

I hauled myself out of my chair, clutching my mandolin like a lifeline, and crossed the stage. The orchestra cleared the way like I was infected but I ignored them, kneeling by Molly's chair.

A perfectly manicured hand shot out and grabbed my collar. "I saw him!" she hissed.

"Who?"

"Kris Carter! The orchestra leader!"

"Just now? Because I —"

She shook her head furiously and pulled me even closer to whisper to me. "When I started the society. The *night* I did. I thought it was all a dream—I woke up and he was playing my violin! He said he'd been waiting for *so long*. I haven't been able to get the songs out of my head since!"

"You told me you didn't —"

"I know, I know. I lied. I was scared! I thought if—if I just played the songs—he'd leave me alone."

"Is he hurting you?" I asked urgently, shifting my grip on her hands where I'd just been trying to stop her from strangling me to try and feel her pulse. She looked pale and horrendously tired.

"He wants us to finish playing."

"Yeah, but —"

"Ally, you're all in danger and it's my fault. I have to finish this."

"I did a spell to purify the ghosts away. I don't know why it didn't work... The music went away out of everyone's heads for a few minutes."

"Not mine."

"But we're still getting possessed when we play..."

"Maybe it's just because of me... Because I'm playing. No one else fainted, did they?"

I nodded. "What about you though?"

"We're going to keep on playing." She let go of me at last and I fell backwards, she'd been hauling me forwards so much. I found the others standing in a loose ring around us, all looking very curious.

"The show must go on," I announced, feeling rather ridiculous to have an actual opportunity to use that phrase in the heat of the moment. I got to my feet, sharing one more look with Molly, trying to convey my concern for her, but she looked away and struggled to her feet, seemingly hauled up violin first.

Well, probably *actually* hauled up violin first. It was definitely the thing in control here.

Lucia gestured whoever was doing the curtain for us and we hastily reassembled our group, righting music stands and getting back in our chairs. By the time the curtains opened, to some relieved applause, Molly was standing boldly at the front again, swaying slightly but violin under her chin, her voice ringing out clearly as she announced what we were playing next, her posh tones perfect for conveying that absolutely nothing was wrong.

Once more I disappeared into uncomfortable ghost possession, feeling my hands plucking out the tune with more skill and precision than I could have managed in a year of study, and we powered through another six and a half minutes of music.

No matter how supernaturally good we were, there was no applause when Molly toppled over at the end, going down so suddenly there was no time for the audience to even be sure the song was supposed to have ended.

"There's nine more songs," I hissed to Rose. "This is ridiculous. Will the professors in the audience stop her if she keeps trying? Will the rest of the orchestra?"

Rose shrugged one shoulder.

My mum clambered onto the stage and revived Molly with smelling salts. Alana followed her stage invasion, but while I was busy pretending to have never seen Mum before in my life while she played her "Don't worry, I'm a first aider" card while waving around herbal cures she happened to have in her handbag, Alana came over to Rose and I.

"Did you purify the orchestra?" she asked at once, as if she really believed I would be here rather than queueing at an airport gate round about now if I'd missed my chance and knew it.

"Yeah. It's no good. She's properly possessed. It must be, like, soul deep. Hubris for meddling or something." (I saw Rose fractionally nodding beside me.) "Is there anything you can do?"

"It must all go back to the original curse, and those things need careful treatment. Usually destroying the original artefact is a good start, since curses would obviously be tied to those things, or making ritual amends to the source of the curse, if it was a deity or a spirit with demands. But she never even came in contact with it. Second-hand, there's not much to do before this settles into a thrice-yearly ghost performance in this hall no matter what. Their lot *and* yours if we're unlucky. What we needed is much more time."

And not, I suppose, falling out and messing around and generally failing to get our bums in gear with the ghost thing when Gallows Hill didn't pan out... I didn't say it.

Molly was back on her feet anyway, thanks to something my mum had concocted, and she was loudly protesting that she was fine and could keep playing.

"Let's do the next four songs all together," she said when the stage had cleared and we had our hands hovering in trepidation over our instruments again. That way, we powered through eight of our thirteen tracks. I wasn't even surprised when she went down again at the end of that. Most of the orchestra sunk down in their seats or drooped heads between knees for a moment. The stage was cool, the lights too bright on us, too dark outside that bubble. Molly took five minutes to revive afterwards, and we called another interval.

"Is the stress of watching her faint worth the entertainment of these cheesy mixes?" Rose asked, casting a critical eye in the direction of the audience beyond the curtain as we watched Molly struggle upright again. I was feeling dazed myself from the stress and possession, even if it wasn't draining us in the same way.

I looked down at my mandolin and it stared back at me with judgemental eyes.

No. It wasn't the evil eye. Amir had made sure for me, looked up every type of magical eye symbol. They were protective eyes, watchful for evil spirits so you didn't have to be. The kind of thing a hippie witch mum sends to university with her beloved daughter to look over her.

I stumbled to my feet and dashed across the stage.

"Molly! Molly! Can you play the mandolin?"

She looked at me like I'd sprouted a second head (that is, confused and dizzily over one shoulder, because her eyes were out of focus.)

"What?"

I crammed the mandolin onto her lap. "You need to sit down for the next few songs. Take it easy. Play the mandolin."

"What about you?"

I pried her violin out of her other hand. "I'll lead the orchestra."

"You're kidding me! You can't even play your own instrument!"

"Don't care," I said. "Kris's got this."

"Kris?" Lucia asked, since she was hovering around Molly as well. I shrugged at her. Maybe I could explain this later. Maybe this was just going to get forgotten under all the big drama of this determined presentation.

Amir had been hovering nearby with a bottle of water, and he got the message. He grabbed the back of the chair Molly was on and just scooted it away into the line-up with her still sitting on it before she could argue. The violin section gave me very confused looks, or outright betrayed looks that I'd showed up and taken the main role without a single violin lesson while they had sweated and cried and bled through all the grades and here was some Literature student here on a whim.

I gestured vaguely as Lucia had been doing and it got the curtain rolling up again, so I'd kind of set my fate in stone.

Suddenly I was standing in front of the audience, pretending to be a classically trained violin prodigy who deserved the centre of attention.

"Uh, I… Our next song… hopefully won't be stuck in your heads as long as it's been stuck in mine. I—I hope you know h-how to do the T-Time Warp…"

I idly wondered if it was possible to die of embarrassment and fear and just save myself the entire spectacle, but it didn't happen then and there, so I lifted Molly's bow to the violin to the sound of gentle laughter from the audience—probably quite relieved someone had stepped in to save Molly, if they didn't know anything about me and my skill or lack thereof—and hopefully laughing at my terrified attempt at humour.

I felt the bow jerk under my hand, the violin shift in my grip, held suddenly like I actually knew what I was doing, and I watched in amazement as the fingers of one hand made the notes, the other drew the bow across the strings and *actual music* poured out, the rest of the orchestra filling in the accompaniment.

I hoped someone was filming this, because to be honest, I would send a video of this to Teb with no context provided just to make her think that I was a virtuoso out of nowhere, and I have no shame for wanting to do that.

I dreaded the end of the set, but maybe I hadn't been consumed in the same way as Molly had, or maybe the hunch about the purification was right, but when I stopped I felt only the need to take a huge gasp of air like I hadn't breathed the whole time I was playing. Perhaps I hadn't. I immediately looked over my shoulder to see that Molly was upright and clutching the mandolin. She nodded to me. Permission.

I didn't stop to listen to the still going applause (it was all for Kris anyway). I just cleared my throat and started announcing our final three songs right into my parents' gleeful cheering.

I was finishing this.

As Kris played I felt him leaning in closer to the living world, pushing through that veil. I felt his excitement growing as he worked his way through these final songs. If I had gotten fed up of these corny music choices over a single semester, how would he—and all the ghosts—feel about being doomed to play them possibly forever? No wonder he had been pressuring Molly to get it done. I'd have been borderline murderous after years of despair that we'd never be able to stop playing it. It was probably a good thing that, in the real world, ghosts didn't seem to work like in horror movies and just start indiscriminately murdering people.

That understanding powered my mysterious perfect playing all the more, and I gave myself over to the final song, letting it flow through me with fear and relief and Kris's iron certainty that he'd let nothing stop him from finishing his performance. All the ghosts around me were playing with the same intensity—objectively this was probably going to be the most passionate version of Thriller (orchestral) ever played. If that happened very often or anyone cared to measure it.

I recognised the final bar coming up and tried to breathe for the first time in minutes.

Instead, everything went black.

# Judgement

There was a merciless white light above me, like the spotlight I'd been standing under but much, much colder.

I was sitting on a spindly wooden chair like the ones we'd had on the stage, but there were three in a little cluster, Molly at the edge, hands folded over her violin, eyes downcast, and sitting between us was a lanky ginger boy with long musician's fingers and watery eyes. Kris. I recognised him instinctively after he'd possessed me. You get the measure of someone pretty quickly when they do that. He gave me a small smile.

Behind us, when I craned over my shoulder, were more chairs—a shadowy orchestra, if the silhouette of a certain cello in their line-up was a reliable clue. The other twelve ghosts then.

The pool of spotlight might not have stretched to them, but it was growing outwards another way, bringing in a sight ahead of us: opposite our little group were three more figures, seated behind a black velvet-draped table. The figure at the far end opposite me was a female figure shrouded in white cloth, from a veil that concealed her face with only lots of long dark hair hanging out the front to the pools of white linen at her feet. Her arms were bare, the only exposed part of her: her warm brown skin was decorated with golden jewellery, winding all the way up her arms, hanging in long loops of beads from under the hood. Her nails were wickedly sharp and tapping on the table.

Beside her the next figure was clad all in grey—a very familiar figure even if I said so myself. His white eyes shone through a grey blindfold—if "his" was even the right word to use for the Piper transcending physical form to a grey-winged seraph. They were still *my* Piper, sprawled back in the chair, huge bare feet emerging from under the velvet on our side of the table, the giant form as awkward to manage as when I tried to cram my boyfriend into a small car. (I spared a moment to be thankful that we weren't wrong about how tall the Piper was.) It was a million times beyond what I had *thought* I had seen in him when I'd got to see him in the fairy world back in those first few days after learning he existed. What I'd basically seen was him but kinda shiny and ethereal. This was an eldritch sort of ancient non-human shiny bright entity that happened to have jokingly called me "Honey Nut Cheerios" as a pet name once.

The third figure I could also have guessed without any clues, like the lyre on the table in front of her, but Rose had the scythe and the black robes and *all* of it except a horse maybe, and it *really* only sank in then and there that I had been accepting cookies from Death Herself all semester. Or at least, Death Herself targeted specifically at my young adult demographic.

"Told you," Rose said, as if this was a chill sort of scenario where you could joke about *anything*, right after she had accused my boyfriend of losing his touch and being unprofessional.

The Piper said nothing.

Her hood turned to me, and a bleached white jawbone flashed from under it as she laughed. She filled the robes as much as she'd filled out her university logo hoodie, even if she looked skeletal when bits of her stuck out from under it. "Well, Ally, congratulations, you just won me a bet."

"What is this?!" Molly asked, finally looking up, her voice shrill. Kris, on the other hand, looked completely resigned to this, even eager. "Are we still on the stage?"

"In a way. This is your final judgement."

I remembered, suddenly, that Molly had spent every interaction she ever had with Rose winding her up and getting really aggro with her play style. Not that Rose had helped, but... My hopes for being able to help Molly began to sink.

The figure in white stirred. "My sacrifice," she said in a booming voice that reminded me of Teb when she was getting righteous about what movie we should pick. Yeah, this was the goddess responsible for the curse.

"W-what did we do?" Molly squeaked.

"Nothing," I shot back at the goddess while pretending to answer Molly. "We played this stupid concert set and got her sacrifice cooties all over us, so whoever this is thinks she gets to steal us away."

The Piper's head turned to Rose and she scoffed. "Fine, but you only get that point because I helped her."

"Was this a test for me?" I demanded.

"Judgement thought it would take your mind off the stage fright," Rose laughed, then immediately corrected herself with a shake of her head. "It was a test for them, not you. Impartiality is hard when you go around making girlfriends and saving their lives."

"So this is about the cultists!"

Behind and never able to catch up, I heard Molly hiss, *What cultists?*

"You are meant to be dead, Ally. This is the reckoning on that choice." Rose said, speaking over her. "You were supposed to die months ago. I pulled up this old haunting since it was related to your extracurriculars, and it would give these ghosts a chance to be at peace and move on. Then all I had to do was throw them at you and let the curse do the rest. You were marked for death the moment you set foot on campus."

I heard Molly gasp, and it pulled a question to the front of my mind that gave me a clarity beyond the screaming panic of the rest of it: "What about Molly? She wasn't supposed to die!"

Rose shrugged. "People die. She made her choice to revive the orchestra. She's here fair and square."

"Excuse me!?" Molly butted in. "I'm not going to die! Are you *punishing* me for playing music? What is this?"

"A trial, of sorts. Minerva has a claim on all your souls after Kris Carter played on a restored artefact in the museum. Can you believe they just let students handle these things? Since the old power structures to arbitrate such things is long gone, we've awoken Minerva to hear her claim in a higher court. Just me, her, and Judgement to say what must be done."

"W-what happens to them—us—if she wins her case?"

"Minerva's afterlife isn't so bad. The instrument that Kris played is tied so intimately to her, those who die by the curse will play for her for eternity at her side, one of the highest honours in her time, even if it has become… a little more of a devouring curse in its hunger over the centuries. Originally it was a blessing, which would come to you only in your natural time of death. People used to vie for a once in a generation chance to play the artefact in question. So you see, even if the final decision is that you must die, it will not be so bad for music lovers such as yourself to be elevated beside a goddess of such wisdom and learning."

I scoffed a little to myself. Also I couldn't play for toffee, so I felt this was not my ideal afterlife. "What's this 'even if', then? Give me some options here."

"Yourself and Molly are still, legally, alive. You have three options: die of Minerva's curse and become a ghost, bound to her spell to play your songs and haunt the university forever; Die, and be claimed as her sacrifice and persist in eternal glory… Or, I suppose, convince Minerva to relinquish her claim on you so that you can return back to life. As for Kris and the choir, he has been chosen to speak for them and may now choose whether they continue on as ghosts or move on."

We all turned to look at the nervously fidgeting violinist. "Move on!" Kris blurted as soon as he'd cottoned on that someone was asking.

"Is that a unanimous decision? You have had two months to discuss it, having been informed of the terms."

There was a murmur of assenting voices from behind us, and I turned to see the shadowy orchestra shifting impatiently. Yeah, I was pretty damn sick of those songs too.

"We're ready," he said.

I thought Rose, who seemed to be chairwoman leading this, and of course, Death, would be the one in charge of what happened next, but she only settled back in her chair further. The veiled goddess rose out of her chair and suddenly raised a hand, pointing it palm outwards directly at Kris (I felt myself leaning a little to the left to avoid it even so).

He gasped, staggering to his feet, spilling white light from his mouth and eyes. A moment later he was all light, and the radiance behind us threw long shadows right across the stage towards the table of judgement, from Molly and I and the empty chair in the middle. When it had faded enough that I could lower my hands from my eyes Kris was gone, and the light behind us faded away and winked out.

Minerva closed her hand into a fist and stayed frozen like that for a long, breathless moment, captivating our attention even in her utter stillness.

She sat back down in one graceful movement, and I breathed out again. It was *over*. Whatever else happened, it was over.

I glanced over at Molly across Kris's vacated seat. "We're free of the curse!" I told her excitedly.

"Are you kidding me?" Rose said at the same moment as Minerva lurched to her feet with rather less poise, the air crackling in wrath. "Free?!" she boomed. "You're mine!"

Molly whimpered in terror. I could *feel* Rose rolling her eyes at me despite the fact this entire creepy committee were hiding their faces. (Well, 'Judgement' was affecting a very neutral smirk. I knew I couldn't assume this but I still felt he was on my side.)

I felt, and trust me on this metaphor, possessed as I rose to my feet, all six foot of me, wrapped in a black and white coat that had followed me beyond the veil. "No," I said, with the calmness of someone who isn't even sure that the words were coming from their own head, so disassociated and scared as I was and so pointed and angry were the words. "*You* are kidding *us* with this."

"You played my song!" Minerva yelled, and the stage shook under my flip-flops.

"We played, on our own instruments, a terrible rendering of thirteen generic famous modern western pop culture songs associated with generically spooky things and Halloween, a cannibalised pseudo-pagan calendar event bastardised into a saints' day by Christianity and further into a horror movie celebration more about silly string spider webs than anything of real substance by our modern culture. None of that goes back to any of your holy days in any tangible way and I can say that without knowing a thing about what those were."

Minerva made a rumbling noise in her throat, and I was so fed up I cut right across her to continue complaining about the *colossally* unfair month I'd had: "I signed up for an orchestra to please my mum about learning the mandolin, and Death sicced the ghosts on Molly, who spread the curse like a contagion to me. That's the only reason it ever came to me. Molly herself wasn't even at the university when your curse happened to the previous society, and until presumably right now she didn't even believe in it and thought the whole thing was stupid and I was being overdramatic. And three years ago I didn't even know magic or afterlives and religions or fairies or *anything* existed. When the original offence against you happened I didn't even know my *mum* was a witch. Those thirteen musicians touched your relic *which still I don't even know what sort of instrument it was* and they succumbed to your curse, but you know what? I protected my orchestra with *ghost* warding. We weren't cursed. We were *haunted*. We were possessed. Your curse had nothing to do with having Time Warp stuck in our heads, and that is *all* I have suffered because of you. It began and ended with those ghosts. And if I hadn't stepped in to play for Molly, she wouldn't have made it more than halfway through the whole show, so I *helped* you by finishing the performance and *bringing* you Kris Carter and twelve other ghosts to serve you, *real* sacrifices. You have no claim on Molly and you have no claim on me!"

I stopped, breathing heavily, and scanned the line of hooded or blindfolded figures that were all somehow staring at me. I swear that *dork* flickered one white eye at me in a brief wink, as much as I could tell anything about what was going on with his appearance.

"Jeeze, Ally," Rose said, sounding actually stunned. "You're not going to let Molly or Minerva say their bits? We had a whole routine."

"Stuff it," I told Death. Death was uptalking at me. I didn't think I was in too much danger.

Minerva turned to the Piper. Judgement. She was bristling with static electricity that made her jewellery lift from her skin a little. "They were touched by my curse! You know they were! You have to hear this fairly!"

"Do you still recognise us as the absolute power in the universe?" Rose asked. "I mean, tough luck if you don't, because remember, *we* asked *you* to come sit at our table and you even got thirteen fresh tributes for doing so. Just making sure you know that three thousand years ago you'd never have even *met* us first-hand, or got this sort of preferential treatment for a squabble about a curse. It would have been an in-house matter for your pantheon. I'm not doing this for you, Minerva. I'm making sure Judgement still works, and everything still gets weighed fairly, so a petty matter over fifteen mortal souls of no particular value and a long-forgotten goddess is small fry for us. I mean, I wanted Osiris because it looks cooler with the scales and hearts and feathers and all, but this is what we had to work with. Just so you understand."

Minerva finally sat back down, chastised. I had a feeling from her folded arms she'd thought Rose had her back here.

I wondered if she had once been a mortal woman, like Teb.

We all looked at the Piper. To *Judgement*. I was not going to give him the satisfaction of that title when we were over this.

Silently he extended a hand, in a fist, much like Minerva had done, but slower, calmer, like one who has all the time in the universe to decide. The hand landed on the table palm up, fingers stretched out. And he just sort of left it there, instead of doing anything cool like the gladatorial thumb up or down. Maybe it was the choice of left or right hand but excuse me for not knowing the code.

"You live," Rose reported, her voice resentful. Not at me—at the Piper, who she was still looking at her, arms folded, leaning back in her chair to get a wider view, like she was checking for a single drop of smugness. I had a horrible feeling we'd failed her test, and that everyone had known it before I even spoke. Before I even picked up Molly's violin.

Maybe around the time he showed up for lunch when I asked him to.

But she said nothing else. A moment later, the spotlight above us clicked off.

# Nope

I gasped awake lying stretched across four chairs. My parents were right there, and Alana bobbing nervously behind them. The Piper was holding my hand, crouched beside me. And Rose, behind him, hands crammed in the pockets of her hoodie, her mouth a flat line.

"Stage fright?!" I blurted at her, as soon as I met her eye. "You did all that for *stage fright*?!"

Rose's face broke into a huge smile and she saluted me with a middle finger. Yeah, we could still be friends if we ignored *everything* else. Like how she'd been actively rooting for the Piper to proclaim that an ancient goddess could steal my soul because it was somehow the more neutral seeming option.

"She's babbling," the Piper said, pressing a huge hand to my forehead. "Perhaps she hit her head when she collapsed and addled her brain."

I shoved his hand away, struggling to sit up as Mum and Dad leaned in to fuss around me.

The Piper blocked them: "I think she needs to go back to her room and lie down for a while. The performance has clearly aggravated a nervous disposition, like poor Molly's."

"We're really not built for this performance malarkey," I groaned. "Though we're not fainting Victorian women."

"You went down like dominoes," Alana commented, her voice a weird croak.

"I don't know, I think you played very well," the Piper said with a smirky smile he had clearly been holding back the entire confrontation. Oh yeah, sure, he was just playing the relieved boyfriend in front of my parents. With his back to Rose so she couldn't see how relieved he was that I'd browbeaten her and Minerva without making it personal about me and him and given Rose what she wanted.

(An extremely unfair trial, so, you know. He could have let me and Molly off on a technicality at that point but it would have looked garbage, I suppose.)

"When did you learn to play the violin like that?" my father demanded.

"Shh," Mum chided. "Talent runs in the family. I told you she'd be a natural."

"That's it, I agree with my boyfriend despite how he's pretending to be a doctor with no formal training. I need to go to bed."

As I tried to leave Molly came rushing over, pinkness restored to her face. "Ally! Wait!"

I let her pull me away from the Piper; she looked suspiciously at him for a moment but maybe didn't see the resemblance. "Ally... I... I don't really know what happened. But, um, I feel like I owe you. Thank you. Um. I'll take a break from Orchestra to focus on my studies for a little while, but I might start up again after Christmas. You're welcome to join."

"I'm all played out for now," I admitted.

She nodded and gave me a stern look that suggested that 'after Christmas' was a much slimmer probability than she was letting on and that my rejoining was also way less optional than it sounded.

The good news was that we were alive to continue this argument.

*

I got back to the halls and went to have a shower, then it all hit me—all that fear from facing down Minerva, having her gunning for my soul—and I threw up down the drain. I crawled back to my room not long after that and found Alana sitting on my chair, the Piper sitting on my bed.

"Sent your parents off for you," Alana said.

I waved vaguely at her and got into bed still just wrapped in my damp towel. The Piper folded himself warmly around me, and I fell asleep.

*

I woke up around four am. Alana was curled up on the comfy chair the Piper normally favoured, her feet on my desk chair. The Piper's coat was spread over her like a blanket. The Piper himself immediately opened his eyes when I poked him in the cheek with my sharpest fingernail.

"Are we in trouble?" I hissed at him. "With Rose."

He nuzzled in closer to my ear so he could talk without waking Alana up. "Honestly, I'm one of the most powerful things in the universe, and I couldn't tell you. Rose has given us a stay of execution and my word on what is fair is still legally seen as absolute, even if I may have concluded the trial far too quickly for her liking and been, frankly, embarrassingly indulgent towards you. I knew Minerva's side of it. Rose knew what you said was all true enough. We could have fought for days, but I knew you were right. And I'm so proud of you."

"I don't think she cares about that. What happens next?"

"What happens next? There are only three of us who are more powerful than I am when it comes to the matter of a final word, as they knew the final word before it even happened, and guide my actions as firmly as anyone else's. It will be left to Fate what is to come."

I sighed. "So you're as oblivious as the rest of us right now?"

He cracked a smile against my neck. "Yes. I'm slumming it for the time being. Isn't that how you like me best?"

I shivered as it caught up to me that I'd been sleeping burritoed in a damp towel. "C-can you not look for a minute while I put some pyjamas on?"

He laughed into my neck, but then the grip on me loosened and he rolled over to face the wall. I glanced over at Alana, but she made an undignified snore, so I figured she was well and truly out of it.

Wearing warm winter pyjamas, I crawled back into my bed with my phone and winced at the brightness of the screen. I had a message from Mum to make up for my rushed goodbye—

"You were so brilliant!!!! I know it was just the ghosts but your dad is v. proud of you for playing the violin & I am so proud of you for getting rid of the ghosts!!!!! See you tomorrow? We're giving Alana a lift to the airport. Maybe we can go out for breakfast? Let me know!! Love you!!! Mum xoxoxoxoxoxoxox"

And a notification from Facebook messenger—Teb wishing me luck and hoping that Alana wasn't being too much of a pain and that my three am phone call from the night before had just been me trying not to get a stress ulcer and that she was very sorry that she had missed the call but she did still sleep.

Under that, a reply from Tanya. My heart skipped. I opened it to see that it was from barely twenty minutes after I sent my apology.

"Ally! You are going to be FINE, trust me. (Why are we doing ALL CAPS? Is this a thing I missed?) I have to say you do not strike me as a competent violinist but hey ho things happen. (Yes I know you play the banjo. Shush.)
But seriously, I put you in danger and made the Piper save you! It's MY fault and I understand why you froze me out. It's been HAUNTING (haha) me too. Maybe this ghost thing is the SPECTRE of our guilt? Trust me, Ally, things always work out. You might not notice all the

time but you have a charmed life.

Hope you can stop freaking out and accept you're in the hands of fate (but she isn't always cruel!) and your performance isn't a total disaster.

I'll phone you tomorrow maybe so we can catch up.

I dyed my hair blue and regret it but I think you should do something with yours.

Laterz, Tanya.

(PS: Ghoooooosts. Srsly how do u do it??!)"

I typed back "MANDOLIN" and grinned at my phone until I caught the Piper giving me an adoring look. I had to shove him away. "Shh," I said.

"I'm just happy for you," he said.

"Oh, don't you start."

He pulled me in closer, and I let him do it, relaxed and sleepy and warm as he tucked me up against him.

"Go to sleep," he mumbled, and I suddenly realised that for the first time in weeks I didn't have any song stuck in my head at all. When I closed my eyes, that blissful quiet was all I needed to drop off and officially draw a line under my music career.

9 781913 387105